Ron and Bruno

Against the Doctatorship

A Novel by
Don Milton

Copyright 2024 All Rights Reserved Don Milton
ISBN 978-1-61191-013-1

Acknowledgements

Age before beauty:

John Whitten

Ron Morrow

Jen Milton

Dedicated to those whose lives, families, and businesses were destroyed by the doctatorship.

&

In memory of those who died alone, because nurses, doctors, guards, and hospital workers followed orders.

&

In memory of those who were killed by so-called vaxes so doctors and hospitals would qualify for financial incentives.

&

In sympathy for those who were injured so badly by the vaccination that life remains a daily struggle to survive.

And in defiance of the doctatorship!

Whoso sheds man's blood,
by man shall his blood be shed:
for in the image of God made He man.
Genesis 9:6

Sic Semper Tyrannis

About the Author

Don Milton's love for stories began the same way as for most of us, with bedtime stories. Then a speech impediment in 1st grade turned into a blessing. The pronunciation drills his teacher taught him gave him a love for reading aloud to others. By the end of 1st grade, his teacher was using him as a motivational reader for 2nd graders. She'd sit him down in front of the 2nd grade class and he'd read: *What Fox Did Not Know*. This was one of the many books his parents gave him to improve his speech. Speaking and reading in public came naturally after that and was never one of his fears. Adventures such as Marco Polo, Lewis & Clark, and Robinson Crusoe were his favorites. By age ten, he was telling his own stories to friends in the neighborhood. In the summer before 7th grade, he began studying French using Berlitz LP records. He'd hoped it would improve his ability to *pick up girls*. And it did, along with playing guitar. But tragedy struck when he was 16, his brother, who was also his best friend, died. Grief-stricken, he dropped out of school. But he returned after a month. His teachers did all they could to help him catch up. His creative writing teacher even promised him that if he could get an A on his class poetry project, she'd pass him, despite missing over a month of classes. When he got an A, she still failed him. She accused him of stealing his own original poems from Robert Frost, Longfellow, and others. He didn't even know who those other poets were. So he challenged her to find any poem that was plagiarized. She couldn't, and she had to admit, he indeed had written the poems himself. Shortly after graduation, he took his first shot at writing for a living. He put placards on telephone poles advertising poems made to order in the tradition of Cyrano De Boujerac. A Seattle TV station caught wind of it and with the backdrop of Seward Park and Lake Washington, they did a segment on him. Don graduated from Ron Bailee School of Broadcasting a year later. But instead of pursuing life as a DJ, he put out his thumb, hitchhiking from Seattle to Vancouver, then all the way across Canada and back. He earned enough playing guitar on street corners and cafes to cover the costs of food and youth hostels. *And* he was finally able to practice his French with native speakers in Quebec. There wasn't a province he missed. There still isn't. His next venture into the art of language was to study Tagalog, the Philippine national language, then Mandarin, then Spanish. Don earned his BA in Linguistics at the University of Washington and then opened an insurance agency. But it was the ads he wrote for his insurance agency that first got him serious attention. His ads were a hit, and his agency became the most profitable Allstate agency in the state of Washington. He'd marketed his agency as That 255-7799 Guy, a ploy that assured KISW radio listeners would remember his number, a must, in the era before the Internet and smart phones. But after 10 years of selling insurance, he grew tired of the repetitiveness of insurance and sold his agency to move to the Philippines. The ill health of his parents, however, brought him back to Seattle where he was blessed to be at his mother's side and then his father's side as his parents went on to be with the Lord. Since then, he has published eleven books, and authored three. Don lost his firstborn to the doctatorship, the organization whose reckless health directives have killed millions. He hopes this book will lighten the hearts of those who've suffered similar losses and give them a sense of closure. Don now lives a quiet life with his wife, Jen, and their two young daughters.

A Picture of the Author

Contents

Chapter 1

Me and Bruno

Bruno and I have known each other since our twenties. If you'd met us during the first few years of our friendship, you'd never guess we knew each other. Bruno wore jeans, a Pendleton, and army boots, while I looked like I'd just walked out of a business meeting. And our differences didn't end there.

Bruno's knowledge of the darker side of Seattle brought me to a more skeptical view of the world, a world of cronies and criminals. Maybe he got his information from overhearing the bosses down at the union hall, or from the regulars at the *Doghouse Restaurant and Bar*. Fact is, it could have been any number of places, Seattle has a large underbelly. But the stories he told me? I'd rather not have heard. It felt like my ears were burning, hearing the evil of the city just north of our suburb. But they were stories I needed to hear. Leave it to Beaver was a TV show. America was not like that. The America I thought I knew was a creation of Hollywood. Oh, there's a good Old America, hidden in small towns, independent churches and families where people read the Bible and pray. But Bruno's frankness about the world opened my eyes to the fact that there is a hidden government in every big city, one that cares more about political donors than citizens. Bruno knew of the corruption that was taking place in Seattle, even before the grand jury indictments of the 1970s. At least 260 *so-called* cops were indicted. *So called*, because wherever there is something of great value, there will be counterfeits. And a real cop certainly *is* someone of great value. A dirty cop isn't a cop at all. A dirty cop is a fake cop. Just like a lying reporter is a fake reporter. The only thing real about them is their prop: a camera for a *fake news reporter,* a badge for a *dirty cop*, and now an FBI badge for a stooge of the Communist National Committee. Oops, I forgot. They like to be called Progressives.

But I made up for my ignorance of political crimes with my

1

knowledge of street crimes. I'd been driving taxi for years and had come across my share of criminals, of which Seattle had no shortage. And every so often, I'd share one of my stories with Bruno. Here's one of them.

"So, me and my passenger are standing next to the cab and I'm waiting for him to pay me, but instead, he pulls out a chain. So I pulled out my .38 and say, 'You just gave me permission to shoot you.' Then he drops his chain and I say, 'Take off your shoes.' 'What?' He says. Now my gun's still in my hand and I say, 'I respectfully request that you take off your shoes.' So, he takes 'em off, and I say, 'Walk that way and don't turn around.' So, he hunches over as he walks in the direction I pointed, as if I'm gonna shoot him in the back. So I pick up his chain. I get in the cab. I put it in reverse. And I slowly back it around the corner. Then quietly I drive away. He doesn't see me. He doesn't see my cab. He doesn't see my cab number. Who knows what that creep would have told the cops. No sense calling them. You know the rules. *Never assume the cop will believe your side of the story.*" Then I took out the chain to show it to Bruno and said, "I think he'd been a lot worse off if he'd pulled this chain on you."

Bruno replied, "You're not kidding! I'd a let him swing that chain around my wrist and used it to jerk his scrawny face toward me. Then I'd smash it in!" We both laughed. Bruno had a knack for delivering a clear and concise message. I'm sure he'd have done exactly that if he'd been the driver.

So that was me and Bruno in our twenties. By the time we were in our sixties, he'd been married once, and I'd been married twice. But a funny thing happened, rather than become more jaded, we'd become more idealistic. Seeing Trump turn our Nation around was not just heartening, it was exciting and fun. We loved the way he handled the fake news. And the more the fake news attacked him, the more we trusted Trump. It was a sad day when we all had the election stolen from us.

It had been over 20 years since I'd moved away from Seattle, but Bruno and I kept in contact with frequent phone calls. It was just a 3-hour flight from Phoenix Sky Harbor to SeaTac, but this was my first trip back.

I hated Seattle, but Bruno's mom had passed away and I was flying up to help him with paperwork. I was providing moral support more than anything.

Now that you know a little bit about Bruno and me. I'd better introduce you to who I am today. I'm Ron, Ron Miller. I haven't driven taxi in 35 years, and I don't miss it. I write Christian stories that teach children good morals. I've had major tragedies in my life but my trust in God has only gotten stronger. The Bible is my reference book and guide for how I look at everything in life. I read it daily. I'm a sinner saved by grace, and I pray like I talk, a lot. So, here's my story.

Chapter 2

SeaTac Airport

Bruno met me at the airport. He knew I'd need guidance since they were under lockdown. It was the first time I'd been anywhere that had a population of obedient maskers. I was used to defying lockdown orders. I never wore a mask. I wouldn't get vaxed. And there was no way I was going to supply *papers* to any government official.

"You'll need to put on a mask." The security officer at baggage claim said.

Bruno could see me from where he stood on the other side of baggage claim. He was shaking his head and putting his finger over his lips shushing me. But when it came to my freedoms it didn't take much to set me off.

The security officer asked me again. "Mask?"

"Oh, you mean *the Mask of the Beast?*" I said.

He just looked at me, silent. I put on my mask which had large red letters that spelled out Lamb of God in Hebrew.

"What's that say?" He whispered to me.

I figured since he whispered, he wanted to keep it between the two of us, so I whispered back.

"It says, Lamb of God, in Hebrew."

Still whispering, he said:

"There are supposed to be 144,000 of us. I've been reading a lot about that. Do you have an extra?"

I handed him one.

"God bless you." He said, no longer whispering.

"I'll take that as a real blessing." I replied. "Remember me in your prayers. My name is Ron"

"Okay, Ron. Just call me Hank. Looks like you got a friend waiting for you in baggage claim."

"Yeah, Hank. I better be going. Nice meeting you."

I nodded my head to Hank as if tipping a hat, a custom I'd

picked up in Arizona. Then I walked over to where Bruno was, but not before getting a good look at Hank's name tag: Captain Henry Lewis. I repeated the name in my head and to remember, I associated it with John Henry the hard driving man and Joe Lewis the champ. You never know when you might meet a person again. Remembering a person's name is an act of neighborly love.

Bruno was nervously pacing at the baggage claim.

"I thought you were gonna get yourself arrested." He said.

"As if what you thought wasn't obvious." I replied. "I saw you pacing back and forth like a guard dog locked inside a junk-yard fence."

"Got any other poetry for me?" Bruno asked.

"Well, I got the best book of poems right here."

I held up my Bible and smiled, looking around me as I said it. A woman with cropped hair and overalls glared at me across the concourse.

"Ah, Seattle. Good to be back where the women hate me and aren't afraid to let me know."

"So why'd that cop stop you for so long." Bruno asked.

"He wanted to know what my mask said and then asked for one."

"So, what does it say?" Bruno asked.

"It's Hebrew. It says, Lamb of God." I said.

"And what's that mean?" He asked.

"The Bible says about Christians in the end times, that *they shall see His face, and His name shall be between their eyes.*"

I paraphrased the verse.

"Better give me one too." He said.

Once we exited the airport doors, I expected to see people walking without masks. But there wasn't a person in sight without one. Even the maintenance workers on the tops of buildings were wearing masks.

"Tyranny!" I shouted to Bruno.

"It's the shits." He replied.

"No, it's not the shits." I said. "I think Jesus is coming soon and that's fantastic."

"Well, you can think whatever you like, Ron, but today, it's the shits."

And Bruno was right.

Chapter 3

The Taxi

We jumped in the taxi, both of us wearing masks.

"What's with the masks?" The driver asked.

"You mean we don't need them in your cab?" I said.

"No. You don't need them in *my* cab but the *rest* of the drivers? They're *nuts*. Maskers! All of them. But I'm curious. What do the letters on your masks spell?"

"The letters spell Lamb of God in Hebrew." I said.

"You don't… happen to have an extra one, do you?"

"Sure, I've got an extra."

I handed him a dozen masks and a self-inking stamp so he could make some of his own. Then he introduced himself.

"My name's Diego. Diego Armandia"

"Nice to meet you, Diego. I'm Ron and this is Bruno."

"Nice to meet both of you. My wife will be so happy. We've been talking about masks like this in our church."

"Your church is open?" I asked.

"Not our *old* church. We have our *own* church now where we meet secretly. That's the only way you can do it without covering the image of God with a mask."

"Now that's one I even know." My friend Bruno said. Then he quoted, "*In the image of God created He them.*"

"Well, Bruno," I said, "I'm glad to know you're still listening to the TV preachers, even if it's just to mock them."

"Oh, you do that too?" Diego said. "When they didn't speak out against the masks, I knew them for who they were."

"'*And no marvel, for Satan himself is transformed into an angel of light.*'" Bruno quoted the Bible again.

"This guy's good." Diego said.

"See that, old Ron? Takes a stranger to appreciate me." Bruno said.

"So where are we headed?" Diego asked.

7

"Here, this is the hotel."

I handed Diego a brochure I'd been sent by the hotel staff.

"It's close to the hospital where we're going." I said.

"I hope everything's alright." Diego replied.

"As right as anything can be considering the times." I said. "It's just a paperwork thing. The doctor has to sign off on some forms for my friend here. His mom passed away last year."

"She didn't *pass* away!" Bruno erupted. "They killed her! She was a perfectly healthy senior citizen that tested positive on their fake Covid test. Then they kidnapped her. They claimed it was voluntary. But when doctors tell us we need to be admitted to the hospital, is it ever voluntary? They did it to get their blood money, $13,000 from the Feds just for admitting her! And on top of that, the insurance company still paid all her bills. The Fed money was bonus money raining down from taxpayers. We were paying doctors to lock up our parents. Oh, but do you think that was enough? No, they had to triple their money, $39,000 in Fed money if they slapped her on a ventilator. And justifying it was easy, just put her in a filthy room and she'll have pneumonia in 24 hours. Have you seen what the hospital rooms look like now? They're empty except for patients. The workers who refused the jab were fired. There's nobody left to disinfect the equipment. And the doctors, under orders from, well, may his name not be praised, forced her to die alone, without family. Maybe mom thought I was the one who forced her to die alone. I don't even know if they told her that I was kept out. What kind of subhuman tormentors are those doctors! Tell me!"

Bruno's anger was the only thing that kept him from sobbing. But he continued railing.

"And they kept that ventilator crap stuffed down her throat for weeks. I know who killed her and why. Doctors killed her! And since they didn't speak up against their paymasters, they were part of it, as one by one, they willingly took part in one of the largest mass murders in history!"

Bruno's rage was a combination of anger and pain. Had his personality been different, he would have been in tears. But when Bruno hurt, he wanted to pummel someone. But there was no one to pummel, just a nameless bureaucracy of doctors on the dole. Even so, his words landed like punches. It was hard seeing my old friend suffer through his grief.

"I know, Bruno, it's crazy. For so long I thought it was God's doing, that God was exercising judgment on the world by confusing our leaders. How could the governors be so stupid as to lock down their own countrymen and bankrupt them! Still, it might just be God's will. But Bruno, you're right. I think the world was in shock when they saw Governors across the United States destroy life, liberty, and the pursuit of happiness. Where the hell did the patriots go!"

"Ron, don't take the name of a place nobody should want to go and use it as an expression." Bruno quoted what I'd said to him years before.

Bruno had a memory for anything that could be used against those with faith. But now, I was starting to think Bruno had his own type of faith, and a discerning spirit that could weed out those who weren't what they put themselves out to be.

"I know, Bruno. Leave it to you to correct me with my own words. We need to pray for those governors. It must be a huge burden for them to know that they..."

"Screwed America!" Bruno finished my sentence. "And then screwed the world! With their lockdowns and mandatory vaxes the politicians starved and literally put our people on the street. And despite the rising deaths from *unknown causes*, they keep pushing those crap phony vaccines that by now have injured and killed more people in the world than Mao did with his great leap *backwards*."

"I can't disagree with you." Diego said. "The hospital did the same thing with my little cousin, wouldn't let any of us go to him during his last days. He was hit by a car. No covid, nothing, but

9

they wouldn't let anyone into the hospital who didn't work there. I think he would have survived with moral support. And I think his not getting moral support was what killed my aunt."

"Was she vaxed?" Bruno asked.

"No, none of my family got vaxed. She died of a broken heart. She blamed herself for my little cousin's death. She said she must not have tried hard enough to get into the hospital, that she should have at least tried to sneak past security. We all felt guilty that we didn't defy the hospital authorities and just march on in there. And we're still asking ourselves, how much longer are we going to put up with this? And to this day, the media won't report the fact that vaxes have killed tens of thousands of Americans, if not hundreds of thousands, not to mention the millions of vax injuries. I don't get it."

"All of it's bad." I said. "And then they used fear to usher in cheat by mail, stealing not just the presidential election, but a ton of local ones."

"It's sad to see all this." Diego said. "Anyway, you guys have a hard road getting into a hospital. They're so locked down in Seattle. I don't know how you'll get in to see a doctor to sign forms, unless you got someone on the inside. I'll pray for you."

"On the inside." Bruno retorted. "Sounds like a prison."

"Got that right." Diego said.

"So how many masks you got in that suitcase?" Bruno asked. "I don't know. I've got a few thousand." I said. "And you can breathe right through 'em."

"Oh, *you know*, Ron. He counts everything, Diego. Ron's got some odd thousand minus what he gave out today. How many you got, old Ron?"

"Okay, I've got twelve thousand minus the ones I gave out in the last half hour. I got some self-inking stamps too."

"I like this guy." Diego said to Bruno.

"Yup, not a superstitious bone in him." Bruno chuckled.

"Superstitious or not, Bruno. There's something happening

today that's beyond what our eyes can see." Diego said.
"I'll agree with you there." Bruno replied.

Chapter 4

Pill Hill

Diego pulled into the driveway of the Sortida Hotel. It was just outside of Seattle's *First Hill District,* also known as Pill Hill for all its hospitals and clinics.

"I hope you won't mind if I give Hank a call to let him know I got you here okay. You know, Hank, the cop you met at the airport. He's the one who called me to pick you up in front. Drivers aren't allowed to pick up there, but since we're both believers, he helps me out once in a while."

"Yeah, tell him you got us here." I said. "Maybe we can all go to your secret church together. I'm thinking meeting you and Hank may turn out to be a heavenly coincidence."

"Serendipitous, as the secularists would say." Bruno quipped.

"Yeah, my cousin married a commie professor." Diego said. "He loves using that word. I suppose it's serendipitous that we ended up on the only planet in the universe where more than nuked cockroaches can survive. I had to look up the word, and once I knew what it meant, I decided to pray for whoever used it. I know you're a man of faith." Diego said to Bruno. "But I'll pray for you anyway so as not to break the habit."

"Good to know you're praying for me, Diego, just so you don't mistake me for a commie professor. If I recollect right, the last time someone prayed for me, I twisted my ankle. Couldn't walk for a week. I just hope the result of your praying will be a bit more gentle than Ron's. But thanks for the ride."

"Yeah, Diego, thanks for the ride." I said.

"You're welcome. And thank you both. Stay free."

Diego bid us goodbye, handing each of us his business card as we got out of his cab.

"Vaya con Dios." Bruno said.

We waved as Diego drove off. Bruno's favorite restaurants were Mexican, so he'd picked up a bit of Spanish over the years.

To the staff, he was a welcome face, and not just for his friendly attitude and good tips. But because they could depend on him to subdue unruly customers. His bellowing voice and fists pounded on the table were usually all it took. If that didn't work, Bruno was willing to take what he called *corrective measures*. He liked to say that he preferred iron fists to steel bullets. I'd never had the pleasure to witness Bruno dishing out *corrective measures*. But knowing his knack for words, I'm sure every punch came with a punchline.

The last time I'd been to the Sortida Hotel was to dine at the Sortida Back Room, a five-star restaurant on the top floor. It had a fabulous view of Puget Sound and Downtown Seattle. For $9.95 they served a full course meal that included Prime Rib. Let's see, that was 44 years ago, when I was just 25. My date was Vilma, my Filipina girlfriend. She paid for our dinner. I didn't find out till years later that in the Philippines, if the girl is rich, she thinks nothing of footing the bill for her less financially fit date. My contribution was my two-for-one dinner discount card. There must have been some marketing benefit for a five-star restaurant to include itself on a discount card. You'd think. But it sure was a benefit to us. After deducting one meal, adding coffee for me, and a drink for Vilma, plus a 20% tip on top of the total before discount, the cost was still less than twenty-five bucks. Maybe I should have paid for the meal myself, but my date had just gotten lucky on coffee futures. She'd put in five-thousand and gotten back twenty-five thousand. She netted twenty thousand in less than two months. She was the only smart gambler I ever met. It was her first and last bet. It tided her over for a few years on top of what she was getting from her well-connected father, or was it alimony? Being the 80's, and my having no interest in a serious relationship, I didn't ask where all her money came from.

But there was one thing about Vilma that she couldn't hide. I arrived one night at her apartment to find a *friend* of ours coming out the door just as I was about to knock. I found her *lying* in bed.

13

And yes, I learned later, the dual meaning fit. There were cough medicine bottles strewn all over the bathroom and towels with blood. She was very pale. For someone who normally had a dark complexion this was a dire warning. I wrapped her up in a blanket and put her in my car, then drove to Harbor View Medical Center. I parked as close as I could to the emergency entrance, then picked her up and bolted through the double doors. There were two police officers standing next to a table between the first and second set of doors. One of them waived a nurse over who was standing next to the ER desk. She pointed to a stretcher. I laid Vilma on it and the nurse rolled her inside.

"You packin?" The officer asked.

I nodded.

"Leave it on the table. You can get it on the way out."

There was another pistol in its holster already laying there.

"That belongs to the cab driver delivering blood" He said.

I did as I was told, then walked over to where the nurse had rolled Vilma.

"My girlfriend's hemorrhaging and losing blood fast." I said.

The nurse got Vilma's insurance card and handed it to the person behind the ER desk.

"Have a seat here in the lobby." She said. "Only relatives can go where I'm taking her."

Except for cab drivers, she might have said. Because for the next hour, cab drivers kept going through the heavy double doors that divided the lobby from the patient rooms. They were delivering packages labeled blood. A few hours later and the doctor called me in to see Vilma. She was back to normal. The color had returned to her face. She was alert and seated in a wheelchair.

"She's good to go." The doctor said. Then looking at me with all seriousness, he stated. "Your baby didn't make it."

Vilma, my now ex-girlfriend looked at me. I remained silent to protect the guilty. I had a vasectomy. But I didn't blame her for straying. Ours was an on again off again relationship. I took

14

Vilma back to her apartment and sat in a chair to keep an eye on her. It was my day off. Staying up while she slept wasn't anything heroic. I worked the night shift. I'd have been up till 6am whether at her place or mine. And when she woke up, I left.

I didn't hear from Vilma for years after that. Then out of the blue she calls me up to help her move out on her fiancé, on the very day she'd moved in with him. I had a talk with her soon to be mother-in-law. She said her son was crazy about Vilma, and that she was too, and that she loved her like a daughter. I never found out what caused Vilma to call me that day. Maybe she had to be sure we really were over. But I hadn't given it a second thought after her self-induced abortion.

I know it's a lot to think about in the seven seconds between my getting out of the taxi and turning around to find Edwin, the bellhop. But the Sortida Hotel had lots of memories for me.

"Hi. Sir Ron?" The bellhop asked.

"Yes, I'm Ron." I replied.

"We've been expecting you." He said.

Still true to my new habit, I looked at his name tag. He had the same last name as the girl I'd just been reminiscing about, Santos. It's one of the most common Filipino names, so it was unlikely he was related to her.

"Please excuse the workers." He said. "They're testing all the hotel security cameras today. I'm sure they'll be finished by evening."

"*Walang suliranin.*" I replied.

Which meant, *no problem,* in his language. With Santos for a surname, and his pronouncing f's like p's, it didn't take a linguist to know he was Filipino.

"Oh, you speak my language!" He said.

"Yes, I happen to be one of the few old white guys who can speak Filipino, other than Mormon missionaries. But I'd bet you speak a few of your own languages, plus English."

"Yes, I speak my mother's and my father's languages and the

15

two national languages, Filipino and English. Plus, I'm learning Spanish from my fiancée." He said.

"Oh yeah, I'd forgotten how English is one of your national languages. Kind of amazing how it's yours but not ours."

"Oh, really, Sir Ron. I didn't know that."

"By the way, Edwin. How'd you know my name?"

"The bellhops are the first ones to see the guest itinerary and your reservation profile included a picture, Sir Ron."

"That's good. I was just wondering because I ain't wearing a name tag and I ain't famous."

"Yes, you are not famous." He said.

There was an odd tone to his voice when he said it. But it was an hour past nap time for old Ron, and everything gets a bit odd when I'm late for my siesta.

Bruno didn't have a bag except for the wrinkled grocery bag he was carrying. He'd be heading home after he got his form signed. It was just a ferry boat ride and a short trip by taxi to his place. I remembered the story my dad told me about a ferry ride with my nephew. They were standing on the top deck and all of a sudden, the horn blasts. My nephew about jumps out of his socks. Then he looks up at my dad and says: "Do it again, Grampa, do it again!"

As usual, my mind was everywhere but where I was. The bump of my bag on the cart brought me back to the present.

"By the way, Edwin, this is my friend Bruno." I said. "We've got a form to get signed over at the hospital. He's just hanging out till we get it taken care of, then we'll celebrate."

"Nice to meet you, Edwin." Bruno said.

"Nice to meet you too, Sir Bruno." He replied.

"Welp, I told you my family descended from the Knights of the Round Table, old Ron. See how he called me Sir Bruno?"

"Oh, sorry sir. It's our custom. I just came back from a trip to my country, and all my old habits have returned. I'll try to re-member next time, Sir Bruno, I mean, Bruno."

16

"Oh, it's no problem, Edwin. I'm jousting a bit with my old friend Ron." Bruno said.

"Oh, jousting." Edwin said. "So maybe Ron's a knight too."

"This kid's got rhythm, Ron. But I'm not surprised. He's a workin as a doorman at one of the most exclusive hotels. I can imagine the kind of pull Sir Edwin must have."

Bruno took a stride like a warrior king as we entered the Sortida Hotel, cradling his well-worn MAGA hat like a knight's helmet.

As we proceeded through the doors of the elegant Sortida, I forgot for a moment that I was one of the detested class, an old, straight, white man. Funny how they'd substituted the word privileged for detested and felt that gave them permission to treat us like second class citizens. Well, I didn't put up with it. I was vocal, and so were my friends, few of whom even belonged to the detested class. But now we were being treated like royalty, guests at the Sortida Hotel.

"So Bruno, the stairs or the elevator?" I said.

Bruno noticed Edwin's nervous glances toward the front desk. It might have broken protocol if Edwin's guests, who were to receive five-star service, bounded up the stairs of the hotel. But I must admit it was tempting.

"No, Ron. I think I'd rather enjoy the fine service this young man is providing. His service is every bit as elegant as the hotel."

I could see the relief on Edwin's face. His home country was one where authority was honored. Even if the desk clerk hadn't minded, Edwin would never have felt comfortable with guests bounding up the stairs at the Sortida.

Edwin held the doors open as we stepped into the elevator. The mahogany panels oozed nostalgic reminders of the Sortida that once was, and the famous men who'd dined at the Back Room Bar on top. We were only going to the second floor, but I planned on going to the top later, to see what memories I might awaken. Memories have so many doors. Open one, it leads to more. Ha, I was already daydreaming in poetry. Now, I knew I'd find a tale to spin about this place, even if only for a children's story.

Edwin followed us into the elevator with the luggage cart.

"I have your check-in information here." He said. "You're booked five nights in room 211, isn't it?"

"Yes, five nights. And 211, *it is*." I said.

It was déjà vu when Edwin said, "Isn't it?" That's exactly what Vilma, my ex-girlfriend, would say. I'd never heard it used prior to meeting her. It's simply not American English. But for Filipinos it makes perfect sense. It's a direct translation of their phrase that turns any statement into a question. It was Vilma's nonstandard English, contrasted with her high intelligence, that turned my once snobbish attitude about proper English, into one of accepting the way a person speaks, as long as they're able to make their point.

When we arrived outside Room 211, Edwin looked up at the closed-circuit camera on the ceiling. There was a monitor connected to it so that anyone entering would know they were not anonymous. It was flickering like an old black and white TV and then went off.

"Ever since CHAZ." Edwin said. "You know, the Capital Hill Autonomous Zone. Since CHAZ, we've implemented strict security protocols. Don't worry, I'll report that camera. We're only eight blocks from where the takeover happened. You've heard about CHAZ, right?"

"Yes, yes, we've heard about CHAZ." Bruno answered, with contempt in his voice.

"I don't like them either." Edwin said.

Edwin unlocked the door to my suite and handed me the key. The lights and heat were already on.

"This is your suite. And this door opens to your bedroom." He said.

Edwin opened the door to my bedroom. It was reminiscent of pictures I'd seen of the bedrooms of kings. The bed included a headboard that rose five feet behind its satin pillows. Ornate carvings of flowers, leaves and branches were cut into its ebony stained hardwood. Heart shaped leather insets were nested within an embroidered braid of vines. See-through curtains created a dream-like effect as the chandelier reflected off its threads. Finely upholstered chairs were on each side of the bed. Matching armoires stood with doors open, robes hung on wooden hangers and slippers leaned against their base. Valet stands were placed like guards next to the armoires and a padded chest was at the foot of the bed.

I didn't deserve this room. Nor did I *reserve* this room. But I was anxious to find out who did. It was a gift from an anonymous donor. Why I'd received such a gift, I was to find out. At least, according to the letter I'd been given along with the reservation.

Now this, was a room! I'd never imagined such a room, let alone been in one. I was tempted to take a nap just so I could wake up in that majestic bed.

Edwin's voice brought me back from my, well, how would you describe it, from my immersion in the room.

"So, you like the room, isn't it?" He said.

"Yes, it *is*, a *fact*, I *love* this room! Why would anybody give me such a gift? I really think it's some kind of strange mistake, like somebody with tons of money put the room in the wrong name, and after they'd mistakenly given me the reservation, didn't want to take it back for fear of bad publicity. If that's the case, and you know who it is, just tell me, and I'll get another room. I won't tell anyone about it."

"Oh no, Sir Ron. It's not a mistake. It was wonderful seeing your reaction to it."

Edwin handed me his business card which included his cell number and the extension for the concierge.

"Well, this is great." I said. Then I handed him a tip.

"Thank you!" Edwin said. "And by the way, Diego wanted me to text him when I got you to your room. Yes, Sir Ron. I know

Diego and Hank, both of them. I've attended Diego's secret church too."

"That's good to know, Edwin. If it weren't for that, I'd think you were all Feds by now."

"Feds?" Edwin asked.

"No worry, it's an inside joke, Edwin. I'm too worn out to explain it now. And yes, go ahead and give Diego a call. He's a brother."

"In more ways than one." Edwin replied. "I'm engaged to Bella, his sister. She works at the hospital. Diego said you might need help to get in. She can get you in and make sure you see the right person to sign your form. Take that nap you've been looking forward to. I could see in your eyes how much you wanted to try that bed. Then after you're rested, I'll take you to the side door of the hospital where you'll need to enter."

"Wow, that's, that's a blessing. This is going to be a lot easier than either Bruno, or I thought. Right, Bruno?"

I looked to where I thought Bruno was standing but he was already sound asleep. He was lying on the couch in the main area of my suite. He must have conked out right after we walked in.

"He probably got up really early to meet you at the airport." Edwin said.

"Yeah, well, it's good he's resting. It's never easy to finalize paperwork for a loved one who's passed away. It's like saying goodbye to them all over again. I know. I've had to do it myself."

"Yes, so have I, Sir Ron."

"Edwin, I'd prefer it, if you don't call me Sir Ron. We're both believers. And, as of today we have a lot of friends in common. Now, what was it you wanted to tell me?"

"Well, I figured out what you meant by your joke about the Feds, but that's not what I wanted to tell you. It's just that, I've got one more heavenly coincidence to tell you. You see, I am here because of you."

"Okay, so what's going on, Edwin?"

20

"Well, Mr. Miller. Sorry, I, I just don't feel comfortable calling someone older than me by their first name."

"That's okay Edwin. My kids wouldn't either, *and* I wouldn't be happy with them if they did. So, what's this you want to tell me?"

"Um, Mr. Miller. I have something to finalize too. It's the last request of my mom. She passed away a year ago."

"Oh, I'm sorry to hear that, Edwin. Grieving is a difficult thing to deal with."

"Yes, but I was at her bedside when she died, and she was able to share so much with me. I never had a doubt as she left her body behind that she was cradled away in the Lord's arms."

"That's wonderful, Edwin. So, what have you got to finalize? I'd be happy to help you with it."

"Well, Mr. Miller. You're actually the only one who *can* help me. You see, my mother knew you. And she told me she regretted not thanking you."

"So, your mom was Vilma Santos?" I said.

Now Edwin's seriousness vanished as he burst into laughter. "Yes!" He continued to laugh, but still managed to get out the words: "And my aunt was Nora Aunor." Then he laughed till tears filled his eyes. When he regained his composure, he asked: "So, she never told you her real name?"

"Now that you mention it, I must have been pretty dense not to realize Vilma was her nickname. I'd even told her she looked like Nora Aunor, the Philippine actress who competed with Vilma Santos for roles. Chalk it up to my being a shallow young man."

"Yes, I mean, no, No, you were, you were not shallow, Mr. Miller." Edwin began to laugh again. "I'm sorry. I'm rude." He said, barely able to contain himself. "This is not right." He said, regaining his composure. "I should not be laughing when this is a serious matter."

"Don't worry about it, Edwin. You remind me of your mom.

21

She loved to laugh and had cute expressions like, 'What in the worldy pie!'"

"She said that when she was young?" He asked. "I thought she only talked like that because she was my mom, and we were kids. What else did she do?"

"Well, the first time I heard the Filipino nursery rhyme about a bald father falling into a well."

"It was from my mom?" Edwin exclaimed.

He had the biggest grin, and I could see this was giving him a lot of joy, hearing what his mom was like when she was young.

"Yeah, and she sang it with such glee, as if she was five years old all over again, taunting the neighbor kids. She was adorable."

"It's wonderful to hear that you cared about her. Now I must tell you about her, after you knew her. And I must tell you one of her last requests, the one that included you."

"Well, I'm honored, Edwin. Let's take a seat over here at the table."

We sat down and Edwin continued.

"She said one of the things she loved about you was your idealism, and from the way you remember her, I can understand what she meant. You have an idealism that most people lose after they've lost their innocence. But she said that even though you were a disco playboy, that you were the most romantic man she'd ever met. She kept the letter that you sent to her when she was working in the Alaskan cannery, the letter that caused her to drop that job and come back to Seattle to be with you. She confessed to me that every time she was angry with Dad that she'd waive that letter in his face."

"Well, some things don't go the way they're planned, Edwin, at least not the way men and women want them to. What about your dad?" I asked.

"Dad was a new Christian when he married mom, and mom had done a good job of fooling about everyone when it came to her faith. My grandpa and the members of his church, everyone, thought she was a Christian. But she'd never really accepted the Lord, at least not in Dad's lifetime, and Dad knew it, so he left her a letter. And I don't mean any offense by this, Mr. Miller, but the letter that Dad left her made yours look *like filthy rags*, as the scripture goes."

"Yes, I know the scripture, Edwin.

We are all as an unclean thing, and all our righteous acts are as filthy rags, and we all do fade as a leaf, and our sins, like the wind, have taken us away.

Nothing we do in this world, as you know, Edwin, can compare to Jesus' work on the cross. Our works are as filthy rags and that includes all the love letters and love songs that have ever been written. No love story, Edwin, is more beautiful than the real-life love story of Jesus, sacrificing Himself for us on the cross."

"Amen, Mr. Miller. And Dad told Mom everything about his faith, with the letter he left for her, and how Jesus loved mom more than he ever could. And how he would have gladly let her marry anyone in the world if he could only know on his dying bed that she had accepted Jesus. Mr. Miller, my mom got saved that day, the very day that my dad went to be with the Lord."

"That's a wonderful story of God's grace, Edwin, *for by grace we are saved through faith, and that not of ourselves: it is the gift of God.*"

"Yes, and I'm so thankful. because when Mom died, she was more in love with Jesus than with Dad, or you, or all the money and jewelry she'd accumulated. And that was no small amount."

"Yes, Vilma was blessed with an ability to accumulate wealth. I'm glad she finally put her trust in God's treasure, His own Son."

"Yes, Mr. Miller. But I better tell you Mom's real name, so I don't start laughing again when you call her Vilma. Her name was Victoria. She signed V. Santos, so it was only natural that Filipinos would kid, 'Let me guess, Vilma?' And she'd giggle and say, 'Yes.' When you admitted her to the hospital, that may have even happened. There are so many Filipinas that work as nurses in the U.S."

"Which hospital?" I said, still covering for her indiscretion.

"Mr. Miller, all my family knows what happened and about the hospital. My mom told us about all of that in the days before she died."

"She didn't have to do that." I said.

"That's what she said you'd say."

Now Edwin teared up from emotions, but he continued.

"You know, Mr. Miller, part of the reason Mom wanted me to contact you, was so to tell you that she'd come to know the Lord. And that she'd see you on the other side, as one of your Christian friends."

"I'm so happy to hear that, Edwin. I look forward to seeing her and so many more of my friends and family when it's my turn to die. It took a lot of life's punches to get me on my knees before God. And it's beautiful to know that the Lord has a mansion with many rooms where my Christian friends have already taken up residence, and that they'll be there when I arrive."

"Amen, Mr. Miller. So as you know, after my mom accepted Jesus, she was a new creature in Christ. And she kept a daily log of what she must do to serve God. Her final confessions, and last wishes, were in that daily log. Her death was quick. The Lord was gentle with her. My dad did his best to get his whole family saved but he wasn't successful during his lifetime. Mom was Dad's last convert, but as I've said, that didn't happen till the day he died. But when she did accept Jesus, something happened to her, and to everyone in the family. God's spirit worked through her, and then through each one of the family as they experienced God's calling. So, when we read her log, as she requested that we do in her will, we were shocked to learn that she killed her first baby with cough medicine and that you saved her life."

"Now, wait a minute, Edwin. I don't think I saved her life. If that guy who was visiting her didn't know I was coming, I'm sure he would have gotten her to the hospital. But he knew I packed a gun. He probably figured I'd be angry if I found out that he had something to do with her drinking that cough medicine."

"Mr. Miller, I respect you. But I can only tell you what my mom wrote in her daily log. She said that man, I won't name him, was cursing her, and telling her he wished she was dead, for no reason at all. She called you because she knew he was leaving. But when you got there, she was afraid to say anything to you, because she knew you were against abortion. That's why you got a vasectomy, isn't it?"

"Well, Edwin, that's only half true. Sure, I didn't want any woman to kill my kid. That was part of it. But I still thought it should be legal for others. Then a few months after I'd had my vasectomy, I was reading my favorite filthy magazine, they may still sell it today, it's called Hustler. Well, in that particular issue, the publisher, Larry Flint, allowed both pro-abortion and pro-life arguments to be presented. The pro-life argument included pictures. After I saw those pictures of babies developing in the womb, and what they did to them at the abortion clinics, I could never say I was against abortion for me but not against it for others. That's a condescending elitist view, and it's wrong. Because if abortion is murder when it's my kid, it's murder when it's your kid too, unless for some elitist reason, your kid's inferior to mine. But the only favor I knew I'd done for your mom, was to keep quiet when the doctor thought the aborted baby was mine. Oh man, I didn't mean to let that slip."

"Don't worry, Mr. Miller. You haven't revealed any secrets. She wrote in her log that she was nearly as thankful that you were the kind of man that would not shame a woman in public, as she was that you saved her life. And me, my brothers and my sisters, and my nieces and my nephews, not one of us would be here, if you hadn't saved her life. That's what I meant when I said, I'm here because of you."

"You're going to have to stop, Edwin. You don't know all the sins I've committed in my life." I said.

"Mr. Miller, we both know that when you were saved that every sin you committed was forgiven, past, present, and future. The Lord already knew everything about you."

"I know, Edwin. But there's no good deed that can make up for all the sins a man commits. Our Lord died for our sins. His blood is on our hands."

"And praise God, our Savior Jesus, *that loved us, and washed us from our sins in his own blood. He loved us so much that He gave His life for you and me while we were yet sinners.*"

"Amen." I said. "So, has this discussion of ours taken care of your mom's last wishes?"

"No, Mr. Miller, it hasn't. You see, my dad was onboard a fishing boat along with my uncle when it sank. The waters were so cold that even though they had life jackets, they'd gone to be with the Lord before anyone could pull them from the water. My uncle was my godfather. My uncle was godfather to all of us. And Mom's last request was that you become our godfather and god-father to all the Santos family."

"I don't know what to say, Edwin. But of course, whatever she wanted is fine. I'd be honored."

"I'm glad you've accepted. My sister gave birth this week to a baby boy. She'll be so happy to hear that you can be there for his dedication, and to be his godfather. It's this Sunday."

"Where will the dedication take place, Edwin?"

"It will be here, at the hotel. In fact, that's how you got your room. We reserved the banquet hall as if it were for a wedding. The wedding package included some rooms."

"Well, thank you for the room, Edwin."

"Oh, don't thank me. I'm simply doing what my mom would have done. You know, she was always extravagant. This is what she would have wanted. But I'll go for now, Mr. Miller. I'm sure you'd like to rest before going to the hospital to get Bruno's form signed. It's still early."

"Thanks, Edwin. I will."

Chapter 5

Siesta

After Edwin left, I walked back into the bedroom, looking beyond the furnishings to the memories that might have been. I could imagine Audrey Hepburn shyly looking across the room at Gary Cooper, a scene from the movie, Love in the Afternoon. Or was it Audrey Hepburn with Humphrey Bogart in a deleted scene from Sabrina. And yet, I saw Victoria in my imagination, and I was the debonair, older man. She hadn't aged a day. Her playful eyes and spontaneous smile contrasted with her designer clothes. And was that a smudge of food on her blouse? Such details in a daydream! But that was Victoria: natural, trusting, loving, and... Had I really loved her? What an odd flash of imagination. Well, as the wise King Solomon said, "It is not good to look on days past, but we must put our hands to the day's task." And this would be a busy day.

My thoughts were interrupted by a knock at the door and a voice.

"Food service."

That's odd. I just checked in. I opened the door, and a young woman greeted me.

"Mr. Miller?"

"Yes, I'm Mr. Miller. But I didn't order food."

"Oh, this is complimentary." She said, rolling a cart with trays into the room. "It's included with all the bridal suites."

She was dressed in the same kind of outfit that might have been worn when the Sortida was established, over a century ago. She reminded me of an old picture of my grandma when she was just 18, around the opening of the Sortida.

My grandma worked in the ticket booth of the Moore Egyptian theater. That's where my grandpa played piano for silent films. He was as close to a star as my grandma ever met. He was a tall man for the times, but even in high heels, Grandma stood over a foot shorter than him. I would have liked to hear their love story but that was all I knew. I was too preoccupied during their lives to ask. I met Victoria shortly after Grandma passed away. Seattle sure had a way of bringing back old memories.

The young woman waiting with the food cart was Carmelita. It was her hair woven into a net that made her look like the picture of Grandma in my scrapbook, otherwise, there was little resemblance. Carmelita was curvaceous, and despite her outfit looking like it came from another era, it couldn't hide what was underneath. And let me state, there's nothing vulgar about anything or anyone that God creates. He has created us to be who we are. Carmelita was created with just a little bit more of who she was.

"My order says there are two guests."

She glanced to where Bruno was stretched out on the couch, still asleep.

"Oh, that's Bruno, my friend. He won't be staying the night. We'll be taking care of some business later." I said.

"Bruno?"

She smiled.

"Yes. Is there something I don't know?" I asked.

"Oh, no, I just *love* the name Bruno. It sounds like the name of a bold man, a say whatever you feel like kind of man."

"You got that right." I said.

She spoke with a thick Spanish accent and kept looking at Bruno, as if hoping he'd wake up. She was noisily arranging the dishes on the table, so I shushed her.

"Please, I think he needs the rest."

"Oh, sorry sir." She said.

She quietly placed the rest of the contents of the cart onto the table. I put a tip on her cart, and she rolled it out of the room.

"Thank you, Mr. Miller." She said.

"Thank you too, Carmelita." I replied

I was still keeping track of name tags. Carmelita Divina, her tag read. I couldn't read the rest. It was smudged. It matched her makeup which looked hastily done. She had a loose tag hanging from the bottom of her skirt. Too bad Bruno hadn't woken up. He would have been nuts about this woman. I knew his type and she just walked out of the room! I felt guilty knowing Bruno had missed out on meeting Carmelita. Well, I'd tell him her name. He could track her down later.

I went back into the bedroom. The food could wait. I was dead tired. My dreams were arriving before my head hit the pillow. "Wow, this is a big party. Nice to meet you." I said under my breath. My dream continued as my head touched that softest of pillows. "Sure, where should I meet you… Zzz"

When I woke up, I was completely rested. I looked at the clock on my phone. I'd managed to get in a quick 30 minutes. Bruno was already eating.

"Where'd you get this Mexican food?" He said. "Es una comida muy deliciosa. I haven't had food like this since before Guadalajara's closed."

"Room service delivered it. They said it was compliments of the house. It's provided with all the bridal suites." I said.

"Bridal suites? What ain't you telling old Bruno, Ron?"

"An old girlfriend paid for the room, Bruno."

"An old girlfriend paid for the room, he says."

"It's a long story." I said.

"So you gettin hitched?" Bruno asked.

"No, I ain't gettin hitched. That would be an odd wedding. She passed away. Her kids got me this room. I'm gonna be godfather to all their family. I didn't even know it till Edwin told me. He's her son."

"Whose son?" Bruno asked.

"Vilma's, I, I mean, Victoria's."

"Make up your mind, there Ron. I know there were a lot of them, but let's have a little respect for the dead."

Now that was the irreverent Bruno I knew. It was good to hear him talk like himself again.

"Here's the deal, Bruno, I thought Victoria's name was Vilma but now I know it's Victoria."

"Oh, Okay, old Ron. Whatever you say. As long as I ain't stuck payin for the room, or for the food."

"Don't worry about that, Bruno. And by the way, the lady who brought the food was exactly your type. But don't worry, I got her name."

"As if you'd know my type, Ron. You know your type, they all look the same, but you don't know my type. I got a particular taste in women, you know."

Now I *knew* Bruno was going to get over what they'd done to his mom. It had taken a lot out of him, but this was core Bruno, sarcastic, quick witted, and edgy.

"Okay, Bruno. Anyway, if you want to check her out. She's probably down in the kitchen. Her name is Carmelita, Carmelita Divina."

Bruno now roared a roar that only Bruno could roar.

"Ron! You let her get away! Oh! She's here! My Camerlita!"

Bruno deliberately mispronounced her name.

"Camerlita was here, and you didn't wake me up! That's her food. That's what she cooked for me at Guadalajara's. They said she went to work in a swanky hotel after the restaurant closed, but I never found out where."

"Welp, she works here, and when I mentioned your name, she purred, 'Oh, I just *love* the name Bruno. It sounds like the name of a bold man, a say whatever you feel like kind of man.' Ha-ha!"

"Oh, she purred, did she. I think she fancies me."

Bruno's crooked smile no longer aligned with his meticulously cut mustache.

"Fancy you?" I said. "She was clanging those plates around so much I had to shush her. It was like she *wanted* to wake you up."

"Now, Ron, don't tell me you shushed my Camerlita."

Just then the room phone rang. I picked it up.

"Hello?"

31

"Hi, Mr. Miller. This is Edwin. I heard Carmelita just took a food cart there. She's my fiancée's cousin. She said Carmelita is crazy about Bruno. I'm supposed to keep track of her. I was the one who told her about the job here. Promise me you won't leave her alone with Bruno. My fiancée's family would be furious with me if she were courted by a man her family hasn't met."

"Just a moment." I said to Edwin.

"Hey Bruno, looks like you're gonna be meeting Carmelita's family. That's the only way you can *court* her, Edwin says."

"Court her, eh? I got no problem with that. So, when's the meeting." Bruno asked.

"Edwin, Bruno wants to know when he can meet Carmelita's family."

"Well, they're coming to the Sortida Back Room Ballroom tonight. It's practice for this Sunday's dedication service. Bruno can meet them tonight."

"Tonight, Bruno. You'll meet them tonight."

"Fine and dandy." Bruno replied using one of his favorite outdated expressions.

"I'll let them know." Edwin said. "And when you two are ready, I'll take you to the hospital to get your form signed."

Between my memories and Edwin's telling me about his family, I'd forgotten he had someone on the inside to help us get into the hospital. God was surely watching over Bruno and me.

"Thanks, Edwin. I'll give you a call in about an hour." I said.

After I'd hung up the phone, I sat down to try some of the food Carmelita had brought.

"So tell me about your Carmelita." I said. "Is there anything in that nickname you've given her?"

"Oh, Ron, do I have to explain everything to you? And you a linguist. Camera Lita becomes Camerlita. She was always takin pictures of me and her food. Genius that I am, I came up with that nickname and everyone at Guadalajara's started using it too. So, what else can I educate you on, old Ron?"

"I'm sure you'll think up something." I said.

"Yes, as surely as professors used to actually teach, before the commies took over, I'll think of something." Bruno replied.

Bruno knew everything about the food Carmelita had brought. He explained which ingredients were used and why, and the ones Carmelita told him improved a man's vitality.

"Oh, so Carmelita is teaching you about vitality? Could be she's worried..." But before I could finish, Bruno retorted.

"Now old Ron, just because you got seven kids doesn't mean you got vitality. And you told me about that doc who sewed you up, reversing your vasectomy. You said he did something extra to your plumbing, kinda turbocharged it. In fact..."

Now I interrupted Bruno.

"Alright, just a little lighthearted kidding, Bruno. You better figure out what you're wearing to meet Carmelita's folks. You got clothes in that wrinkled up old bag?"

"What did you figure I had in this bag? As far as clothes, I'm covered."

Bruno tilted his head and looked at me sideways, as if his pun was worthy of attention.

"Oh, the punster." I said. "I'm sure Carmelita's daddy will be impressed with your one-upmanship. Yes, muy contento having a son-in-law who talks like he's had a few, even though you've never touched a drop."

"Alright, ya got me there. Just pray that I don't screw it up. She's got to have something wrong with her to want me."

"Don't start with the poor Bruno routine." I said, "A woman likes a man who's not afraid to be a man and blusters around a bit. Just be natural with her. And when she looks at her Bruno with adoring eyes, her parents will see they got no choice."

"Oh, so now I'm takin advice from a man who's just gotten his, what is it now, third divorce?"

"If it matters, second. But Bruno, I wasn't advising you. I'm congratulating you. You got yourself a young woman after you.

33

How old's that girl?"

"I know what you're thinking, Ron. And she..."

I finished his sentence.

"She ain't young enough to be your daughter. I know, I know, your daughter turned 36 last week. So your new girl is somewhere between 37 and what?"

"Between 37 and an old maid, Ron. Can't you see, I'm a saving her from a life of shame."

"Ha! Okay. Old Bruno is a saving the *damsel* in distress."

"Now, old Ron. You know I ain't a racist, and I ain't a sexist, well, not in a bad way, and I certainly ain't an ageist. And I will not make age an issue in this relationship. I'm not going to exploit my girl's youth and inexperience for any purpose."

"Well, Bruno, Reagan won an election against Mondale with that quip and I'm certain you'll win the hand of your Carmelita, quip or no quip. So, congratulations in advance."

"Congratulations? Win the hand? Now, wait a minute. We don't need to be talking about any hand winning around here. It's just a simple introduction to Camerlita's folks. So stop your congratulating. That's code for gettin hitched." Bruno objected.

"Well, Bruno, why do you think Carmelita's folks need to meet you before they'll allow her to be *courted* by you?"

"*Courted* by me?" Bruno half roared, then said. "You know, I could do much worse, *muchisimo peor*."

"Bruno, I don't think you could do any better."

"Welp, I hate to say it, Ron. But this might be one of the rare times you're right. What is it they say about a broken clock?"

Bruno and I had finished eating every chimichanga, tostada, and enchilada on the plates, as well as the other tasty dishes that Carmelita had prepared. There was nothing left but a few drops of salsa and that was only because we ran out of tortillas to wipe them up.

"So, you got a routine?" I said to Bruno.

"What do you mean a routine?" He said.

34

"You know, so you don't get fat, eating like this every day."

"I ate like this every day at Guadalajara's. You're looking at a fine specimen of humanity."

Bruno smirked his signature smirk as he boasted.

"Yes, Bruno, as long as Carmelita sees you that way, you're a blessed man. Well, time to text Edwin so he can take us across the street to get your form signed." I said.

"Edwin?" Bruno asked. "What's Edwin got to do with it?"

"While you were sleeping, Edwin told me that they're locked down over at the hospital. But his fiancée works there, and she can get us in."

"Okay, let's get this over with." He said. "You don't know how much this kills me, not having this all behind me."

Then he looked at me, remembering how many griefs I'd been through, and said:

"It's just an expression, Ron, just an expression."

"Yes, I know. It's a burden having unfinished business when it comes to a loved one's passing. We both know."

"Maybe that's Edwin knocking on the door now." Bruno said.

I opened it.

"C'mon in, Edwin. Bruno and I have to get our lines right, before we walk to the hospital and talk to the doc."

I took out the form that we wanted the doctor to fill out.

"Are you good with what you're gonna say to the doctor, Bruno?"

"Yeah, 'I got a comorbidity form, Doc. Can you sign it?'"

"Well, that may be all it takes." I said.

"Okay, let's get on with it." Bruno said.

Then he turned to Edwin.

"I'd like to thank you for helping us, Edwin."

"Oh, you're welcome, Sir Bruno. Carmelita told me about you. She says you're a *get things done kind of guy*."

"Let's hope so, Edwin. I don't really need this form signed. It's just that I'm responsible for taking care of my mom's estate, and I wouldn't feel right if I let one penny go unaccounted for."

"You're an honorable man, Sir Bruno."

"You can drop the Sir, Edwin."

"Okay, Mr. Hartman." He answered.

"Now on second thought, Edwin. Mr. Hartman does sound a little stodgy. But Sir Bruno kind of rolls off the tongue."

"I think so too, Sir Bruno."

Chapter 6

Dr. Jensen

Edwin left his bellhop cap and coat in my room, and we walked down the hall and out of the building. A few blocks and we were at the loading dock of the hospital. Edwin's fiancée was waiting at an employee door beside the cargo door.

"Get in. Get in." She said.

Then she rushed us down the hall and into a storage room.

"This is my fiancée, Bella." Edwin said.

"So why are we here?" Bruno asked.

"This is the only door in the building without cameras." Bella replied. "Here, get into this."

She handed us some hospital gowns and masks.

"Now wait just a durn tootin minute." Bruno objected. "What is all this stuff?"

"The hospital is on total lockdown. This is the only way you can gain entry." She said.

"So this ain't on the up and up?" Bruno said. "I'm all in! I'm sick of these lockdowns anyway."

"Make sure to put on the gloves too." She said.

"So this is gonna be a fight?" Bruno quipped.

Bella scolded. "Now let's be serious, Bruno. Carmelita told me about you."

"And what did she say, pray tell?"

Now Bella coyly smiled and said:

"Carmelita said she *fancies* you."

"Now *there*, wha'd I tell you, old Ron. Camerlita fancies me. That's all I needed to hear. Let's suit up."

"And put this on too." Bella said, "Nobody will be able to recognize you. They'll think you're from the hazmat team."

Bella handed us hazmat suits that looked like the gear firemen wear. Now Bruno objected.

"I ain't a gettin into one of those contraptions." He said.

"Is there another way?" I asked.

Bruno was claustrophobic, and anything that covered him so completely was out of the question.

"Oh, well yes." She said. "The other way is to send the paper you want signed through a courier, then wait till it gets to the doctor's desk. Then wait till he decides to sign it. Then wait till he sends it out. And by the way, this doctor you want to see, this Dr, Jensen, well, the courier service told me…"

Bruno was looking for anything that could keep him from putting on the hazmat suit, so he cut in.

"I see, the courier service told you. I thought you were our contact on the inside?"

"Oh, no." Bella said. "I would never get the jab. Everyone on the inside has gotten the jab and some have died."

"So are you're telling me this is all guesswork? How are you gonna get us on the inside?" Bruno asked.

"My cousins provide food service here with their food truck." She answered. "They've been providing temporary service for the Sortida and the hospital as well. I just load the carts that go into the cafeteria. Housekeeping rolls them in. My cousin Julio drives the food truck and my cousin Carmelita cooks."

"Well, since you're Camerlita's cousin, and we're all in this together. Okay, and gracias. I'll just think of her when I'm under this shroud and it'll get me through." Bruno said.

"Carmelita will be delighted to hear how you say that." Bella replied.

Bruno's face was still glowing from hearing that Carmelita fancied him, and I could see his courage building back as Bella said that Carmelita would be delighted at his words. As the wise King Solomon said: *The way of a man with a woman, who can understand?*

Bruno had been a firefighter for 44 years. He could have retired early but felt it his duty to fight fires as long as he could. Then the worst apartment fire he'd ever fought put him in the hospital for three months. He said wearing masks brought back memories of the screaming kids who couldn't be saved. Still blamed himself. But if he'd stayed another moment, he wouldn't have survived. Said he lost all his toes on one foot to burns. But I knew Bruno. Had to be way worse than that, for him to admit anything. Bruno didn't like being treated special. He saw doing what's right as doing what's normal. The injury is what gave him his swagger. He wasn't trying to act tough. He was tough.

We continued putting on every piece of equipment that Bella gave us. After almost 10 minutes, we were all suited up.

"Let's go put out a fire!" Bruno exclaimed.

"Amen." I said.

But Bella wasn't through explaining how we'd get to the doctor's office.

"You see how your suits have a patch that says, 'Hazmat Security?' You have authority to enter any part of the hospital. But there's one more thing you'll need."

She handed each of us a hazmat materials bag. Mine contained an assortment of soft drinks and a cake with the words: *Happy Birthday Princess Cassandra*. Bruno's contained his form for the doctor to sign.

"What's this?" I asked.

"It's a distraction." She said. "I overheard the couriers talking about the Charge Nurse on the 5th floor. Today's her birthday and her husband is always sending her some kind of gift."

"Old Ron, are you starting to hear the music for mission impossible?" Bruno said.

Bella cut in. "I know you're anxious to get this over with, but there's just one more thing. You'll go through the first doors you come to after we leave this storage room. There's an elevator just inside. Take it to the 5th floor. When you leave the elevator, go to the left. Then go through the double doors. That's where you'll see a small table for packages. It's the only table when you come through the doors. Drop off the birthday treats there. Then walk straight past the nurses' station to Dr. Jensen's office. He's all the way to the end of the hall."

"Thanks for your help," Bruno said. "I didn't expect all this. It's such a blessing."

Yes, I thought to myself. Sneaking into a hospital in hazmat suits. What a blessing. But despite my sarcastic thoughts, I knew it was a blessing that Bruno and I didn't have to go this alone.

"So how do you come by so much inside information." Bruno asked Bella.

"Oh, I just stand out here. This is where all the staff takes their breaks. So many people in Seattle smoke now. It's the only way we can remove our masks. I just use non-nicotine vapes. I hear everything that happens in this hospital." Bella said.

"And I thought Filipinos held the record for gossiping." Edwin objected.

"Who do you think I get the information from?" Bella said.

"Good to know we still hold the record." Edwin replied.

"Okay, are we set to go?" I asked.

"One last detail." Bella said. "You'll need to know this more than anything else, how to get out. Just come back down the way you go in, but when you go out that door, the one you came in, you'll crouch down before you open it, so that you can't be seen above the food truck. Julio will be parked there waiting. Then crawl down the loading dock and go underneath the truck. It has a trap door. It's for running out the hoses to recycle the stove oil. Climb through the trap door and into the truck. Then take off your hazmat suits. There will be some plastic garbage bags for you to put them in. My cousin Julio will be the driver. He'll take you to your hotel just like he drives there every day. And that's it. Easy as rolling out a tortilla."

"Now you see, Ron? It's as easy as rolling out a tortilla. Let's roll." Bruno beat me to the punchline.

Then Bruno put on the last accessory of his hazmat suit, the shroud. That's what he called the head covering he once wore as a fireman. I could barely see him through the hazy plastic. For sure, nobody would be able to identify us.

"Oh, one more thing." Bella said. "Dr. Jensen isn't expecting you, but Hank's been paying him to smuggle in relatives of patients. Hank said to just tell Dr. Jensen that Hank has a patient form to be signed and that Hank will cover the cost."

I put on my shroud, and we all exited the storage room. What once would have been an impossible entry, was made easy, by the fear and submission that the CDC had conditioned into the public. Anyone in a hazmat suit was automatically given carte blanche. Before the CDC had seized control, we were able to easily see our loved ones. We only had to abide by visiting hours. But now, the CDC with its insidious mind control, had power over all but the most fervent people of faith. How else could you account for more than half the population poisoning themselves. It was, after all, gene therapy disguised as a *vaccine*. I hadn't been inside a church since they'd begun to cover the images of God, our fellow humans, with masks. So much for people with fervent faith.

*In the **image of God** created He him, male and female created He them.*

I hoped I'd get to visit Diego's secret church before returning to Arizona. Yeah, I have a habit of thinking of everything but the task at hand when the stress gets high. But I set my mind back on our task, getting the signature Bruno needed.

Bruno and I waddled through the first door. Then I pushed the elevator button. Bruno looked at me like he used to on the Fourth of July, just before he'd light off a quarter stick of dynamite. I enjoyed fireworks, but to risk my hand? Not a chance. But Bruno was a risk-taker. And he ratcheted up his risk taking when he became a firefighter. I couldn't imagine the nightmare of running into a burning building, but to Bruno, it was a sweet dream. It takes someone special, with guts, and a lifetime dream of becoming a firefighter. Yes, Bruno was more than bluster. He was exactly what Carmelita said he was, and then some. He was brutish like an animal when it came to saving the lives of those who couldn't save themselves. His faith was primal, and it was strong. How else could you run into a burning building? His was the kind of faith few of us will ever know.

The elevator door opened, and Bruno and I stepped in. I pushed the button for the 5th floor. The elevator inched its way up, then the doors burst open. Not really, but that's how my gut felt. I'd never trespassed before, at least not as an adult. We turned left and went through the doors. Bruno stood still for a moment between me and the nurses' station as I put the cake and soft drinks on the table. Next, we walked past the nurses' station. Then one of the nurses screamed. I about jumped out of my haz-mat suit. She'd found the cake and soft drinks.

"Casandra! Casandra." She said. "Your Don Juan husband has left you a cake and soft drinks!"

A nurse's aide asked Casandra, "Are you really a princess? It says you're a princess on your cake."

"Well, of course." Casandra said. "My father didn't approve of my marriage and so he banished me from our kingdom. Ever since, I've been telling my husband that he must make up for all the treasures I left behind."

"And has he?" The aide asked.

"I'm not sure." Casandra said. "I'll find out when I get home. He's got a lot of dishes to wash, laundry to do, diapers to change and clothes to iron."

Then she cackled more like a witch than a princess. In unison, they cackled too. Did they have a choice? She *was* the charge nurse.

As Casandra and the other nurses enjoyed their cake and soft drinks, Bruno and I kept walking down the hall. The last door would be Dr. Jensen's. Just a few more steps and... the door was open.

"I've been expecting you." Dr. Jensen said. "Come in, come in, and shut the door behind you."

Maybe Hank *did* get a chance to tell him we were coming. Dr. Jensen paced in front of the window behind a mahogany desk. It had a protective glass top and underneath there were greeting cards from past years. One was signed, Dr. Tony Fauci. Another was signed Dr. Deborah Birx. There were a few from Congressman This or That and a signed letter on the wall from a governor. This guy was connected, unless it was all puff, just phonied up stuff to make him look important. But if they were real, why was he here? And why would this guy take the time to see a couple of unknowns like us?

Dr. Jensen was pacing back and forth with his million-dollar view of Puget Sound behind him. He had one of the windows wide open, enjoying the rare Seattle sun. Seattle was having an Indian Summer, that's what locals call the spate of warm weather that arrives just after the kids get back in school. I remember as a kid, there'd be no sunlight for the entire summer and then finally, after we were back in school, the sun would come out. They used to say it was an Indian curse on the children of settlers. Probably just a story made up by one of the teachers.

"Ah, beautiful day." Dr. Jensen said. "And to make it even better, I've got *visitors*. So, what have you got for me?"

He was in an awfully good mood for someone being met by complete strangers. I wondered what Hank must be paying to get relatives in to see patients.

"So, what have you got for me?" Dr. Jensen repeated.

Bruno held out the form.

"What's that?" He asked.

"Mr. um..." Bruno couldn't remember Hank's last name.

"C'mon, speak up!" Dr. Jensen spoke gruffly.

Oops. One of the *others* just spoke crossly to Bruno. That's what Bruno called anyone who didn't know him well enough to verbally joust with him. But amazingly, Bruno kept his cool. Then he remembered the name.

"Excuse me there, Dr. Jensen. Hank, er, Captain Henry, sent

43

us with this form for you to sign. Nothing special. If you'll just sign here, we'll get out of your way."

"A form!" Dr. Jensen bristled. "A form is all you got. That does it. Tell *Hank,* or whatever his real name is, unless I get cash, I'm not signing anything else. I thought you two jokers were from the new vax company. They're bringing cold cash. You think we'd push clot shots without getting paid?"

Bruno maintained his composure. He'd clearly set his mind on completing our task.

Dr. Jensen was still pacing in front of the open window to enjoy the sunshine of an Indian Summer.

"You see that Mercedes?" He said, pointing out the window. "That used to be mine. Now it's my wife's. She didn't even have the decency to divorce me. She filed for *separation.* And when I objected to the amount of alimony? She requested my bank records. Now, I can't have her or anyone else snooping around my financial transactions, can I? So, I'm here, a really nice guy. And I'm just stuck. So, pardon me, fellas, if I'm not in the best of spirits."

Bruno was still determined to get his form signed so he made an offer.

"What say you, Doc, if next time, we bring cash. Sounds like Hank owes you and we have experience in collecting debts, if you know what I mean. Hank needs to learn a lesson in honesty and who better to teach him than me and my buddy here. We just got out of the joint and we learned a lot about how to make a man honest."

Dr. Jensen had been listening while polishing his shoes with his electric shoe buffer, one of those fancy ones that has a button on the top of a long handle, the kind you can use while standing up. He let go of the button on the handle, and said,

"I like you. Yeah, let's do business. But I gotta get you guys outta here. The two hazmat Harrys that I mistook you for are coming soon. They're with... well, we don't need to name names, but

44

he doesn't like competition. But with you two onboard, it looks like I might be able to double my take. Hand me the form."

Bruno held out the form to him. Comorbidities was written in big letters across the top, followed by Bruno's mom's name and her patient information. It was an affirmation that she died from Covid, not comorbidities. If Dr. Jensen signed it, the Feds would reimburse Bruno for the cost of his mom's burial. It's the least they could do, considering it was their policies that killed her.

"So, this is for, wait a minute now." Dr. Jensen paused. "This is for Emma Hartman? You, you're Bruno Hartman?"

"And you're that damn doctor that kept me from seeing her on her death bed! I didn't recognize you in street clothes. Sign the damn form!"

The only thing that prevented Bruno's roar from being heard down at the nurses' station was their partying, and the hazmat suit that muffled his voice.

Dr. Jensen reached for the form to sign it. But he'd lost his balance. He steadied himself on the handle of his shoe buffer. Then he slipped again, this time stepping on the buffer. He gripped the handle even tighter. Wheeze, the motor maxed out. His foot shot out from under him. He reached out to grab onto Bruno, but it was too late. His hand caught hold of the top of the form ripping off a piece of it as he fell out the window. Bruno and I ran to the window to see what had become of Dr. Jensen. He lay sprawled on top of a truck in the alley, still gripping the piece of paper he'd ripped off Bruno's form.

"Not to make light of what just happened," I said, "but we don't wanna be blamed for an accident we didn't cause. Dr. Jensen's gripping a piece of your form in his hand. What does he have?"

"Dr. Jensen's got comorbidities."

"Well, that's good. If he doesn't make it, we can't be blamed."

"Neither can Covid." Bruno chuckled.

"Is that our food truck down there?" I asked.

"Looks like it." Bruno replied.

"Well, we better get outta here." I said.

Bruno put what was left of the form in one of our hazmat bags then we walked out the door. As we passed the nurses' station, they were still partying. We walked through the exit that led to the elevator and I pushed the down button. When the elevator doors opened, the two Harrys in hazmats were standing there, the ones that Dr. Jensen had been expecting. Bruno and I acted instinctively, blocking their exit till we were both out of view of the corridor cameras. This was too easy. Now the nurses would think they were us, going back to get something we'd forgotten.

When the elevator doors closed, I hit the 1st floor button.

"Bruno?" I said.

"Yes, old Ron? He answered.

"In my life, Bruno, I've never met anyone so corrupt as Dr. Jensen. Then like a villain in an old black and white movie, he was gone. I wonder if those two will see Dr. Jensen."

"They're a bit late." Bruno said.

"So is Dr. Jensen." I replied.

My joke about a dead man was deliberate. I was still in shock at how corrupt Dr. Jensen was, and how unafraid he was to tell us. As the slow freight elevator descended, Bruno and I laughed. It was a laugh I wouldn't want to repeat, full of anger, sadness and pain. I'd seen men die violent deaths, but never a man so worthy of the penalty. Dr. Jensen had mandated clot shots for payoffs. Other very well-known people had done the same, profiting from death. They even recommended it for babies, just to make a buck. Even so, to laugh about a man's death was something I'd never done. And I hoped I wouldn't repeat it.

I knew it was too late for Dr. Jensen, but I could never stop praying that the wicked would repent. Nineveh repented on hearing the message of one man, Jonah. But could those responsible for the Covid reign of terror ever repent? If they could, like the criminal on the cross who was crucified next to Jesus, they still had to pay the *penalty in this life* for their *crimes in this life*.

46

By the time the elevator doors opened, we were ready. We ran to the exit, crouched down, opened the door, and crawled across the loading dock. Then Bruno and I slid under the food truck and went up through the trap door. A man was sitting in the driver's seat.

"Julio?" I asked.

"That's me." He said. "Quick, get out of those hazmats and put them in the hazmat bags. Then put the hazmat bags into these garbage bags."

Bruno grabbed his form from his hazmat bag and held it over the gas burner, lighting it.

"Hang on, hang on. Everything nice and orderly." He said.

It took about 10 seconds, but it seemed like minutes. When he was finished, he scooped up the ashes and threw them into the grease vat. Then we used spatulas to push the garbage bags containing our hazmats down into the black grease.

Julio was nervously rocking in his seat. I could tell he hadn't grown up a juvenile delinquent like Bruno and me. Finally, he couldn't hold back.

"I heard a thud like a sandbag landing on top of my truck. I didn't get out since I knew you could be here at any moment. What's going on?"

Bruno got a look on his face that I'd never seen before. Then he commanded us.

"Julio, you don't wanna know anything and you *don't* know anything. Got it?"

"Yes, I got it. Bruno."

Then Bruno said to me:

"You're gonna run halfway up that driveway, then you're gonna turn around and keep your eyes on this truck. If anyone asks questions, don't answer."

I got out of the truck and ran up the driveway. By the time I turned around, Bruno had climbed onto the roof. He was already administering CPR to Dr. Jensen.

Dr. Jensen

Just then, the two Harrys in hazmats burst out of the building and ran to a car that was parked in the driveway, leaving a trail of hundred-dollar bills behind them. They turned around to look but were too panicked to stop and pick up the cash. Then they jumped in their car still wearing their hazmats. As they scrambled to find the keys, two cop cars boxed them in. Once the officers had them cuffed, they cut them out of their suits with shears borrowed from the medics who were already on the scene.

The medics were the reason cops were there. Seattle was a dangerous city. At the hands of the *homeless*, Seattle medics and firefighters averaged 10 assaults against them per month. So, when cops heard an aid car, they followed, *to serve and protect*. It's beautiful when it happens. And it happens every day in every city.

Bruno had by now revived Dr. Jensen and was waiting for the medics to get him down from the roof of Julio's food truck. Dr. Jensen looked up to the window he'd fallen from, then down at the cash strewn in the driveway. I don't know if his groans were more from injuries, or from seeing *all his cold cash* strewn in the driveway.

By now, a TV crew had arrived and had their cameras pointed at their on-site reporter. She was describing the scene when one of the medics who'd just arrived yelled up to Bruno.

"Is that you, Bruno? I haven't seen you since the 4-alarm fire. Still saving lives, I see."

"Yeah, yeah, get this guy outta here. He fractured his ribs but he's breathing now."

"How'd you get him up there?" The medic quipped.

"Har har." Bruno replied. "You remember what we do with wise guys, don't you?"

"Yep, clean up. But with all these hundred-dollar bills lying around, I won't mind cleaning up after we're through here. But no joke, Bruno, how'd that guy end up on top of a... food truck?"

"I guess he was hungry." Bruno said.

Then we all laughed, including the TV crew and reporter.

"And another thing," the medic asked, "how come we got a message from your mom's emergency clicker, and it pinpointed her right here in the driveway."

"Emma won't be needing it anymore. She won't be having any more emergencies." Bruno said.

"Sorry to hear that, Bruno. I mean, you know what I mean."

"Well, good to know these things actually work." Bruno said. "I figured it was the quickest way to get you guys here."

I wondered if Bruno was thinking the same thing I was. The device meant to save the life of his mother, was used instead to save the life of the man most responsible for her death.

The camera crew was scrambling to broadcast what had just taken place. I could see one of them jamming the thumb drive he'd just pulled from the camera into a broadcast terminal inside their van. This was the kind of human-interest story that every reporter longed for: a real-life John Wayne. An anchor was already introducing: Breaking News, then the reporter showed up complete with intro, which quickly cut to Bruno. He was the star. They got everything on tape. Then they cut to an "exclusive" interview. It was obviously recorded right after the 4-alarm fire with one of the firemen who'd seen Bruno's heroics. I wondered why they'd buried it till now. Bruno saved 17 lives in that fire, but he'd never talked about it. All he said was that wearing a mask reminded him of the screaming voices of those he didn't save. The fireman described the 4-alarm fire as if he'd seen a ghost.

"The fire was chasing Bruno. It was hideous. The flames rose like fiery whips. I'd never seen anything looked like that, and I've handled the pumper truck for 30 years. But Bruno's been running into burning buildings since I was in grade school. And at 66, he's still running into them. There's nobody better. I don't think the devil likes it, and I think the devil was in the building during that 4-alarm fire."

Now the station cut to another interview. He continued where

49

the first fireman left off.

"Each time Bruno went in one door, he had to come out another. The flames seemed to chase him, but he kept outrunning them. He'd come out with two or three kids and then run in for more. I heard it was a drop house for human traffickers. But Bruno got all the kids out, all 17 of them."

Did I just hear all 17? Then why did Bruno think there were kids left behind? What happened to him in that hospital that made him think he'd abandoned children? And why was an obvious hero so isolated? I wonder if his burns would have healed more quickly, if only he'd had the moral support of those who knew him. The nurses wouldn't allow any of us in to see him during his nearly three months in the hospital. They wouldn't even allow his mother to visit. And it wasn't because of his burns. It was because of the lockdowns. Worse yet, the nurses treated him like a criminal for refusing to comply with the covid tyranny. He refused to wear a mask. So, they isolated him even more.

It would be easy in that isolation to dwell on regrets, and to think your own sins were the cause of your situation. But Bruno had gotten all the kids out. What regrets could there be? And why didn't anyone tell him that he'd saved them all?

The medics had lowered Dr. Jensen to the driveway by now and were loading him into the back of an ambulance. But before they shut the door, I heard the driver say:

"You're lucky Dr. Jensen. In less than two minutes we'll be pulling into your own ER."

"Not my ER!" He said. "Not mine! Take me to Swedish!"

"Sorry Doc. We can only take you where we're dispatched. We can't remain here. The cops want us to clear the area. Just let me get you over to ER and you can change your destination there. We're less than a minute away."

Before the doctor could object again, the driver took off. The reporter heard the same fear in Dr. Jensen's voice that I heard, and she and her crew took off just as quickly to chase the ambulance.

"I've got to see this!" Bruno said.

"Me too!" I said.

We ran around the corner to the hospital ER where the ambulance had pulled in. By now, another reporter was on the scene, competing for a chance to ask Dr. Jensen what had happened.

"Dr. Jensen. Dr. Jensen." Both reporters vied for a response.

One of the two nurses who'd come out to admit Dr. Jensen intervened.

"I'm sorry, Jessica, Brad. All of us here at the hospital love your Covid reporting but we're on full lockdown. You'll have to forward your questions in writing. Or we can do a Zoom call later. Dr. Jensen will be in the hospital for at least 10 days per admission guidelines."

"I'm, I'm not even checked in." Dr. Jensen objected.

"Is Dr. Jensen checked in, Anne?" She asked the other nurse.

"Yes, Casandra. I scanned the patient code on his wrist."

"Thank you, Anne." She said.

"Don't roll me in here, Casandra!" Dr. Jensen objected.

"Now what did the recent memo say about unruly patients, Anne?"

Anne replied. "'Upon scanning patient code, if patient history doesn't indicate drug interactions, sedate the patient from the approved list of medications.' Cassandra, his history indicates no drug interactions whatsoever. He's not on any meds. In fact, he's not even vaccinated."

"Not vaccinated?" Cassandra said, "Well, alright then, Anne. Sedate Dr. Jensen, then segregate him with the anti-vaxers."

Then Cassandra walked back into the hospital while Anne verified some information with the ambulance medic.

"I see you've already got an IV inserted into Dr. Jensen. Was his blood pressure low?"

"It was low just after resuscitation. But it's fine now." The medic answered.

51

Anne turned back to Dr. Jensen.

"Okay. Dr. Jensen, follow the doctor's orders." She said.

"What orders? What are you talking about?" Dr. Jensen said.

"Let's see, let me read this memo. Whose signature is that? Can you read that, Dr. Jensen?"

Anne showed him the memo.

"Well, yes, that's... that's my signature, but..." He objected.

"You know, Dr. Jensen. I'm not much for quoting the Bible, but I know this one. *'Physician, heal thyself.'*"

Then Anne inserted the syringe containing the sedative into the injection port of Dr. Jensen's IV solution bag.

The poetic justice of Dr. Jensen being involuntarily admitted to his own hospital wasn't lost on us. Nor was it lost on the TV crews who had their cameras aimed the whole time. And even if the Covid censors cut it out, it would be archived and brought out later, just like the two witnesses to Bruno's heroics.

Chapter 7

17 Missing Kids

As Bruno and I rounded the corner back to Julio's food truck, we expected to find a forensic investigation in progress. Instead, we found what looked like a Mexican block party attended by Filipino nurses. Julio was taking their food orders and Carmelita was cooking as fast as she could. Bruno's reaction at seeing her was the opposite of what I'd seen just before he resuscitated Dr. Jensen. He stopped for a moment, staring at her from a distance, then all the creases in his face, the furrow in his brow, and his frown disappeared. It was replaced by one giant smile.

"Camerlita!" He shouted.

When Carmelita heard Bruno's voice, her demeanor changed too. She went from fry cook to voluptuous temptress in a blink. She grabbed a napkin to dab the drops of sweat off her upper lip, accidentally smudging her lipstick. But was it an accident? Or did she know how to drive Bruno wild by adding a bit of tawdry to her smile?

"Brrrruno!" She purred, making his name sound more like a Mexican dish than someone who'd just become a TV sensation.

"Yes, Camerlita?" He replied.

"You're famous! Did you know that?" She said. "I'll finish these orders, then we'll talk."

"Fine and dandy." Bruno said, unaware of what she meant.

After Carmelita completed her last order, she showed Bruno the clip of the local news. By now, it had gone viral. It included the part where the fireman said Bruno saved every kid from the fire. Bruno could hardly believe it.

"There were no other kids? Not one left behind?" He asked.

"Nada!" Carmelita answered. "Oh, Bruno. I loved you even before I knew this. Don't forget me now that you're famous."

"Of course not, Camerlita." He said.

But Bruno's mind was elsewhere. I don't think he even

noticed Carmelita had just said she loved him.

Julio instinctively knew what was troubling Bruno, so he held up his phone and turned it off, signaling we were about to discuss America's enemies. Then he opened a container most patriots had come to know, a Faraday bag. It was a broadcast proof bag where these diabolical phones had to be stored. Yes, the off button was in name only. Just because it says off, doesn't mean it turns it off, any more than putting a vaccine label on poison, turns poison into a vaccine. We put our phones in the bag, then got into his food truck. It was just me, Julio, Bruno, and Carmelita. Julio drove a few blocks away and parked on an empty street. Then Diego, the taxi driver, pulled in behind us. After he got into the truck with us, he told us what happened to the 17 kids Bruno rescued.

"Bruno, right before the fire, there were adults in that building. They left before it blew up in flames. The fire was lit to destroy evidence, and the evidence was the 17 kids. They knew too much. But the ones who lit the fire hadn't planned on you. And when you saved the kids, you were marked for death. To them, it was nothing personal, just a matter of principle: Mess with their plans, you die."

"Whose plans?" Bruno asked.

"The ones who lit that fire." Diego said. "Call them whatever you like, human traffickers, black mailers, Deep Staters..."

"I'll call them filthy bastards." Bruno said.

"Yes, and we knew they'd block us in the courts." Diego said. "So, we took matters into our own hands. The kids were under observation in the hospital after the fire. And we knew that if the outfit responsible for them got them back, it would be the end of them. So just before they were to be released, we grabbed them. We figured those who wanted them dead, would think someone else who wanted them dead, did away with them. And listen to this, Bruno, there hasn't been one news story about them since the fire. 17 missing kids and not one story? But today? Your story went viral, and *#17missingkids* is trending on every social network. That tells me that our initial fears were correct. Somebody very deep wanted them dead. But we already knew that, or we wouldn't have hidden them in the first place."

"What made you suspicious that someone was out to kill the kids?" Bruno asked.

"Well, Bruno, my wife and I were watching the news. And there was no mention of adults in that fire. It seemed obvious that someone had planned to kill them."

"So, based on that, you kidnapped 17 kids?"

"Ha! It wasn't that simple." Diego replied. "We could see that the media wasn't doing its job. So, we decided to do our own investigating. It had been about an hour since the news had reported that the blaze had been doused. So, we drove to the location of the fire. By the time we arrived, the camera crews were gone, and the fire crew was packing up. So me and my wife, Tessie, parked our camper van down the street from the scene. After the fire crews left, it was quiet. There wasn't one investigating unit there. In fact, for the next 24 hours, we didn't see any traffic except for lost drivers making U-turns. It was dead-end."

"In more ways than one." I said.

"That's right." Diego replied. "And we stayed there another 24 hours and watched, but still no inspectors. And the news blackout continued, until today."

"So, where are the 17 kids now?" Bruno asked.

"They're safe." Diego answered. "And their guardians are home schooling them. The youngest is now 8 and the oldest is 14. The lockdowns made it easy to hide them. People were so dazed by fear-porn that they were incapable of noticing any activity outside their own households. And masking started right when the kids were released. It would've been difficult to find them, despite the fact that the ones that started the fire had photos."

"So, immigration never looked for them?" Bruno asked.

"Well, you and I both know that immigration is over-worked, and officers are attacked simply for doing their jobs. But immigration had nothing to do with these kids. They were all born right here."

I wasn't shocked. I'd heard rumors of child trafficking taking place right under our noses. So the rumors were true.

"Ever wonder why the list of frequent visitors to Epstein's not so secret island has so many redactions?" Diego asked.

"Well, most of us have assumed it's because powerful people don't want the details known." I said. "Is there another reason?"

"There were also videos." Diego replied. "And they included those kids with powerful men. Thank God nothing happened to any of those kids. The videos were Epstein's insurance policy. He made it look like something was going on, and in the case of these kids, more than actually was. But from what I've learned, the kids were about to enter an intense grooming phase of their captivity. It was a heavenly coincidence for these kids that just then, Epstein was killed. But after that, it didn't take long for those associated with him to want to torch any evidence of that association. Including those kids. Then a second heavenly coincidence arrived."

"What's that?" Bruno asked.

"You, Bruno. Any other fireman would never have gone into that building. Any chance you can tell us about that?"

"I didn't go in there on my own." Bruno said. "This has only happened to me a few times, but something grabs hold of me and lifts me toward the flames, then I feel a cool breeze around me. I felt it that night, but more, as if my feet weren't even touching the ground. Now I know what those screams were. I wasn't able to make out their faces till now. It wasn't anyone I'd left behind. And I can now see the hands of the angel who was carrying me. I don't know why I'd forgotten. He took a shield and held it up against the flames." Bruno was overcome with emotion but fought through his tears to tell his story. "The angel held up his shield against the flames that the demons were throwing like darts. Then something like a river flowed out from his shield and it was as if the demons were washed out of the doors by a flood of light. They were crying out in agony. It was their cries that I heard." Then Bruno cracked a smile and said: "First time I've actually enjoyed hearing someone cry."

I was always amazed how easily Bruno turned from serious to jovial.

"Bruno." I said, "There's a verse I'd like to share with you, but my Bible is in my phone."

"I've got a Bible." He replied.

Then Bruno handed me a half-scorched Bible he had crimped into his pocket. It was the tiniest print I'd ever seen. But I could read the words inscribed on the front: *The Fireman's Bible.*

"This is unique." I said. "Where'd you get it?"

"My grandfather gave it to me. He was a fireman too, and a Christian. But he rarely talked about it. He said his job was to save people from small fires so that someone else could save them from the big one."

"It's good to hear he knew his calling." I said.

I opened Bruno's Bible to the verse I wanted to show him. Then I noticed it was already highlighted.

"Bruno, have you noticed this verse before?"

I handed him back his Bible.

"Let's see now." Bruno said.

Then he read it aloud:

"'Above all, taking the shield of faith, with which you shall be able to quench all the fiery darts of the wicked.' I remember seeing this. But it didn't get through my thick skull till today!"

"But it got through!" Carmelita said.

Diego began to pray. "Lord, on the night of the fire, You sent an angel with Bruno. Few can know, like Bruno, what it's like to be protected by an angel. You've protected Bruno for a purpose. We pray that he'll find that purpose and that your path for him will be clear. In Jesus' Name we pray."

We joined Diego in saying: "Amen."

"So, what do I do now?" Bruno asked.

"What do you wanna do?" Diego replied.

"I wanna get baptized."

"Well, let's go! I've got a baptismal at my place." Diego said. "Julio knows how to get there. I'll be waiting."

Diego got out of Julio's food truck and took off in his taxi.

Chapter 8

The Secret Church

It only took a few minutes to get to Diego's place. It was an old three-story building on Yesler Way. The double door garage made it look like it had once been an auto repair shop. When Diego hit his remote, the doors rolled up together. My hunch was right, it *had* been a garage. Diego pulled his taxi into one of the garage bays and motioned Julio to pull into the other bay. Then Diego hit the remote again and the doors closed behind us.

"This is our home." He said. "As long as you have lots of fire sprinklers, *and guns*, it's safe."

The greasy steel door that led from the garage to his building was heavily weighted, like those found in government buildings. He pulled it open, and we found ourselves inside a large foyer. It was like passing from one century to the next. And it wasn't just that Diego's place was newly renovated, it was luxurious. Once inside, there were three more doors, each with a plaque. One of the plaques had a painting of a kitchen, another, a living room, and the third, a chapel. We entered the chapel door. Diego motioned for us to sit in front. Then he spoke through an intercom.

"Hi, Tessie. We have guests."

"Okay, Diego. Give us a few minutes."

Diego left us for a few minutes and returned with more guests. There were a couple dozen kids and nearly the same number of adults. One of the guests was Hank.

"This is my beautiful bride, Millie." He said.

After I'd greeted Millie, the other guests took turns introducing themselves. Once we'd had a chance to meet, we went back to our seats.

Diego handed Bruno swim trunks and a baptismal gown, then led him to a changing booth. By the time Bruno had come out of the booth, Diego had already removed the cover of the baptismal.

"I'd like to introduce you to Bruno." He said. "Bruno is the

59

fireman who saved the 17 missing kids..."

But before Diego could finish his sentence, there were gasps, then cries from the children, joyful cries that they would finally meet the man who saved them.

"Bruno, these are the kids you saved. I'll introduce you to each one of them in a few minutes."

When Diego stepped into the baptismal, Bruno followed. Then Diego took hold of Bruno's elbow with one hand and put his other hand on the back of his neck, dunking Bruno in the water.

"I baptize you in the Name of the Father, and of the Son, and of the Holy Spirit." He said.

When Bruno came up for air, we all shouted:

"Amen!"

Bruno was wet from the water and his tears, but he was smiling as I'd never seen him before, even at the site of Carmelita. It was a blessed smile and a blessed day. My old friend Bruno had finally come to terms with the faith that was woven into his daily life, a faith that came by hearing the Word of God, even as a spectator of the hypocritical televangelists. As the saying goes, *it's not the messenger, it's the message.* And the Word of God had become real for Bruno, not only after the realization that an angel had directed his steps, or even in the weeks and months before his baptism, but as far back as the blaze, Bruno's walk in God's Word had begun. But today, his mind and spirit were one, fixed on his precious Savior, and the fellowship that everyone in that room now shared with him.

None of the children waited for Bruno to get into dry clothes. Like bees they swarmed him, hugging him till there was not a proverbial dry eye in the chapel.

It was a beautiful sight. But I couldn't help wondering, with Dr. Jensen's fall, and the news coverage of the 17 missing kids, would we now find ourselves in the Fed's crosshairs.

Chapter 9

Back to the Sortida

Following our afternoon of fellowship, Diego took us to the hotel. There was no small amount of activity when we arrived.

"I figured they'd be waiting for us." Bruno said.

"Me too." Diego agreed.

As we pulled in, a man in black directed us to a parking spot. Bruno rolled down his window and said.

"Fancy seeing you here, Chet."

"Yeah, fancy." Chet replied. "And I suppose you'll give me standard Bruno if I ask you any questions?"

"That's... what I'll give you, standard Bruno. And these are my friends, standard Ron and standard Diego."

"Oh, so that's it." Chet said.

"On orders." Bruno replied.

Bruno rolled up the window, then gave us some advice.

"Feds. Never talk to 'em about anything. They record everything. They'll charge you with perjury for saying a girl's pretty one day and beautiful the next. And you can go to prison for lying to 'em. But they can lie to you, or even deceive the President of the United States, committing treason, without any repercussions *what so ever*. Well, I'm preaching to the choir. You two already know that."

"The whole country knows." Diego said. "If the cook, the driver, the maid, the food truck vendor, and all the other people with names like mine know, then everyone knows."

"Couldn't have said it better myself." Bruno replied. "Welp, we'll hear the Feds' lies on TV for the next week. I wonder what nonsense they're leaking on Dr. Jensen and the Harrys in hazmats. Whatever it is, you can be sure it's deception straight from the serpent's mouth."

"Looks like Edwin's getting a little bit antsy over there by the door." I said.

61

"Looks like it." Diego said. "I'll say goodbye for now. Don't forget, Bruno. Carmelita and her folks will be in the banquet hall later, it's Ron's practice session for becoming godfather."

"How could I forget." Bruno replied.

"Got it, Diego." I said.

Edwin held the door for us as we got out of Diego's cab. He was acting like a stuffed shirt, which wasn't hard, considering he was a bellhop at a five-star hotel. But he was hiding something with his rigid manner. He signaled with his eyes in the direction of our room on the 2nd floor, while handing Bruno a package with a note.

"Someone left this for you. Sir Bruno." He said.

His formality clued us in that something was up.

"Why, thank you, young man." Bruno replied.

It was obvious Edwin was signaling us and the package had something to do with it. I figured Bruno took it the same way: our room was bugged. When we got to the room, Bruno started walking around with his hand in the paper bag. Every so often he ripped a bug from under a table or beneath a cabinet. After a few minutes he had barely enough room in the package for all the bugs he'd removed. Then he said:

"Look at this one. Looks like it's got two sets of prints on it."

I played along with his ad lib, figuring Bruno was indicating there was still one bug left to hear our words.

"You brought a fingerprint kit with you?" I asked.

"Oh yeah, you never know when a dirty cop might try to frame you. My dad passed me down a database of dirty cop prints." Bruno messed with his phone for a second, took photos of the fingerprints, and then said:

"There, these oughta be out to a few thousand people within seconds. The Feds can't hide evidence if all the world has it."

Now, I wasn't sure if Bruno was kidding or not. And if I couldn't tell, the Feds couldn't either. Bruno's knack for mind games with cops was unmatched. I wondered if his detective dad had been teaching him this stuff since he was a toddler. Bruno sure loved his dad. It was hard to see him grieve when he lost him. I think that was part of the reason he kept to a script whenever talking with cops, to honor his dad by putting into practice the things he'd been taught. Now don't get me wrong. I love good cops, and obviously Bruno did too, his father was a good cop. It's the counterfeits that should never get respect, the ones who become brown shirts overnight when the orders come down.

"Hey Chet," Bruno yelled at the coffee table. "Any of your prints on these illegal bugs?"

I was as certain as Bruno, that Chet, the Fed we spoke with at the entrance, had heard every word we'd just exchanged.

"What'll we do with these bugs?" Bruno asked.

"To the evidence room with them." I said.

"Just what I was a figurin on doin." Bruno replied. "I'll make sure to send one to each of dad's favorite police chiefs."

Now, neither of us were ad-libbing. Bruno opened the app he'd been using for delivery of legal documents for his mom's estate. In a few minutes, there was a knock at the door. The first delivery driver had arrived. He had a pouch. Bruno dropped one of the bugs in it with a note. A few minutes later and another driver appeared. Bruno had another bug and another note. They kept arriving till all the bugs except the one under the coffee table had been sent. Bruno made sure to speak directly to it.

"My dad knew lots of police chiefs." Bruno said. "And Dad told me, 'Nothing can keep you safer than evidence on those who wanna put you in a cage.' I'll take that advice, Chet. Oh yeah, he also told me it's a felony to interfere with evidence sent to law enforcement, not to mention, it's obstruction of justice. So, what do you suppose Chet's up to, old Ron? Why are they trailing us, considering we're just a couple of old white men?"

"Hmm, Chet? I can't recall that name. And are you talking to a coffee table, Bruno? I don't think either of us are competent to be answering any questions at our age. Did you introduce me to someone named Chet? My memory isn't what it used to be."

"Now that you mention it, old Ron. I can't recall either. So, what was the question?" Bruno asked.

"I can't recall. It must not matter." I said. "Besides, I gotta eat my oatmeal and take a nap. I can't even remember what we ate for lunch. Can you? Did we already eat our oatmeal?"

"Well, here's my answer."

Bruno signaled me to turn off my hearing aids, turning off his as well. They doubled as ear plugs when turned off, diminishing anything we might hear to no more than muffled gibberish. Then Bruno hit the remote for the TV and maxed out the volume.

Yeah, being deaf has its perks. The Fake News was spewing out the Feds' spin and neither Bruno nor I could make out a word. Now I don't know how well the Feds listening on the other end of the bug could hear, but after the sound blast Bruno gave them, I doubt they could hear at all. Such a shame, the best anchors money could buy and the Feds who bought them couldn't hear them spinning. Then Bruno grabbed the bug from under the coffee table, flushed it down the toilet, and said:

"There! Now they can get their news straight from the source."

Chapter 10

The Sortida Ballroom

Bruno rarely dressed to match his triple pension and well invested assets, but today he was a suitor, meeting the parents of
his beloved Carmelita. He wore freshly pressed slacks, a white
shirt, and Tony Lama boots.

"You ready, old Ron?" He said, stepping into the elevator.

"To go home, yes." I replied.

"Yeah, it's gotta be tough, no family around."

"Look who's talking." I said.

"Welp, at least I got potential. So old Ron, when's the last time
you dated?"

"Bruno, you know I don't date."

"Yep, old Ron, you just marry the prettiest girl at the ball before Cinderella's coach turns into a pumpkin. The problem is you
never sold shoes. You keep thinking you got Cinderella, just to
find out the shoe didn't fit. You keep getting the wicked stepsis-
ter, not Cinderella. But if Solomon can't figure you out, neither
can I. *The way of a man with a maiden.*"

"You're right, Bruno. You're right." I said.

When the elevator reached the top floor, the doors opened to
the Sortida Ballroom. Our hosts were waiting. Edwin was there
to introduce me to my soon-to-be godchildren, his brothers, sisters, cousins, nephews and nieces. And Carmelita was waiting to
whisk Bruno off to meet her family.

Now I missed my kids even more. All these people, and not
one related to me. Edwin's extended relatives were there too, plus
the family of Bella, Edwin's fiancée. And Carmelita had an end-
less lineup of relatives waiting to shake Bruno's hand. I felt ut-
terly alone for the first time since I'd gotten on my flight from
Phoenix to Seattle. And now I was beginning to think I'd finally
cracked. The stress of the last few years had been huge, but I'd
never lost touch with reality. And yet, here I was, staring at

Victoria as she looked 40 years ago. I closed my eyes for a moment and prayed. When I opened them, Edwin said.

"I knew you'd notice her. She is my cousin. She looks…"

I finished his sentence.

"Exactly like Victoria."

Man was I glad I wasn't going nuts. I went from thinking I was losing it to, well, something entirely different.

"We thought your reaction might answer a question for us." Edwin said. "And it has. You loved my mother."

Gazing at Edwin's cousin, my eyes grew misty. I felt a déjà vu, but it was more than that. She didn't just look like Victoria. For a moment, she *was* Victoria. She stood in front of the same window that framed the same Seattle sunset, just a memory ago. The chandelier twinkled in her dark eyes, as if signaling to skyscrapers now lit with reflections of the city lights. The commuter ferries on Puget Sound were lit up too. Yes, it had been over 40 years since we'd dined at the Sortida, but my heart was just twenty-five tonight. And my desire? Haven't I said it already? This was Victoria in the flesh. I had to know more about this intergenerational twin. I wasn't shy, so I approached her.

"Everyone's been waiting to see my reaction to you. Well, I know you're not a memory. I'm Ron, and you are?"

"Mika. Nice to meet you, Ron. And yes, I know. I look like my aunt, but I'm jealous of her."

"Jealous? Why is that?" I asked.

"Well, how many women die having been truly loved by two men? The one who married her and the one who never got over her?"

"You've got a point." I said. "But I really didn't love her. At least not the way a husband does. You see, love is a verb. And I was only with her for a few months. How much could I love her in that amount of time?"

"Ron, I know the whole story. You loved her with a love that few women can know."

66

"Thanks, Mika. I'll take that as a compliment."

"And it is." Mika said." "Men aren't complimented enough."

"Your husband must be a happy man." I said.

I used the not-so-subtle Filipino ploy to see if she was married.

"Oh, I'm not married" Mika said. "I'm NBSB, no boyfriend since birth."

Had I been of today's generation, I might have been shocked by her placing a value on chastity. But some of us still value it. I knew that among traditional Filipinos, if the father was actively involved in the raising of his daughter, she'd take to heart the old-fashioned values he taught. One was to have no boyfriend till completing college.

"So how long have you been in Seattle?" I asked.

"Only a year." Mika said. "I just graduated from Seattle Pacific University."

"Congratulations!" I said. "Do they have a satellite program in the Philippines, or was it a transfer-in?"

"Oh, it wasn't a transfer-in." Mika said. "I was expecting to enter their PHD program. But when I got here, they told me they wouldn't accept some of my credits, even though I'd earned my Master's in Christian Music Ministry."

"Oh, that must have been really disappointing." I said.

"Yes, it was. But I was brought up to make the best of things. And since my father had paid all my school fees, including the dormitory, I just took up another Master's, this time in Early Childhood Education."

"You say it like it's so easy, Mika, you *just took up another Master's*. Then you completed it in a year? You're obviously very studious."

"Not really, Ron. It's just that I knew this might be my last chance to study in the states, so I made the best of it."

"Well, whoever marries you will be a very fortunate man. You're smart *and* you've kept yourself pure for your future husband."

"Ron, men here might consider themselves fortunate to win my hand in marriage, but in my country, as you know, women like me are a dime a dozen. And by our standards, I'm already an old maid."

"Women like you? An old maid, Mika? I don't see you as an old maid."

"I'm sorry, Ron. I'm normally not so pessimistic. I guess it's just my nerves at meeting you."

"No worry, Mika. And if it means anything. I had butterflies in my stomach walking over to meet you."

"Really, Ron?"

"Honestly, Mika? No. But I won't tell if you don't. So, was there something that prevented you from finding a husband at Seattle Pacific University?"

My brutish teasing worked. Mika retaliated by taking our conversation to the next level.

"My aunt warned me about you, Ron. You never talk about what you're really after. But she said if you fall in love with a girl, she'll have you for life, as long as she doesn't betray you. Is that what my aunt and your wives did to you?"

"Let's not go there, Mika. I'm talking to a girl like few I've met. I'd rather not be distracted by all that."

"Oh, where is that girl you're talking to? Like few you've met, huh? Does she give you butterflies?" Mika said.

"There's that fire." I replied. "So, was there something that kept you from finding a husband at Seattle Pacific University?"

"Well, yes." She said. "I didn't have a PHD."

"Wow, a PHD is now required to get a husband? I didn't realize things were that tough."

"Ha-ha, yes, Ron. The dating apps all require that now. Silly. You probably know why. My *Daddy* required it. But now he says he'll waive the PHD requirement on one condition."

"And what's that condition?" I asked.

"I'll answer that later, Ron. But for now, I'd like to introduce you to the rest of my family."

I was surprised at how easily I could converse with Mika in a large room full of people. She even understood my kidding. Better yet, I understood hers. Normally, the background sounds would have made a conversation impossible with my hearing aids. Then I realized, the room had been silent. We had an audience. Mika's relatives had been listening to our entire conversation. And according to Philippine custom, my ploy to find out if she was married was taken as a sincere interest in courting her. And as soon as she said: *I'd like you to meet the rest of my family*, the interest was considered mutual. So, I wasn't surprised when the first introduction was to her father, Cesar, Edwin's uncle.

"My name is Cesar and I'm Mika's father. So good to meet you, Ron. You're very popular."

"As he should be." Edwin said. "He is the guest of honor, and the soon to be godfather of the Santos family."

"I'm honored by all of this." I said. "And Cesar, meeting your daughter was a once in a lifetime treat."

"Once in a lifetime, Ron says. You see the impression my baby has made on Ron?"

Cesar's voice bellowed as if he were on stage. And he could have been. He was the only one speaking. He looked at his daughter, Mika, with a smile, then looked at me with a grin.

"You're the kind of man we like, Ron. And as our beloved Dolphy, our most famous comedian, once said, *Age does not matter, as long as matter does not age.* And I can see from your health that your matter has not aged. From your feet to your shoulders, you don't look a day over twenty-five. Now, from the neck up, that's another story. But seriously, Ron, I kid you as I would kid a family member. Just take my frankness as an acceptance of the reality. My Mika has fallen in love with an old man, and I approve."

Wow did that come out of nowhere. Cesar was telling me his daughter had fallen in love with me. I wasn't shy, but a slight blush came over me. I knew that in the Philippines a marriage with such an age difference wasn't out of the question, and that sometimes a foreigner would marry a Filipina within a couple of weeks of their first meeting. Both my marriages had been exactly that. But now, we were in the *United States*, and I'd just met her. Even so, customs are hard to buck. And for traditional families in the Philippines, there is no such thing as dating. There is only courtship. Not to mention, for Christians like me, the same applied. A best-selling book among Evangelicals is even titled, *I Kissed Dating Goodbye.*

Mika continued where her father left off.

"Ron." She said. "I was the one who my Aunt Victoria put in charge of finding you. And I ended up knowing more about you than she did. And the more I learned, the more I understood what my aunt saw in you. The opportunities you gave up, just so you could be with your children, the losses you suffered, but overcame. I... I respect you, very much."

"Well, thank you, Mika, but isn't that what all men do as they age? Any family man is going to do his best to keep his family together."

"Yes, Ron, that's mostly true. But we both know there's more to your story than that."

"As much as I enjoy compliments, Mika. I'd rather hear about you. I walked out of that elevator one man. And now? I've aged backwards 40 years. And the reason isn't because of your resemblance to a woman I once loved. No, it's you, Mika. You're full of life. You're confident. And you've dedicated your life to Christian ministry, which makes you eligible for any Christian man's love. But the reason I feel my clock ticking backwards is because no other woman, not even your aunt, stepped right into my heart and took up residence the way you have just now."

Until that moment, everything about Mika was serious. But now, the seriousness vanished as her playful eyes lit up her face.

"Did you hear that?" She said, searching my eyes. "That was

me bolting the door of your heart and swallowing the key. Now you'll never get me out of here." She pressed her hand against my chest. "Oh, it's really beating now."

And it was. But instead of reminiscing how similar she was to Victoria, I couldn't help but immerse myself in the moment. I needed healing. And this was a healing as few men know. They say a relationship will never be any better than it is at the beginning. Well, it could be 10% of what I'd just experienced and that would be enough for the rest of *my* life.

Our audience, which had been silent, now erupted in laughter, then applause. Then they did something I'd only seen at Filipino wedding banquets. They clinked on their glasses with spoons. This was the signal to the bride and groom to kiss. Mika's father diplomatically interrupted. It seems his relatives were too rushed even for his fast-paced idea of engagement.

"There will be plenty of time for clinking of glasses when there is a real wedding." He said. "Tonight is the practice for our guest of honor, Ron, who will become godfather to most of our family on one blessed day, this Sunday. Now, please, I encourage all of you to get to know Ron. Mika is anxious to introduce him to you."

Mika took me around the room introducing me and telling her family things about me that I'd even forgotten. I hadn't realized I'd been through so much. The hand of God heals. And more than ever, I had needed His healing hand over the past few years.

After the introductions, Mika took me aside to one of the private conference rooms that were adjacent to the banquet hall. It had thick glass windows like a recording studio. And though we were behind closed doors, Mika whispered.

"Ron. I know this all seems too fast, but my family is crazy about you. They say you're my perfect match, a Christian author who writes storybooks for kids and who already has connections to our family. But... it's not too fast for me, Ron. I... I... well, there's time for that later. But there's something else."

71

Mika continued to whisper, this time, right next to my ear.

"We got a tip. The Feds are going to question Bella, Carmelita, and me about everything we know about you, Bruno, and Edwin. And you know there's only one way to stop them, the same way that real criminals stop them. That's for Bruno to marry Carmelita, Edwin to marry Bella, and you to marry me."

I whispered back in Mika's ear.

"Mika, you know this is nuts."

Mika nodded her head. Her glistening black hair caressed my cheek as I continued to whisper in her ear.

"And you realize you just proposed to me."

Mika nodded her head again. My mind was beginning to drift as I felt the warmth from her cheek, but I kept my focus.

"And since you've investigated everything about me, you know I don't have any regrets about my past marriages, and that I believe each one, for whatever reason, was what God wanted for me at that time."

Mika nodded once again. This time lifting her hand to gently stroke my beard.

"Now this, Mika, I doubt you knew. But before marrying each of my ex-wives, I laid out a fleece. I requested a sign from God that it was His will that I marry them."

"I knew that too." Mika said.

"Wow, Mika, you really know me!"

"Yeah, Ron, ha-ha!"

"Anyway, Mika, I'll lay out a fleece. I can't say yes or no to you without God's consent. You just proposed to me. So, here's the fleece I'm laying out. If Carmelita proposes to Bruno, and Bella proposes to Edwin, then I'll take it as a sign from God that I must accept your proposal."

"Yes, yes. Ron. We'll leave it up to God!" Mika said.

Our private discussion was now over, and Mika and I left the conference room. It worried me that the Feds were planning to grill the girls. I hated worry. I liked everything to be orderly, or at least, not chaotic. And I could think of no greater chaos than to see people I loved grilled by the Feds as if they were criminals. And in less than 12 hours, *people I loved*, had increased more than at any time in my life. We're to love our brothers and sisters in Christ and this is no chore, no difficult command to follow. I did love these new brothers and sisters in Christ.

Alejandro, Carmelita's father, now stepped up to the banquet hall stage where a microphone was waiting. He whispered into the mic to test it, then began.

"As you know, my daughter, my Carmelita, is a Goldstar Wife."

Applause erupted as everyone stood to acknowledge Carmelita's loss. Her father continued.

"In the seven years since her husband gave his life in the call of duty, my Carmelita has raised her three children well. All of them now have their own families. After her loss, my daughter waited tables at her uncle's restaurant till it closed due to the lies of the last few years. And it was while she waited tables that she met the man who I *hope,* will ask me for her hand in marriage. That man is Bruno, the man who saved the 17 missing kids from that blazing inferno three years ago."

There was now a hush as all eyes were on Bruno. There was no spotlight on him, but it was as if there were. He clumsily put away the handkerchief he'd been using to wipe sweat from his face. It wasn't like Bruno to sweat, at least not out of his fireman's uniform. So I was just as anxious as our new found families to see what would unfold.

Alejandro motioned Bruno to step up to the stage. It was a slightly raised platform with an old-fashioned mic. Bruno swaggered to the platform, then one stair at a time, he ascended with heavy steps, as if dreading what was about to happen. Then he spoke into the mic.

"Alejandro, I can't ask for your daughter's hand in marriage. There's something wrong with her, damaged goods."

Alejandro's demeanor went from happiness to burning anger in a millisecond. But Bruno wasn't finished. He pulled up his pant legs and unzipped his Tony Lama boots to reveal there was nothing inside, except for his prosthetic feet. He'd lost both legs from the shins down saving the 17 missing kids. Then he said:

"I'm damaged goods, Alejandro. There's got to be something wrong with any woman who wants me."

Alejandro's anger was extinguished as quickly as it had been ignited and he was quick to reply.

"I was happy, at first, to know my Carmelita had found a man she could love. But now? I'm overjoyed at how wisely she has chosen: A man who will *surely fill the boots* of her late husband. Carmelita, come up here."

Alejandro now placed Carmelita's hand in Bruno's and said, "You no longer need ask for my daughter's hand in marriage, *I'm asking you to take it*. And Carmelita, it is honorable that you should propose to Bruno."

Carmelita got down on both knees and grasped Bruno's legs, what was left of them, and while looking up at him, said in a thick Spanish accent.

"Bruno, there is no better proposal that I can give than this, I just *love* the name Bruno. It sounds like the name of a bold man, a say whatever you feel like kind of man. And you've said what you feel like today, my Bruno. Take me as your wife, for a day or for life. I am yours just the way you want me."

The applause was so loud that if it weren't for the mic, even Bruno's bellowing voice would have been drowned out when he said, "I will."

And that was more than Bella, Edwin's fiancée, could bear. This was not the composed mastermind who'd planned our entry into the hospital. This was a sweating, twitching, wild eyed girl out of control. Her lip curled and her eyes squinted to keep back tears. She couldn't even speak, but she could scream.

"Daddy!"

Her father, Sergio, who'd been standing next to Alejandro and her other relatives on stage, quickly grabbed the mic.

Just as quickly, Bella pulled out a compact, powdered her face, and glossed her lips. Composed again, she nodded to her father.

"Ahem," Sergio now spoke into the Mic. "My daughter has caught the attention of a young man who deems her both honorable and worthy to follow him in marriage, and I approve. Please come up here Edwin."

No sooner had Edwin stepped up to the platform than Bella kneeled next to him at Carmelita's direction, who by now had her camera ready and was directing the shots. Bella posed while she put her arm around the back of Edwin's legs and leaned the right side of her face against his left thigh in perfect selfie style. Then she gazed lovingly at Edwin, and she repeated the words that Carmelita had spoken to Bruno.

"Edwin, take me as your wife, for a day or for life. I am yours, just the way you want me."

Mika pulled on my arm indicating she wanted to say something in my ear. Being much taller, I leaned down so I could hear her.

"I'm shy to do what Carmelita did, Ron, but Carmelita's words were so beautiful that I want to say them to you before I forget them. You already heard my father say he approves of you, just like Carmelita's father approved of Bruno and Bella's father approved of Edwin. So, I'll propose to you now."

"Take me as your wife, for a day or for life. I am yours, just the way you want me."

"I will." I answered.

Neither Mika nor I realized she'd been shouting. I'd removed my hearing aids since they'd begun to interfere with my hearing in the banquet hall, and Mika knew it. So she shouted so loud that *even the helpers in the kitchen could hear.* Then *they* and all our families joined in applause, for us as well as for the other couples.

But Carmelita, Bella, and Mika weren't finished. They began

taking turns reenacting what Carmelita had started. It made me wonder how much the craze for selfies had reduced the opportunities for paid models. These women looked like brides on their wedding day. And yet, none wore makeup except Carmelita, who used it more to smudge than out of necessity.

While the girls were doing their reenactments, Diego arrived.

"You missed a lot." I said.

"I didn't miss nothin." He whispered. "Carmelita went live just before her proposal. And it's gonna drive the Feds nuts."

Carmelita looked over to where Diego and I were standing as if waiting for a signal. Diego gave her the thumbs up. Then she ceremoniously touched the screen of her phone.

"There." Diego continued to whisper. "She just tweeted for 250 million X users to see. If going live didn't send the message to the Feds. Elon will."

"What message?" I asked.

"That we've got them in check. If they don't move fast, it's checkmate. *Isn't this fun?*"

Fun? Maybe the question should have gone to Bruno. Bruno loved messing with cops. But maybe I could acquire a taste for it. My fight or flight reaction hadn't hit these levels in years and my clarity of thought was euphoric. The Feds were now certainly in a rush to grab the girls. But if Bruno, Edwin, and I had a chance to marry our now fiancées, before the Feds got to them, any leverage they had with threats of contempt would vanish. A wife doesn't *have* to testify against her husband. And these girls had tons of stuff on us. Bella had gotten us into the hospital with Edwin's assistance. Carmelita was there too. And Mika? She knew more about me than even my best friend Bruno. And I was beginning to suspect that she was the one who reserved my room. She wanted a wedding, why wouldn't she want a wedding suite? But now, the Fed's goldmine of possible witnesses was about to collapse, *if only we could be wed before they caught up with us.* Despite my concern, humor had an odd way of creeping into my thoughts. The irony of Carmelita burning up the Internet hit me. Bruno was famous for putting out fires and here he was, about to marry the Internet pyromaniac. First, Carmelita goes live, then she tweets, starting an Internet fire that would burn for weeks.

All this prompted me to check my phone. #bruno, #17missingkids, and #dirtyfeds were all trending. And here we were, about to put a brick wall in front of the Feds investigation, right when the creeps giving them orders must have been increasing the pressure. Yes, Carmelita had lit a fire, and I was loving it. And I could see in Bruno's eyes that he was loving it too.

I'd officiated at Bruno's first wedding, so I knew there was a three-day waiting period between getting a license and getting married in Washington. So there was only one solution: Las Vegas. Diego held out a Faraday bag to drop our phones in, signaling we were on the move. He'd already proved to us he was a genius at escape, having moved 17 missing kids into hiding. And like those kids, we had no choice, we had to escape. And the only way to escape legally was with a quick trip to Las Vegas. We had to be married before the Feds could grab us. Then I realized, I wasn't the only one who knew we had to get out of there. Our fiancées' families had closed ranks around us. And Diego, Bruno, Edwin and I, along with the girls, were slowly being pushed to the exit.

Chapter 11

In Flight

We quickly made our way down the seven flights of stairs to the 2nd floor. As we passed my room, Edwin glanced at the ceiling camera. It was still on the blink. He spoke silently. Bruno and I read his lips.

"I'll tell you about that later." He said.

We continued down the side stairs from the 2nd floor, exiting the same way as when we'd gone to the hospital. This time, a van was waiting for us.

"Vamo nos!"

The driver spoke silently. How did he know we were deaf? Or was it that I'd forgotten to turn my hearing aids back on. Either way, I understood his words. We all got into his vehicle, and he headed in the direction of the airport. Driving quickly, he made every light on the way to the 6th Avenue on-ramp. In five minutes, we exited to Georgetown.

Shortly after merging onto Airport Way, we turned into one of the flight centers at Boeing Field. We'd remained silent the whole trip. We knew the Feds could have bugs anywhere. Our driver pulled up next to a small jet poised for take-off. He motioned with his chin, letting us know the jet was for us.

A stewardess was waiting for us at the top of the stairs. She took us to our seats. Each couple had an elegant table with chairs to match. Just then, Tessie, Diego's wife, popped out from behind the curtain that covered the galley. She placed pairs of mono-grammed *his* and *hers* napkins on each of our tables. Mine read RM. Mika's read MM.

So I was right. We were on our way to Las Vegas. Mika Santos would soon be Mika Miller. And after we and the rest of our en-tourage were married, the Feds couldn't charge any of us with contempt for refusing to talk. Everyone in Diego's church was married, or minors. And if the minors refused to talk, what could the Feds do, lock them up? How incriminating would that look, not for us, but for the Feds. Nope, all the Feds' questions would be worthless once we were married.

And were there ever questions, we all knew about the 17 missing kids, as well as the *crime* of keeping them safe. The kids had even been at Diego's church for Bruno's baptism. We could all be charged with conspiracy... *if* the Feds found out. Yes, conspiracy to protect the kids from the villains the Feds worked for. But without proof of a crime, what could they investigate? Yes, Dr. Jensen might be willing to say something about our visit. But was he going to open his mouth just so we'd be charged with the misdemeanor crime of bypassing security? I'm sure he and the two Harrys in hazmats just wanted everything to go back to the way it was, before they'd been caught, caught fleeing the scene of what didn't have to be a crime. If Dr. Jensen admitted he fell out the window, what crime had the two Harrys in hazmats committed? Was running out of the hospital with cash falling out of their pockets a crime? No. Was it suspicious? Of course. *But when was the last time a hospital official had been investigated? As far as I know, not since the lockdowns began.* The easiest thing for Dr. Jensen to do would be to say exactly what happened, but without mentioning me or Bruno. After all, me and Bruno wouldn't have any problem blabbing about Dr. Jensen's crimes. And we could point to the cash on the two Harrys in hazmats for proof. No, it would be better for Dr. Jensen, and his two accomplices, if he told the truth about how he fell out the window.

"I fell out the window when my electric shoe buffer got hold of my foot and sent me flying. My attorney has already filed suit against the manufacturer."

But it's fairly certain he'd be keeping his mouth shut about us. Two ear witnesses to his careless bragging about his crimes would put him in more trouble than he already was with his wife. Poor Dr. Jensen, his estranged wife had attached his assets and by now had possession of his beloved Mercedes. Should I pity him?

Nah.

So here we were, in a private jet on our way to Las Vegas, about to use the same scheme the Mob used to hide crimes from the Feds: marriage. And instead of prison, I was about to be sentenced to life in Mika's embrace. I hoped this time it'd be without parole.

Yet our soon-to-be marriage was more than just a scheme. We were matched as few couples can boast, despite the fact that our courtship had barely begun. Add to that, we were simply following orders. Jesus said, *"Behold, I send you forth as sheep in the midst of wolves: be ye therefore, wise as serpents, and harmless as doves."*

Wolves described exactly what the Feds had become. What else would you call those acting on orders from child traffickers. How could it be anything else? 85,000 unaccompanied minors and counting. Senator Josh Hawley even called it *the largest child trafficking ring in American History.* All released without any method to keep track of them after they'd crossed the border into the United States. With numbers that high, it's obvious that Epstein was simply a shiny object used to distract us from the bigger crime. It had all been theater. Then the Feds assured the public that Epstein had hung himself. But nobody believed them. And the most famous coroner in the country stated that Epstein's injuries were such that they could *not* have been self-inflicted. Or was it Epstein? Was a DNA test done?

While I mused about our situation, the jet's monitors popped on with one of the Fake News channels. As might be expected, they were busy weaving their tangled web of deceit. As usual, it was on behalf of the Feds. It wasn't easy to remain silent hearing their tripe, but we did, to keep the Feds from tracking us via voice prints.

Bruno grabbed all the remotes that were in slots next to our tables. And one by one, he turned them on to see what was on the other news channels. It was eerie. Each monitor had a different anchor, but they were all parroting the same lines.

"The FBI has a name for the pair that pushed Dr. Jensen out his window: *The Comorbidities*. It seems the two men who are being held for attempted murder, left a calling card of sorts. Dr. Jensen was clutching a scrap of paper when he was admitted to the hospital. On it, was a single word: *Comorbidities*. The suspects are believed to be members of a radical insurrectionist group known for their white supremacist beliefs. They're being held without bail in an undisclosed facility. What would we do without the brave men and women of the FBI?" And like a musical round of row your boat, the anchors on each one of the monitors ended with: "What would we do without the brave men and women of the FBI?" "What would we do without the brave men and women of the FBI?" "What would we do without the brave men and women of the FBI?"

It was uncanny. But the local reporter *did* have something to add. And as I listened, I thought to myself, *"There goes her career."*

"We have a scoop." She said. "But I must clarify, these are still unconfirmed reports. But our sources say, the two suspects found running from Dr. Jensen's office in hazmat suits, might not have been the only ones who entered his office before he was pushed out the window."

"How's that Mary?" Her sidekick asked.

"Well, Bert, our sources say, both men claim that as they were about to exit the elevator onto Dr. Jensen's floor, two other men in hazmat suits stepped into the elevator, blocking their exit momentarily. And now we have security video that may support that claim. Let's take a look."

The video was edited down to five snippets: Bruno and me stepping out of the elevator, Bruno and me leaving Dr. Jensen's office, Bruno and me going into the elevator, the two Harrys in hazmats stepping out of the elevator, and finally, the two Harrys in hazmats running out of Dr. Jensen's office, past the nurse's station, and into the elevator.

"Well, Mary, it looks rather incriminating to me. It's as if the two suspects were leaving, and when they got into the elevator, they changed their minds. Then they went back to Dr. Jensen's office and pushed him out the window."

"That's exactly what I see." Mary replied.

They'd seen no such thing. Bruno and I were witnesses to the entire event. There were no cameras in Dr. Jensen's office when he fell out the window. What man on the take would allow his every move to be recorded. And yet, without showing a clip, they were trying to spin the narrative that Dr. Jensen had been pushed. They were gas-lighting. There was no scoop. The clips were simply an attempt to get viewers to think they saw a clip that didn't exist, one of Dr. Jensen being pushed. These *news* anchors were no different than dirty cops that plant evidence, but the *news* anchors' method, was to drop biases into the minds of viewers.

Bruno and I exchanged knowing looks. These two propagandists weren't risking their jobs, not even close. Left wing *news* anchors, and they all are, take the side of criminals, *unless* they're following orders from the Fake New Department.

Yeah, there's a Fake News Department. How else could the FBI and the CIA have convinced the American public that the assassinations of the 1960s were just coincidences. Four American leaders were assassinated in five years. First, there was Medgar Evers, a civil rights leader who because of ongoing threats to his life was protected by the FBI, a protection that ended shortly before he was assassinated. And he was assassinated the day after then President John F. Kennedy, delivered a major civil rights speech. But of course, that had nothing to do with it, nor with the assassination of the president himself, just five months later. Kennedy was killed *by a lone gunman.* Really? Next came Martin Luther King Jr. His family finally sued, and won, proving it was a conspiracy, and that the convicted gunman wasn't even the triggerman. Finally, just seven days shy of the five-year anniversary of Medgar Evers death, the most likely man to become the Democrat nominee for president, Robert Kennedy, was assassinated. Whether there was direct FBI or CIA involvement, nobody knows. But their influence over the media had begun long before that with the OPC, the Office of Policy Coordination, aka, Official Propaganda Department.

Then there is the strange case of Dr. Fauci, the highest paid government official in American history, whose financial transactions have come under no scrutiny whatsoever by Legacy Media. Yet, according to another doctor, Senator Rand Paul, *"Fauci is a traitor to his country by ordering the production of a super-virus."* And Congresswoman Marjorie Taylor Greene says, *"He should be tried for mass murder and crimes against humanity."* Yeah, they called it Gain of Function until they remembered Gain of Function was every bit as illegal as a super-virus.

Well, from the anchors' spin, it was clear that the Feds were stirring the pot, hoping Bruno and I would react to something that came out on the news. Maybe they were trying to get us to feel pity for their *suspects*, so that we'd confess, and the two Harrys in hazmats wouldn't be charged for something we did.

Well, Bruno and I didn't commit a crime. Dr. Jensen slipped. And if they were going to charge someone falsely, better it be Dr. Jensen's corrupt cronies in hazmats than us.

Besides, the very Feds who were on our trail were likely in on Dr. Jensen's cash deal with the two Harrys in hazmats. It was federal policy that began the payoffs for clot shots in the first place. *Health* insurance companies were incentivized, hospitals were incentivized, and with a combination of incentives from both of those, doctors were incentivized. Not to mention, doctors had long been receiving direct payments from Big Pharma to kill for profit. They call them consultation fees. The nation's addiction epidemic is fueled by prescriptions for opiates and amphetamines such as Adderall. They are recommended for doctor profits, not for patient health, in *consultations* with Big Pharma marketers. On top of that, the United States is one of only two countries where Big Pharma can advertise their drugs direct-to-consumer on TV, Radio, whatever. The elites have already admitted they want to decrease the population. That's called genocide because they're not talking about 30 years from now, they're talking about today. And they're intent on profiting from it while killing our children. Who knows which of the elite and globalist interests are benefiting from it all, but the Feds are their lapdogs. What a name for wolves! They're more like hyenas than the wolves Jesus warned us about. They scavenge for a bite of the action wherever they can. Who can say which agents are literally on the take. But those at the top of federal law enforcement are obviously interested in something other than fidelity, bravery, and integrity. Whether they're working for elite globalist friends or to get petty cash under the table, it's clear something horrendous is going on. And the ones doing it aren't doing it for free. Most men won't murder their fellow citizens, or anyone else for that matter. But the ones who will, wanna get paid. And the Feds know the shots kill. They have friends in the military just like the rest of us. They know the statistics on navy pilots having heart attacks. After the forced vaxes, the heart attacks among pilots increased to nine times the normal rate. Nine times the normal rate and these so-called brothers in arms, the Feds, don't give a hoot in... Well, vengeance is mine sayeth the Lord. I wondered if it would ever be ours.

So, the media was up to something with this story about *The Comorbidities, a white supremacist gang.* Ha! I guess that term now covers Blacks, Hispanics, Filipinos, and all the races of the 17 missing kids. But some of us don't care what race someone is. And for that, *we're* called the racists.

But the media's race-baiting will never stop. Every media personality, also known as propagandist, is the same as a *made-man* in the mafia. They can't have opinions other than the crime boss's opinions. And there's no way to leave, let alone, expose the organization without losing income, family, reputation... and possibly their life. Epstein's list was created to ensure that the Feds would have the same power as the Mob to frame, imprison, and thereby assassinate by proxy, anyone who didn't submit to their control. And now that the list is out, you think anyone on it will be prosecuted or even sued in a so-called civil court? The victims won a $75,000,000 settlement from Deutsche Bank for handling what were alleged to be illegal transactions. What about those who participated in the abuse paid for by those transactions?

So now that Epstein's Lolita Express was no longer around, what would happen? Well, in some form, it is still around, at least for the purpose it was put together: a CIA blackmail scheme for the Feds to hold the Senate, House, Supreme Court, Administration... and if need be, Hollywood, and *all the media*... hostage. But I don't know if you can call it hostage taking. Whores will let you tie 'em up for the right price. And from top to bottom, the power elites don't care what they have to do for their money. As long as they've got those gold rings through their snouts, they've got access to the feeding trough, a trough full of taxpayer dollars.

Bruno turned the channels on the monitors, sparing us from any more Fake News. With a few clicks, he converted them all into aquariums with swimming fish, *instead of talking heads*.

Mika had been silently sitting across from me, studying my face as I watched the news anchors who were joyously licking the jack boots of their paymasters, their career builders, the Feds.

"You're a book." She wrote on a tablet sized white board we had on our table. *"It's like I'm reading between the lines... on your face."*

I erased what she'd written and wrote back. *"Let's just hope the Feds notice the lines on my face more than what's written between them. I wouldn't want to hurt their feelings."*

Together, we both smiled, just shy of laughing. I pointed to the seat belt sign and we buckled up.

As soon as the jet had cleared the runway, Mika began hand

feeding me from a plate of appetizers. But she was more than nourishing me, she was in a sensuous pursuit where pleasing me was the prize. Neither of us dared speak for fear the Feds would know we were on that plane, and the silence was like dry wood on a crackling flame. *Yeah*, here I was, old Ron, thinking in poetry again. But looking at the other couples at their tables, I could see, we were all poets tonight. They could express more with a pastry and a dab of a napkin than any poem I'd ever written. And *Mika?* She was proving that a straight line is *not* the shortest distance when it comes to reaching a man's heart.

Mika used frosting to paint an outline of a kiss on her wrist, then held it to my lips. She sipped from every side of her glass, then raised it for me, turning it, to make sure each place where her mouth touched, mine would too. Yes, it sounds like kids on their first date. But to Mika, this was serious business. I was her man, and it was her tradition to please. I can't imagine what she would have been doing had we been alone. Well, yes I can. But I don't kiss and tell, even if it's just my imagination.

The silence had been a blessing. It forced us to communicate in a world beyond sound, a world where the hearing rarely venture. I was glad I was able to show Mika my world of silence, a world I returned to each time I removed my hearing aids.

Chapter 12

Wedding Words

When we touched down, a helicopter was waiting for us. We went down the stairs from the jet and right back up the ones for the chopper. We still remained silent, which I'm sure was hard for all but Bruno and me. In the years before technology caught up with my kind of hearing loss, I'd been silent a lot. I'd even stopped talking to myself. Why talk, even if it's just to yourself, if it's a one-way conversation. But I was happy to start talking to myself again when these state-of-the-art hearing aids came out. Not because I loved hearing my own voice, but so I could figure out a way to get rid of my Brooklyn accent. Don't get me wrong, there's nothing wrong with a Brooklyn accent, if you're from Brooklyn, but I'm not. And the deafer I got, the thicker my accent became. My kids said my accent sounded like a guy on the radio who I used to listen to. Maybe his was the last voice I heard before the pain from the radio volume became too much. You see, with hearing loss, it's not how loud the volume is, it's how silent certain frequencies are. If someone is deaf in the high frequencies, and someone turns up the master volume, they'll be blasted by the bass just as much as someone with perfect hearing. And those of us with inherited hearing loss generally loose our high frequency hearing first. That translates to the inability to hear consonants. Try hearing if the only sounds you hear are vowels, just five sounds. That's 21 sounds of the alphabet that disappear. So Bruno and I were accustomed to remaining silent. Why talk if you can't hear the other side of the conversation?

The helipad where we touched down was just a short ride from the Las Vegas Marriage Bureau. But there was one detail to take care of. When the chopper blades stopped and we descended the stairs, we were met by a bevy of tailors waiting to fit us for our wedding apparel. A few minutes later and we were in a van to make the 3-minute trip for our marriage licenses. We signed the papers and were back to the helipad just as the tailors returned. White dresses all around for the women and tuxes for the men. The tailors even had portable dressing rooms. Once we changed, we were up the stairs and into the chopper again. The moment we were airborne, the wedding officiant began.

"Good evening. I'm John Smith. Congratulations to each of you. Diego gave me the Wedding Words, as he called them. Is everyone here okay with that?"

We all nodded. The officiant didn't appear curious as to why we were silent. Maybe that was normal, the chopper *was* loud. But before he began reading the words, he reached above the pilot and turned on a monitor. Diego quickly cast his video chat from his phone to the monitor. Now we could see those back at the Sortida Ballroom and they could see us. But this wasn't an ordinary video chat. Diego had it live streamed on X, and millions had joined to witness the wedding of Carmelita to Bruno, the man who'd rescued the 17 missing kids. We were greeted with loud applause by those who'd been patiently waiting back at the Sortida. The officiant began.

"Dearly beloved, we are gathered to join four couples in civil marriage. A civil marriage is just that. You are joined. Grooms, you may kiss your brides."

As each couple kissed, the shouts and hoots from the families at the Sortida Ballroom drowned out the sound of the chopper. By the time their applause died down, we'd landed next to our jet at the Las Vegas airport.

As we stepped out of the chopper, the officiant gave us our certified marriage certificates. We were set, no more worries that the Feds would wedge family against family, loved ones against loved ones. Not that they wouldn't try, but we were all married now. And we could enjoy all the protection that the Mob had enjoyed for years. We could keep secret the location of the 17 missing kids *and* our failed attempt to obtain a signature from Dr. Jensen, two events, neither of which were crimes. Even so, the Feds

Ron and Bruno

had become such that the innocent were now the hunted.

Chapter 13

Fly Me to the Moon

By the time we climbed the stairs of our private jet to Seattle, Diego had our live stream on the widescreen. The surround sound made it like our families were right there with us. And the X viewers could hear what we were saying and see what we were seeing on split screen. This was the biggest conference call I'd ever been on.

Our tables were set with sumptuous dishes, as were the tables at the Sortida. Some of the Santos family had begun clinking their glasses with spoons, their cue for the newlyweds to kiss. But before my lips and Mika's could meet, Cesar, her father, interrupted.

"Ahem, I believe it's fitting that Diego begin with a prayer." Then he motioned to Diego. After Diego had prayed for each couple, as well as their families back at the Sortida, he prayed blessings on the food. Then there was silence…for about two seconds. And once again, the clinking on glasses began. Mika and I accommodated them. It was her day, and this was all part of a Filipino tradition. The clinking of glasses, followed by a kiss, would be repeated many times throughout the evening. And the other couples got in on this Filipino tradition as well.

As we waited for our jet to taxi to the runway, Tessie placed our phones on our tables. But Mika and I hardly noticed, the connection we shared was stronger than any phone signal.

One of Mika's many cousins at the Sortida began playing the upright piano next to the stage. It was a relic from the era of silent movies. I wondered if my grandpa might have played on that very same piano. He used to get gigs around town on his off hours. And who, but the most famous piano player in town, would the Mob bosses hire to play for their guests at the Sortida. I hadn't thought of it before, but Grandpa must have been privy to a lot of untold stories. Prohibition began in 1920 while Grandpa was still playing piano for silent movies at the Moore Egyptian Theater. Why hadn't it entered my mind till now? Grandpa likely played piano at speakeasies. Well, a lot of things hadn't entered my mind. My life had been one series of poor choices, except for having children. Never did I regret choosing to have my beloved kids.

Then I realized, I've got my phone back. I can text them! Immediately I sent them texts about my new marriage and received back nothing but congratulations. How wonderful to have children who wanted their old man happy. And very soon, I'd have even more children.

Mika had been squeezing one of my hands as I texted with the other.

"What did they say?" She asked.

"Congratulations, of course, and that they're looking forward to meeting you."

I didn't want to get teary eyed, so I altered my mood from deep drama to light and inspirational. Mika noticed.

"How is it you can go from one mood to another in the blink of an eye?" She asked.

"I just do." I answered. "Everyone can do it. They just don't. No sense going where I don't want to go. There's a time…"

She finished my sentence. "…for everything, a time to weep, and a time to laugh. Hahahaha!"

Except for my children, I hadn't heard a laugh like Mika's in over 40 years, not since Victoria. But Mika had inherited her aunt's talent for laughter and then some. Hers was as adorable as it was contagious. If there were such a thing as a professional laugher, Mika would be at the top of the field. But tonight, her laughter, and Mika herself, were mine. I was a blessed man. And I knew our children would be too. How could they not be, with a mother who could create laughter for every occasion, even for no occasion at all. Mika saw how her laughter buoyed me and laughed some more. The joy I felt when she laughed was the same joy I felt with my children, and why wouldn't it be? She was now *bone of my bones, flesh of my flesh*: family.

But it was not their laughter that I remembered now, but the tears we'd shed together when we found my son, their brother, dead. The horror at finding him stiff and cold instead of standing in the door greeting us can't be erased in this world. Bastards that killed him! Murderers! The Pusher Man is no longer a song about back-alley heroin pushers. It's about the money grubbing doctors that live among us, prescribing with no regard for life.

A simple entry on a database can prevent doctors from making addiction easy. But if doctors took that simple step, they'd lose their precious *fifty bucks for an appointment*. At least the back-alley pushers earn big bucks. You have to pay them a lot to murder for hire. But doctors will murder your kid for the price of a repeat customer. And about all the doctor gets, after overhead, is fifty bucks, fifty bucks to send their neighbor's kid to the morgue. Then the doctatorship took over and the doctors must have thought they were in heaven. The Fed's bounty to shoot a kid with a clot shot was 250 bucks, dead or alive. All you had to do to win the prize in this shooting match was to shoot 75% of your patients. The kids dropping dead from heart failure shows how successful the campaign of mass shootings was. Tell the kid he's gonna kill Gramma and he'll let you kill him. Nice trick there, *doctors. First, do no harm?* Yeah, sure.

Good thing my anger brought me back from my funk. Mika's eyes, as usual, had been reading my ups and downs between the lines on my face. And what a roller coaster ride that girl's eyes had been on. But Mika wasn't just an observer, she was a doer. While I was lost between her laughter and missing my kids, she was secretly texting every one of them with a link to join us. Then she whispered in my ear.

"I got you a wedding gift. Take a look up there."

Mika pointed to the widescreen. My kids and grandkids were all on X live. They appeared in boxes that formed borders in

92

between and around the two split screens. Then I realized, *Diego* wasn't the one handling this. One of the X influencers was up in the corner of the livestream behind a mic. *We* could only hear each *other*, but thousands of viewers on X live were watching us with a play by play of who we were, where we were, and why we were doing what we were doing.

The X influencer obviously knew nothing about Bruno and me entering Dr. Jensen's office. But he did know the association that Bruno had with the 17 missing kids. And he knew of Bruno's mistreatment at the hands of jack-booted thugs: the nurses and doctors who enforced orders to keep those who could offer hope *away* from those who needed it most. *"Need not even try"* was their answer to loved ones who asked if they could visit their child or parent, brother or sister. At least that's what they said to me when my son was hospitalized, not just once, but twice. And it wasn't even for Covid, the mild disease that killed the gravely ill and morbidly obese. It was for Covert Intentional Death by any means possible. They didn't care if you were in for a few stitches, an OD, or your final battle that would end in death. You were going it alone. Now why hadn't I thought of it till now? Had one of those bastards talked my son into taking the jab at his lowest point, saying he should take it for the sake of his dad? The evil of sacrificing the young for the old, Molech by any other name, is still Molech. Well, we were living in a country of idolaters. Is it any wonder that they'd taken over the medical profession? The Bible says evil men will take over the positions of pastors, why would the profession of doctor be any less susceptible. One deals with your spiritual life, the other deals with your mortal life.

And no marvel, for Satan himself
is transformed into an angel of light.

The fact that Bruno was the reason for the popularity of our X livestream was not lost on his now wife, Carmelita. She came out from behind the galley curtain having redone her makeup. As always, she was 99% perfect, but it was the 1% that drove Bruno wild. This time, she came out with eye shadow to make Blac Chyna blush and a price tag hanging from the back of her gown. Normally, the tag would have been just the kind of imperfection Bruno would have loved, but not with millions of X members watching. So before she turned at an angle where the camera could have picked it up, Bruno snatched it off. But the audience saw it as an ass grab and their comments flew across the screen faster than Dr. Jensen flew out the window, and down to the roof of Julio's Food Truck. Man would I be happy when we could talk openly about everything again. What a happy day when we could use the expression, *faster than Dr. Jensen flew out the window and down to the roof of Julio's Food Truck.* Would future generations even know he wasn't on his way to get a bite? For sure, Mika's laugh juice must have gotten to me. I wondered if it was spread by kisses. With the clinking of glasses, we must have shared a few dozen of those. I know, I don't kiss and tell, but she must have read an instruction book somewhere to kiss like that. Her kisses were therapeutic.

Meanwhile, back at the Sortida, Mika's piano playing cousin, Raul, was just warming up. And as if timed, the seat belt lights went off and Edwin stood up to sing: *"Fly me to the moon, let me play among the stars."* His table with Bella was next to a window, and as he sang, the stars and moon shone behind them in the black Nevada skies. He reproduced the sounds and gestures of Tony Bennett, as only Tony Bennett could, but it was Edwin. When he got to the verse frowned on by me and my fellow Baptists, he changed the words to, *"you are all I long for, not to worship, but adore."*

Maybe this was the reason Edwin hadn't pursued a professional singing career: the idolatry of modern music. He could easily have been a tribute singer, not just in Asia, but anywhere in the world. But nearly all pop songs idolized women. And I hadn't met anyone, not who I'd call brothers, who fell into that trap. *Promise keepers?* I'll call them housekeepers, since unlike a wife, they don't even have a right to complain. Using terms like servant leader doesn't change a doormat into a leader. If a man's wife is in command of his life, then God isn't.

Despite having every part of our wedding festivities sent out to the world on X live, Carmelita was set on doing the work of wedding photographer. Photographer was the only detail Diego had left out. But the girls needed no coaxing to pose and primp as Carmelita directed, nor did the men. It was our wedding too.

By the time the pilot announced our final descent to Boeing Field, we and our families were ready to end the livestream. It had been a long evening. So we said our goodbyes and ended the call.

The last few hours had been all-consuming. It wasn't like me to spend so much time focused on just one person. After all, I had kids who were accustomed to me checking in on them, *despite their having grown up*. Or were they checking in on me and it was just me who was doing the dialing.

I was glad Mika had gotten them in on the livestream. I can imagine her first text to them. "Oh, hi, I'm your new stepmom. I met your dad three hours ago, and now we're married. But the celebration is still in progress. Join us on X live. Here's the link. Hugs and kisses."

But for my kids, such a surprise would *not* be unusual. They were used to me calling them from some remote place and sending them photos of me next to something or someone they could never have imagined. The real and the surreal were never far apart in my world. But Mika had stepped into my life between two equally surreal worlds: one had brought grief, and the other, we could only hope would bring joy and revival. If tonight was an omen, it was a good one. Some who claimed victory in Jesus appeared resigned to accept defeat at the hands of tyrants, but that wasn't in my nature. I was confident we would be kept safe with *the helmet of salvation and the sword of the Spirit, which is the Word of God.* I had my Bible open to this very verse as I pondered it, as I had so many times before. I'd even highlighted it and put a tab on the page for easy reference. Mika was watching as I read it to myself. When I closed the page, she wove her fingers through mine, and said:

"Amen. May God's will be done."

Our jet landed safely at Boeing Field and taxied to the space next to the hangar where we'd boarded. The van we'd arrived in was just outside the fence. When the driver saw Diego, he got out and waived. Then he held up the keys, dropped them on the front seat, and rode off with another driver who'd been waiting for him.

When we opened the door to the van it was full of wedding gifts. There was barely enough room to get in, but we managed.

Chapter 14

The Premonition

When we pulled up to the lobby of the Sortida Hotel, Diego got out and helped put our wedding gifts onto the bellman's cart.

"I'll let the night bellman know to put these in storage for you. I wasn't told about any gifts. They could be bugged."

Then Diego and Tessie bid us goodbye and drove off.

Our new in-laws had already left, and rooms had been reserved for Bruno and Carmelita, as well as for Edwin and Bella. So we said our goodbyes, and left them in the hands of the desk clerks who'd check them in.

I already had the key to my room, the one Mika reserved for me before I even knew she existed. Our relationship was not so unusual. We shared two languages. We had cultural views and religious views that matched. I saw her with the eyes of a young man. And with her knowledge of my past, she saw me both as that young man, and the man I'd become: a man who'd aged more slowly than most, and who chose vitamins over doctor dope. I was blessed. I'd never gone down the path of trusting witch doctors. What else could you call someone who passes out meds like amulets to ward off evil spirits. No, the idolatry of medicine was not one I struggled with. May those who fall prey to its spell, be freed.

Yes, Mika knew all this about me. But what did I know about her? I knew she had two master's degrees from Christian universities. I knew she admired me. I knew she came from a rich family. I knew she was NBSB, at least until tonight. I knew she'd make a fantastic mom for our kids. And I knew... *I wanted her.*

I turned the key and opened the door to the room that Mika had reserved for me, or had she reserved it for us?

The more I experienced Mika's uniqueness, the more I realized, it hadn't been my old flame that I'd visualized earlier. Victoria didn't have a tiny mole on the left side of her mouth, or eyes with tinted circles of golden brown, like halos. The woman I'd seen in my mind's eye just hours before, was like the one I saw now. I perused my memory, trying to remember each facet of the girl I'd imagined earlier, and the more I did, the more I saw Mika. From her dress to her shoes, to her face, to the smudge of frosting that the wedding cake had left on her blouse? *It was Mika!* What I had experienced that afternoon wasn't my imagination, but a premonition of Mika. Now I wondered if Diego had experienced a similar prophetic vision. Could that be why he was prepared for our trip to Las Vegas, because he knew?

I stood motionless, looking at the place next to the bed where Mika had appeared in my premonition. Then the real-life Mika broke the silence.

"It's a beautiful room, *isn't it?*"

"Yes, it is." I said.

"We're not married, *yet.*" Mika reminded me.

She was right. We hadn't consummated our marriage. She was in the language of the King James Bible, my betrothed.

"Excuse me, Ron." She said.

She grabbed both of the robes from the matching armoires and the slippers that were leaned against their base. Then she disappeared behind the bathroom door.

After a few minutes, she shouted:

"You can come in now. Don't forget to leave your hearing aids on your pillow."

When I entered the bathroom, Mika was still in the shower. It was the kind that sprayed water from all sides. There was a keypad on the door to adjust it from a fine mist to a blasting rinse. She motioned me to join her. Then as if to make up for my inability to hear, she spoke to my other senses. And when we moved from the shower to our nuptial bed, though I could hear again, she didn't let up. Mika had learned something from our silent flight. But bound by my custom not to kiss and tell, I can say no more, except that before the sun rose over Seattle, we were indeed,

Ron and Bruno

husband and wife.

Chapter 15

A Welcome Rest

The Ceremony where I would become godfather to the entire Santos family was still two days out. So, Mika texted Carmelita and Bella to bring their new husbands, Bruno and Edwin, to the Sortida Brunch Buffet. The Buffet was in the same banquet hall where our families had celebrated our wedding with us while we were still on the flight back.

The moment the other couples arrived, the girls launched into chatter. Bruno, Edwin, and I excused ourselves to fill our plates with everything from Prime Rib to California Rolls. If it could be found on a Seattle menu, it was at the Sortida buffet. Now it was on our plates. We loaded up with food for our brides as well.

After we sat down, Bruno quipped.

"With all this food, I'd swear there must be food trucks from every ethnicity parked in the alley."

Carmelita held her finger to her lips, shushing him. Apparently, there were! Well, that's definitely a good way to have the best of Seattle all in one spot.

After Bruno shoveled in a few mouthfuls, he asked in his signature slang.

"Ain't you curious why this hotel's called the Sortida, old Ron?"

"Well," I answered. "I was curious, *years* ago. But I'm sure you'll elaborate on anything I don't know. I think I saw that word for the first time in an old mafia movie shot in Corsica. It was posted above all the doors, so I figured it meant *Exit*. Odd name for a hotel. What can you say about it?"

The girls stopped their chattering and were now listening.

"Well, I hear tell." Bruno said. "When a Mob boss had to lay low or was just too old to do his job, the other Mob bosses would get together at the Sortida to plan an exit for him."

If Bruno said, "I hear tell." It meant he knew it for a fact. His dad was not only a former cop, but a former coroner. He'd clue Bruno in on who didn't make it into the news but made it onto a slab at the city morgue. But Bruno wasn't finished.

"So the Mob bosses would gather to plan an exit, a sortida. It would be to someplace where a large Italian community made it easy for a compaesano to fit in. Argentina was a favorite. Sometimes it involved faking the boss's death. But that wasn't difficult. There was a mortuary that offered free cremations to all the John Does at the local morgue. The funeral home got good publicity for it too. But what they really did, was take each John Doe and recycle him as a *Mario Rossi on demand*."

"So let me get this straight." I said. "Instead of getting cremated, the John Doe, now turned *Mario Rossi*, would be buried complete with a crying widow?"

"Not only that." Bruno said as he leaned forward, now lowering his voice. "But she'd join her husband in his new country after the funeral. See that exit light above the door we went out last night?" Bruno pointed to the exit light by the stairs. "Look hard, you'll see the edges of the letters that spell Sortida spilling out from behind it. That was their sortida to a retirement haven."

Bruno was right. Sortida was written in a font from another era, and the exit light box had simply been screwed on the wall over it.

"The old man took me to dinner here even before *you* ate here, old Ron. And he took me down that staircase too." Then Bruno spoke silently so only a lip reader could hear. "And the old man showed me the secret entrance to underground Seattle."

"Well, that's a good thing to know." I said.

"What did he say?" Mika asked me.

"Yeah, what did you say?" Carmelita asked Bruno.

"Look," Bruno said, "I'm sure Edwin knows, but when we're someplace private, I'll tell the rest of you. It's nothing any of you need to know right now."

That satisfied the girls. Besides, they were more interested in their husbands and the food than anything else. Secrets could wait.

Chapter 16

Mika the Detective

When Mika and I got back to our room there was a dessert tray and coffee waiting for us. Halfway through our first cup of coffee, Mika began to talk.

"Some of my family came into the room last night before we arrived. They removed the last of the bugs that the Feds placed. And while we were having brunch, they delivered our desserts and checked the room again for bugs. They've been keeping watch over you, protecting their new godfather. And the hotel staff's relationship is with the guests, not the Feds. Lots of celebrities stay here. The name says it all, The Sortida Hotel. The staff wants to make sure your stay is pleasant, and that you exit without interference, especially from the Feds. The Feds paid a heavy price for bugging this room yesterday. They hadn't entered a Sortida guest room since the 1950s, before the new Seattle Crime Family took over. And the Seattle liberal elites won't let their toes be stepped on without exacting a price. The Feds don't operate as freely here as in other cities. Seattle's politics have always been pay to play and the Feds don't have an exemption."

"How do you know all this, Mika?"

"There's time to discuss that later, Ron."

Mika searched my eyes while she ran her fingers through my beard.

"Nobody can hear anything we say in this room, Ron. Don't you want to know when I fell in love with you?"

"How could I not want to know, Mika? Most men never know what it's like to have a woman fall in love with them. And for sure, not one like you."

"Most men, Ron. But you're not most men. What was it that one of your ex-wives said? That you must be hypnotizing the young women who fall for you? And she said it under oath, in divorce court. Do you hypnotize them? And if you do, how did

103

you hypnotize me before you knew I existed?"

"As funny as it is, Mika, let's not bring up any of my exes. I don't want a nightmare to wake me up from this dream."

"Okay, Ron. I get it. Anyway, when I heard my aunt wanted to track you down, I volunteered. I was the only one who had enough hours left at the end of the day to find you. Besides, it sounded exciting."

"So you had time to track me down while finishing a Master's degree ahead of schedule?" I asked.

"Well, you know how much I love studying about God. So, I was energized by my studies, not drained. And I was done each day by 5pm. Then all over again, I was energized in my search for you. You know, Ron, you've been *around*."

"Ha, and you still fell in love with me?" I said.

"Well, I have to admit, Ron. Your bad boy mannerisms combined with your post conversion personality, *is hypnotic*."

"Now, now, let's not go back to what my ex said. It took me long enough to forget that woman, at least three hours."

"Okay, Ron. I'll try to put it another way. I simply wasn't prepared for what finding you would do to me. Each one of your childhood friends had a unique take on who you were. You weren't famous, but to them you were. You were a survivor, and you were blessed that you came out of it fairly normal."

"Fairly normal, huh. I'll take that as a compliment. But this survivor stuff. What do you mean by that?"

"Ron, please be serious."

"I am being serious. What did my friends tell you?"

"That's exactly you!" Mika said "And that's who I love! I love you so much, Ron. And I know you have a great memory. So let's talk about what you pretend was nothing."

"Okay. But I don't know how my childhood was any different from the childhoods of other suburban kids."

"Ron, I lost my innocence hearing all that happened to you."

"Lost your innocence?" I asked.

"Well, Ron, it was as if I was listening to a series of dramas followed by happy endings. Then the drama would begin all over again when the next friend told his story about you."

"So where am I right now in this soap opera of life?" I asked. "You're in a happy ending faze and I don't want it to end. Oh Ron. Let's not become a drama. Let's be a romance comedy. I know the Lord will grant us this prayer."

"*Where two or three are gathered...*" I quoted the Bible verse. Mika finished it.

"*...together in His name, there He is in the midst of them.* But I still want to tell you when I fell in love with you, Ron."

"Go ahead, Mika. I'm listening."

"Your unexpected good manners are what first got under my skin. Most guys with as much talent, drive, and good looks as you, are such jerks. So at first, I couldn't understand how a play-boy kept ending up the good guy, trying to help others. Then I found out about your childhood and your losses, and how the only way you were able to get past it all, was to pretend that none of it happened. Let me see your nose."

Mika took hold of my chin, moving my head from side to side, inspecting both sides of my nose, then said.

"The plastic surgeon did a good job of excising most of that scar. What about your eye, the one burned by chemicals?"

Now she tugged at my right eye.

"He fixed that nicely too. How long did you have those scars before work was done on them?"

"Look, lots of people get scars." I said.

"Stop right there, Ron! Tell me how long you had those scars before they were fixed!"

"Don't talk to me like that, young lady!" I snapped.

"I'm sorry, Ron. You're right. I came across bossy."

Mika now sat on the footstool in front of me. She took my hand and kissed it over and over.

"I promise, I'll be good. I haven't had any practice being a wife yet. Can we talk about it?" She asked.

"I'm not gonna let you off the hook that easily." I replied.

But it was impossible for me to refuse her. She was all but kneeling at my feet as she sat on the footstool looking up at me.

"Go ahead." I said. "Tell me what you want to talk about."

"I know that from a very young age, you had scars on your face." She said.

"Yes, I had the scars on my nose since I was eight, and I had a droopy eyelid since I was eleven. But I got them fixed when I was thirty."

"That must have been difficult, Ron."

"Actually, not. Guys were afraid of me. They probably figured if I could handle injuries to my face, I could handle them."

"But the girls weren't afraid of you, *were* they." Mika said.

"No, not at all. In fact, my 7th grade girlfriend was the most beautiful girl in school. Girls didn't seem to notice my scars."

"Didn't notice? They noticed. And they loved them. It caused a hunk to become human. Take a good-looking athlete, add a few scars, and you've created a babe magnet. Add to that, the fact that you suffered and identified with underdogs, which led to your helping every kid that was bullied in the school yard. You're in a category few achieve, Ron, famous to your friends, as if you were a celebrity. And it all happened by chance, just like my falling in love with you. Your friends told me a lot worse things happened to you too, Ron. But you'd been toughened at a young age, and you'd become resilient. That is, until the tragedy. I'm so sorry that such things happened to a good boy, and then a good man. But most of all, I'm happy that you're saved by the blood of our Lord Jesus. And between seeing your childhood pictures, reading your Christian story books, and hearing about your custody battles to keep your kids, I fell in love with you. You're a survivor, Ron."

"Well, I'll let you say that because you're my wife." I said.

"But it's true, Ron."

Mika barely got out the words, then sobbed.

"I love you so much Ron. You know about rich girls. They get what they want, but they're not so lucky in love. You're the only thing I ever wanted but couldn't buy. I'm so happy I got you!"

Mika fell in love with me, the *survivor*, before I knew she existed. And I took her as my wife on the same day I met her. We were definitely a pair, and I was glad. Three is a charm. I prayed that this, my third marriage, would be a blessing. A blessing of many years of life, of love, and of children. *Happy is the man whose quiver is full [of children.]* But most of all, I prayed that the Lord's will be done.

Chapter 17

Newlywed Glow & Espresso

The excitement of being newlyweds did little to fend off the
sleepiness caused by our midday desserts. We fell asleep in each
other's arms within seconds of laying down. I felt sorry for our
elegant bed. It must have been envious of the power of sweets to
bring on slumber.

Mika was still sleeping when I got up to answer the door. It
was room service. We'd been asleep since noon. The retro clock
on the wall said half-past-five.

Mika and I had ordered our dinner in advance. It was my favorite: slow cooked beef shank, jalapeno peppers, and huevos
rancheros. The meat was still in its cooking pot. The eggs and
salsa were on the side. I lifted the lid. The smell of beef, spices,
and peppers filled the room. That was enough to rouse Mika. She
hurried to the bathroom to hide her post slumber face. In a few
minutes, she came out.

"Freshened up, are you?" I said. "*My turn* to get fresh."

I grabbed her and we exchanged newlywed greetings. I was
happy to forget the food, but Mika's stomach let out a growl.

"I think we'd better eat." She said.

My appetite was more for Mika than the food, but I gave in to
the growl of her stomach. We were about to spend another night
getting to know each other. The energy from a full dinner would
do us good.

Mika sat across from me and we prayed, not just thanks for
the food but for the blessings we'd received in the past 24 hours.
I pulled apart the beef shank with a fork and spoon to show Mika
how tender it was. Then I poured the broth full of fat and spices
over our huge bowls of huevos rancheros. It was a specialty
of the Sortida. I placed the pieces of beef on top, as the waiter had
done for me many years before. Amazing how much further
money had gone 40 years ago. I drove cab in my twenties but

could afford to eat at the Sortida. Even more amazing, the menu was the same. If it ain't broke...

"So, this is how you stay young." Mika said, pointing with her lips, Filipino style, to the food on the table.

"Hey, don't waste your pucker on a plate of food." I scolded.

"Yes, sir." She said, then kissed me. "So is this your fountain of youth?"

"Do you object?" I asked.

"Oh no." She said. "I love fatty foods and I distrust doctors. I distrust them as much on food as I distrust them on vaxes."

"That's saying a lot." I said.

Then I shoveled in a mouthful of beef, eggs, and salsa, topped with a slice of jalapeno.

"And Ancel Keys?" She said. "He was just one man, but he outdid the doctatorship in the number of deaths his recommendations caused."

"I'm glad you know about him. Yes, he was a villain." I said.

Then I took another bite of my food.

"Imagine," Mika said, "with his cherry-picked Seven Countries Study, Keys got the U.S. Government to publish guidelines that were the exact opposite of a healthy diet."

"Yes, he was a monster." I said. "He's probably responsible for more deaths than Mao, Stalin, and Hitler combined."

Mika finished what she was chewing and then leaned forward as if she were about to share a juicy piece of gossip.

"And the irony, Ron, is his cousin, I shouldn't laugh, but his cousin, was Lon Chaney Jr., who *played* monsters in movies. But *Ancel Keys* was the *real-life monster*."

"Wow, I hadn't realized his cousin was Lon Chaney Jr. They used to play his old movies at double features when I was a kid. He was the first Wolfman."

"Yes, Ron. And what I think most people in America still don't know, is that diets high in grains are what's killing them. Ancel Keys' fraudulent Seven Countries Study convinced

America's medical regulators to side with sugar over fat, and grains full of pesticides over meat. And look what it's done."

"I'd rather not." I said. "I'm not a chubby chaser."

"Hahaha!" Mika broke into one of her melodious laughs. I could have watched her joyous face and listened till she ran out of wind. But she stopped after one stanza.

"Ahem. Sorry for that." She said. "But I hadn't heard *chubby chaser* till today. But I love it, Ron. How dare you criticize people who are going to drop dead from diabetes by following their doctor's advice. That's like telling a drunk they need detox. In today's America, we're supposed to let them keep killing themselves by taking advice from the doctors whose advice made them fat."

"Yes, and Ancel Keys' victims don't even know his name or even of his existence, talk about a silent killer. There were three fat kids in the three sixth grade classes at my elementary school, Mika. That was back in the day, when meat was the biggest part of what we ate. So one in 30 kids were fat. And I still remember their names: Pat, Bob, and Ross. Today's grade schoolers would have to remember the names of over half the kids in their school to know the names of all the fat kids. But enough of fat talk. Let's get skinny."

It wasn't long before Mika and I finished our food, so I slid out the tray from the cart that contained the second course: herb-roasted lamb. It had been simmering on a hotplate. Next to it was a basket of mint sauce, egg-lemon sauce, garlic butter, and other condiments. The colorful condiments made it look more like we were finger painting each other's lips than sharing bites. But unlike the feeding flirtations on our wedding flight, we were now alone, and our senses were heightened to a whole nother level. And the bed, fit for a king, was waiting to prove it could awaken our appetites even more than our carnivore platters of food.

The timer on the automated coffee maker chimed like the bell in an MMA match. End of round one. Refresh yourselves before round two. But unlike an MMA match, we wouldn't care who pinned down who.

Mika drained her first cup of coffee as quickly as I did. It made sense. Anyone who's gone to graduate school knows most students would never graduate without high doses of caffeine. This was my first cup since waking up after our nap and it felt great. We drank our second cup slower and talked about things that didn't matter, the color of the curtains, the designs on the headboard, the feel of the carpet. Then Mika reached up to my ears and said:

"May I?"

I nodded.

She removed my hearing aids and placed them in the charger on the nightstand, then she came back and nodded to me.

I didn't need to know sign language. The signal was clear. She took my hand and we walked to the shower that sprayed from all sides.

Our bed would soon get the chance to prove its sleep-inducing effect again. But I was sure it would be powerless over our newlywed glow and Seattle's high-octane coffee.

Chapter 18

It's a Wonderful Life

Mika and I were growing attached to the bed, or should I say, to each other. After all, we *were* newlyweds. But we took a break from our honeymoon fun to watch a movie classic, *It's a Wonderful Life*. It was one of my favorites and Mika had never seen it. In the past, I'd only watched it alone. It was one of those Christmas movies that came on late at night and my kids would fall asleep before the first commercial. Now I was watching it for the first time with Mika. And at every part where Frank Capra wanted you to cry, she cried. Wherever he wanted you to worry, she worried. And wherever he wanted you to laugh, she laughed and laughed and... It was more enjoyable watching Mika's facial expressions, than it was watching my all-time favorite movie. But as the final scene grabbed my attention, it was Mika reading *my* face.

She cuddled up to me more than I'd ever been cuddled. And for a man with seven children and a slew of grandkids, that's, well, her cuddling was on par with her laughter.

And when we got to the part where George Bailey's little girl pointed to a Christmas ornament, Mika said:

"I want one of those."

"A Christmas ornament?" I asked.

"No. I'll show you." She said.

Then she took my hand and led me to the bed.

"I want a baby girl just like the one George Bailey has."

"Well, I can't guarantee a girl." I replied.

"What a shame, Ron. Just promise me you'll get a royal bed like this one and we'll just keep trying. Oh, who needs a bed."

Then Mika threw the sheets on the floor and pulled me down.

"A man's bed is where he lays his wife. Happy bed. Happy man. Don't you agree, Ron?"

What could I say?

Chapter 19

Full Quiver Family

Mika had determined that in our first few days together she'd be pregnant. And just as we'd begun to discuss Full Quiver Family Planning, there was a knock on the door. It was already 9pm, but Mika didn't hesitate to open it. It was her older brother. He handed her a package.

"Thank you, Kuya Marvin. You know Ron."

"Of course, Mika. Hi Ron." He said.

"Hi Marvin." I replied.

"Bye, Ron." Marvin said.

Then he left without another word. Mika closed the door and leaned against it.

"Okay, I get it." I said. "No honeymoon interruptions. What's that your brother delivered?"

"Just some things I ordered to keep us healthy." She said.

Mika opened the bag. It contained health supplements. She went straight for the folate, tore off the wrap, and washed down two tablets with water.

"I've got to double up on the folate for the next few weeks." She said. "If I'd known I was getting married, I would have been taking it for a month now."

I was aware of folate and how it improved the likelihood of a healthy baby. Then Mika pulled out the rest of the supplements.

"I thought you knew everything about me, Mika. I've got all these already."

I reached for my supplement bag that I kept in my luggage and placed each one of them on the counter.

"No wonder!" Mika said. "You've got to be the youngest old man around."

"Well, you never know when some young woman is going to cart you off to Las Vegas on her private jet." I said.

"Oh, so that's what it was. How did you know the trip to Las

Vegas was my plan?" She said.

"Just a hunch." I replied.

"Well actually, I didn't plan it, Ron. But I did dream it."

"I'm glad your dream came true, Mika."

Mika turned her attention back to the supplements I'd put on the counter.

"Wow, you've got all the stuff I got for you, and more. What's this?"

She grabbed my container of Citrulline powder.

"Well, that comes from watermelon. It's an amino acid that improves circulation."

"I see, circulation. And this?"

She held up my vitamin K2-MK7.

"That prevents calcium from clogging my arteries."

"And what about this?" She said.

"That's Astaxanthin. It's a powerful antioxidant. It's for circulation too." I replied.

"What about this potassium? What does it do?" She asked.

"Well, in addition to being an electrolyte, it increases my endurance when I work out and keeps my blood pressure down. But I have naturally low blood pressure, so I go light on that. But when I know I'm going for a long walk, or about to work out heavily..."

"Like last night and today?" Mika interrupted.

"And tonight." I said.

"So, what are we waiting for?" She replied.

"For me to finish off my bottle of water." I said.

Then we tumbled to the floor as we playfully fought to drink the last of my water.

Chapter 20

I Married a Stalker

By the time I put my hearing aids in, room service had arrived with our breakfast. I know, for some men, hearing aids are a taboo subject. But it never bothered me. Maybe it was because all the people I grew up loving needed them. Or maybe it was because I knew that my deafness was not an accident, but a deliberate plan of God, for God said:

Who maketh the deaf? Have not I, the Lord?

My deafness was inherited. So I considered it a gift the Lord had given me at birth, to be opened later.

Never mind the reason, I was grateful to be deaf. It taught me things I needed to learn, and it taught me the hard way. And for me, the hard way was often the only way I could learn.

But so far, Mika and I had learned about each other the easy way. And that was a pleasant change from recent years.

My kids were supportive of their dad's new relationship too. They'd sent lots of texts since the first night, all positive, and would end with something like:

"Please don't respond till after the honeymoon."

That was my kids. They knew their dad. I can't say any of it was my doing. I simply kept in contact and never said a cross word. They were adults. But I prayed for them, and they knew it. I remember how my folks would pray for me. I never saw it, but they told me they did. It gave me peace knowing it. I needed their prayers and I'm sure their prayers saved my life more than once.

Mika had ordered our morning breakfast – 3 sampler platters from the Sortida's breakfast brunch. She picked up a thin slice of watermelon from one of the platters and placed it over my lips.

"Can you get too much of this?" She asked.

But before I could answer, she penetrated the watermelon with her tongue, kissing me. We ate the watermelon together as our lips remained locked in a kiss. When I could finally answer, I replied:

"The question is, can you?"

Mika launched into a one-minute aria of laughs followed by kisses. I had a feeling it wouldn't be long till we returned to our Full Quiver Family Planning, but Mika's mood was for conversation.

"Haven't you wondered why my family knew so much about removing listening devices?" She asked.

"Yes, I have been wondering about that. Tell me, Mika"

"Did it ever strike you as odd, that your dad worked for the wealthiest family in the state as their head accountant? And all his life, every time someone in the family had a problem, they went to him?"

"Well, he was the eldest, and my dad's brothers and sisters were poor, and they weren't good at budgeting." I said. "Besides, how is that odd? It was clear he had money, at least compared to the rest of his family."

"Okay, Ron. You've got a point. But let's go back a little bit further. How likely is it that your grampa worked in speakeasies, and in particular, at the Sortida as a piano player?"

"It's odd you bring that up, Mika, I've been wondering that myself. I'd say it's extremely likely. But how did you ..." Mika stopped me mid-sentence.

"Oh Ron, I'm so happy we're on the same wavelength. It seems I always know what you're thinking. I love you so much. Even before I fell in love with you, I had a stalker crush on you."

"Well, I'm glad to know the title of our love story. *I married a stalker*. But tell me, Mika, what is this secret I don't know."

Mika finished the last of her coffee, then wiped her lips as if preparing to deliver a long speech.

"Our grampas knew each other. And your meeting my aunt was planned, but things didn't go as planned. My aunt's behavior, and your high standards, got in the way. She didn't know your breakup was match making gone awry, any more than you did, match making by our grampas."

"Wow, that is a secret. I sure never heard about it. But why were our grampas matchmaking?" I asked.

"Well, my grampa was my aunt's father, of course. And it's not unusual at all in Philippine culture, for the father to match his daughter to suitors, and then let her choose from those he's already approved. Who better than his best friend's grandson, and that was you."

"Okay, Mika. Now, it makes sense. How did our grampas become best friends?"

"Well, you knew your grampa was a preacher, right?"

"Yes, I knew that by the time he married Grandma, he was."

"Well, as a piano player at speakeasies, your grampa was the perfect guy for the FBI to get as an informant."

"I hope this isn't going where it sounds like." I said.

"Oh, no, not at all." Mika replied. "When the FBI asked your grampa to help them, he refused, and got out of piano playing entirely, except in church. He knew, as long as he got a paycheck from anyone with the Mob, even for playing piano, his ministry would be compromised. That was when your grampa decided to go into full-time ministry."

"Well, I'm glad to hear that. But what about your grampa?" I asked.

"My grampa was in on the early days of the FBI, plus, he was a founding member of your grampa's church. And as you and I both know, the FBI spies too much and fights crime too little. It's been that way since the beginning. So, after about 10 years, my grampa resigned from the FBI and became assistant pastor in your grampa's church."

"Well, it's nice to know that the woman I married just hours after meeting her, has an association with my family that goes back generations. These are the first details I've heard about my grampa's ministry. I knew he handed out tracts to commuters as they arrived on the Seattle-Bremerton ferry, and I knew he was a pastor, but that's it."

"I'm glad you knew about the tracts." Mika said. "Because that has to do with what I'm going to tell you. Your grampa handed out a tract to a very distraught young man onboard one of those ferries. In fact, the young man had intended to commit suicide by jumping off the ferry, but by the time he'd mustered up the courage, the ferry had already docked in Bremerton. He was the first one off, and he took one of the tracts your grampa handed him. But that wasn't enough for your grampa. He spotted something was wrong and followed him to the pier. It was there that your grampa told him about God's love for him. The young man's name was Joey, and that day, he became a new creature in Christ."

"Wait a minute." I said. "Joey? When was this?"

"The same day you took my aunt to the emergency room, Ron. The father of the baby my aunt aborted, the man who gave her the cough syrup to do it, that was Joey. He was your mutual acquaintance who walked out her door as you were about to knock, over 40 years ago."

"So that *bastard* got saved." I said. "Well good. Jesus said *there will be more joy in heaven over one sinner that repents...*"

Mika finished my sentence: *"...than over ninety-nine just persons, who need not repent.* And he truly repented, Ron. He did what Christians are supposed to do. He led others to Christ."

"That is a miraculous story." I said. "If there's joy in heaven over one sinner that repents, and Jesus said there is, then I have reason to look back on that day, a day I wanted to forget, as a day I can remember and celebrate."

"I'm glad, Ron. I knew you'd react that way."

"But, again, Mika, how does this tie in with us today. Or is it just a wild coincidence?"

"Well, your grampa, and my grampa, had a shared destiny. Your grampa couldn't just shut the door on all the people he'd met in his years playing piano. He was the only Christian many

118

of them knew."

"Yes, I see what you're saying, Mika."

"And my grampa still had friends in the FBI, and for them, my grampa was the only Christian *they* knew. So our grampas set out to share the gospel with both groups, one inside the FBI, and the other inside the Mob, and both groups were growing in faith and in numbers. At first, the members in the two groups were suspicious of each other. But then they realized they shared the same mission, to bring those who had been corrupted by the world, *and the underworld*, to Christ – and to keep America out of the hands of tyrants."

"Well, Mika, they failed on that last mission."

"I agree, Ron."

"So where does that leave us?" I asked.

"Well, it's not as simple as that." Mika said. "You see, your grampa and my grampa realized it would be best if Joey married my aunt. After all, he was a new creature in Christ. So, they gave Uncle Joey the position they'd originally planned for you."

"Wait a minute, Mika. What kind of church position goes with marrying someone, other than the missionary position?"

Mika rightly ignored my corny old joke.

"I'll try to explain." She said. "Our grampas had built quite an organization. And to protect the identities of their assets within the deep state, they sought to keep it in the family. Your *father* had been administering it and the plan had been for you to take over so he could retire. And you and Aunt Victoria were the obvious match to keep it in the family. But that didn't work out. So, when Joey came along, our grampas saw it as God's providence. Uncle Joey oversaw the Ministry of Deacons, which included current and former members of the Mob and the FBI. And our grampas ran the traditional ministries. Then as your grampa, and then my grampa, went to be with the Lord, Diego found his calling: to oversee the traditional ministries. But when Uncle Joey died, the responsibility for the entire ministry fell to Diego. He's done a great job, but one man can only run a ministry of that scale for so long. And Diego was father, not just to his own kids, but to the 17 *missing* kids. Brother Henry Lewis, who you've known since your arrival at the airport, has been serving temporarily as Overseer of the Ministry of Deacons. But he has other ministry duties he'll be handling as soon as a permanent Overseer is found. Our grampas had hoped that a family member would oversee the Ministry of Deacons. And they had plans for its direction. To this day, the only person to have seen those plans was Uncle Joey. And he hoped that one day, you would share in the responsibility of implementing them. That's why Uncle Joey willed that you would take over if he died, to keep it in the family. Ministries like these need to be kept in the family. You agree with that, don't you Ron?"

"Agree with what? Ministries like these? I've never heard of ministries like these."

"Well, now you have." Mika said.

"That's all? Now I have? Oh, and some guy writes in his will that some other guy is going to take over *his* position as Overseer of the Ministry of Deacons. AKA, secret Christians among the FBI and the Mob. Well, I guess if anyone *could will that*, it'd be someone who oversaw secret *assets* in the *FBI* and the *Mob*. So is this an offer I can't refuse?"

"No, no, Ron. It's not like that at all. Uncle Joey just agreed with the plan our grampas had, the plan for you to marry into the family and to oversee the Ministry of Deacons. And of course he chose a bride for you."

"Oh, yes, of course. Haha."

"I'm serious, Ron! Who'd know your type better than the man who married your all-time favorite girl?"

"Mika, you're my all-time favorite girl."

"Thanks, Ron. But don't you want to know who Uncle Joey chose for you?"

"Would I still have to marry her, even after you and I have

tied the knot?"

"So you'd marry her?" Mika asked.

"Well, if that's your Uncle Joey's last wish, I better."

"So what happens to our *happily ever after*, Ron?"

"That *is* our *happily ever after*, Mika. I know you'd never tell me Uncle Joey had chosen a bride for me, unless it was you. And he was very wise to choose you. I couldn't be happier."

"Oh, Ron. I love you so much. But I have something I should tell you."

"Oh no, here comes the confession. Tell me."

Mika put her lips to my ear and whispered:

"I've never stopped having a stalker crush on you. I want you now like I wanted you then. I've wanted you for years. And now I have you!"

"For years?" I asked.

"Yes, Ron. When I turned 18, my aunt Victoria called me to visit her. She said that my Uncle Joey had written something for me to hear when I was an adult. She told me a little bit about you and showed me your picture. Then she told me Uncle Joey wanted me to save myself for you, to be your wife. I asked my dad if he knew anything about it and he said, yes, but I could choose any husband I wanted.

But I became obsessed with you. I read every press release for your book signings, and each of your children's stories, as if they were dedicated to me. I was the lovesick princess, and you were the cure. So by the time Aunt Victoria assigned me to find you, I was ready for a *manhunt*."

"A manhunt, she says."

"So now you know why my family knows so much about removing listening devices." Mika said.

"Yes, I do." I replied.

Then I removed my own listening devices and put them in the charger on the nightstand. Taking Mika's hand wasn't necessary. She would've followed me anywhere. But I took it just the same, and walked with my stalker wife, Mika, to the shower that sprayed from all sides.

Chapter 21

Uncle Joey

After our shower and some Full Quiver Family Planning, we sat down to eat the food we'd left on the table. One sampler platter was plenty for two people, but Mika had ordered three, so after we'd had our fill, we put what was left in the fridge.

When the coffee maker dinged, we were ready. We filled our cups then sipped and smiled, enjoying the calming stimulation of the caffeine.

Mika now took time to study something other than the lines in my face. She ran her fingers over the veins in my arms. She examined the barely perceptible scars on my hands. She placed her feet on the footstool, next to mine. She examined the differences in our toes. Then she asked:

"What will our kids look like?"

"Only the Lord knows." I said. "But I look forward to finding out."

"So do I." She replied. "I hope I haven't talked too much in the last few hours. But these family secrets have been bothering me. I don't like secrets. Can I tell you more about Uncle Joey?"

"Sure, Mika. Our families will meet us in heaven. I'd love to know more about all of them."

"That's one of the things I love about you, Ron. To you, family is forever, no expiration date. A lot of people don't think that way. They hold back something, a part of their heart. But you don't hold back anything. Uncle Joey knew that about you, because even though my aunt Victoria didn't deserve to be your girl anymore, you treated her like family. Her health was the first thing you thought of when you saw her lying in bed half dead. You have to consider the contrast between you and Uncle Joey, and the impact that made on him. Ron, Uncle Joey didn't even see you at the door. He was fleeing a crime scene. He left my aunt for dead. He didn't find out she'd survived till he saw her car parked outside her apartment, the same car he stole to drive to the Colman Ferry Dock. Then he started asking questions in the neighborhood. That's when he found out you'd saved her life. You don't think less of me because of what I've told you today, do you Ron?"

"Not at all, Mika, sharing secrets is the best way to get close. Not to mention, I had to be told the things you've told me. It's a blessing that you're the messenger the Lord chose to tell me. And your uncle, Joey? God performed a miracle that day at the Bremerton Pier. He transformed a fleeing felon into a new creature in Christ, *in the twinkling of an eye*. My grampa never told me about that. I wonder why?"

"Well, Ron, he might have felt ashamed that he mismatched you and my aunt Victoria. Or maybe it was that he gave what was supposed to be your job, to Uncle Joey. Or maybe he just wanted to protect you from the tough crowd that were part of his ministry. FBI agents and members of the Mob aren't exactly the stuff of children's bedtime stories."

"You got me there, Mika."

"But Ron, that's your strength. You're a family man. Your stories represent the protective and idealistic side of you. But when pushed, you're like the man who lives under a bridge. If anybody so much as kicks a piece of gravel at those you love, you're all over them. That's the job description for Overseer of the Ministry of Deacons. He's there to protect his brothers and sisters in Christ, who live in the shadows. He's the string puller who keeps it all together behind the scenes. He treats everyone like his favorite son, until they get out of line. That's you, and that was..."

"...my father." I completed Mika's sentence. "So, how long have you known about this?"

"Since I was a little girl." Mika replied.

"Aye, aye, aye! So our grampas really did try to arrange a marriage between me and your aunt. And your uncle Joey really did arrange our marriage. Well, at least you're young and hot, and

I'm divorced out, so you're stuck with me."

I was teasing Mika, but I was teasing her with the truth.

"Now, wait a second, Ron. *I do love you.* Whatever I've told you, just remember, I had no idea that the man I'd actually fall in love with, stalker style, would be the same man that my family had planned for me from the start, and your family too."

"My family?" I asked.

"Yes, your dad didn't quit being godfather to the Santos family just because he handed the position of Overseer to Joey. You see, we all had a godfather chosen by my grampa. My grampa chose your grampa first, and after he died, grampa chose your dad. It was just coincidental that your dad was Overseer of the Ministry of Deacons when he was chosen. Your dad was at my dedication and became my godfather too. It was at the time of your second divorce. And your dad prayed that I'd grow up to be a woman, worthy even of his own son. Then before he died, your dad said to Uncle Joey, 'That niece of yours is the perfect match for my son, Ronnie.'"

As odd as it might sound, I wasn't surprised by anything that Mika was telling me. I'd grown to expect surprises on a grand scale. And now, I was being told that the writer of Christian story books for kids, that's me, would be Overseer of the Ministry of Deacons, a ministry made up of members of the Mob and the FBI. And that this very same position had been held by my dad.

"So, Mika, tell me if I finally get it. My dad wanted to retire from his position as Overseer of the Ministry of Deacons. So my grampa and your grampa, try to match-make me and your aunt. When that didn't work, Joey takes a ferry from Seattle over to Bremerton, gets saved, marries your aunt, and becomes the new Overseer. Then when you turn 18, your aunt informs you that you're going to have an arranged marriage with me, someone you'd heard about but never met. Then I don't know how many years later, but while you were still enrolled at Seattle Pacific University, your aunt appoints you to do a manhunt for me, your future husband. And by the time you graduate from college with your, what is this, your 2nd or 3rd degree? Anyway, just as you tire of going to any more school, Bruno and I come along, Dr. Jensen falls out the window, and you cart me off to Las Vegas to make me your husband, less than an hour after meeting me. Is that about right?"

I'd temporarily forgotten about Mika's gift for laughing, but the moment the first ha-ha exited her mouth, I knew I was in for a long one. And her laugh was so contagious that our tears and shortness of breath continued till we nearly passed out.

"Ron!" Mika gasped after catching her breath. "I don't know how you do it, but I'm worn out. Let's take a rest."

Mika led me to the bed, my mind now cleared of the fog that had begun when we exited the Sortida on our way to Las Vegas. I looked around me. The room was reminiscent of pictures I'd seen of the bedrooms of kings. The bed included a headboard that rose five feet behind its satin pillows. Ornate carvings of flowers, leaves, and branches were cut into its ebony stained hardwood. Heart shaped leather insets were nested within an embroidered braid of vines. See-through curtains created a dream-like effect as the chandelier reflected off its threads. Finely upholstered chairs were on each side of the bed. Matching armoires stood with doors open, robes hung on wooden hangers and slippers leaned against their base. Valet stands were placed like guards next to the armoires and a padded chest was at the foot of the bed.

I didn't deserve this room. Nor did I reserve this room. But now I knew who did. It was a gift, or should I say perk, from the Ministry of Deacons.

Chapter 22

What's on the Menu?

After our midafternoon nap, we pulled out the sampler platters from the fridge and sat down to nibble from them.

"What should we do for dinner?" Mika asked.

"Well, Mika, you know I hate Seattle, *but I do love their food*, and there aren't many things as fun as tossing fries to the seagulls while dining on Codfish at Ivar's."

"Oh, that sounds fun, Ron. Who's Ivar?"

"I think it's better you read about him from the placards at his restaurant. We'll eat there first."

"First? You mean, we'll be eating twice?"

"No, not twice, we've got to hit at least three places. I'm thinking Ivar's first, then a little Italian restaurant near Yesler. And after that, we'll go to Chinatown for late night dim sum."

"Maybe we oughta save some space for all that food." Mika said.

"Yes, maybe you should." I teased, moving the platters to my side of the table.

"Oh, I was thinking more of you with that fine-tuned vitamin filled body." Mika replied, moving the platters back to her side.

We fought for what remained on the platters, playfully sharing, after we'd gotten the first bite of our favorites.

"Ron?" Mika said.

"What's that?" I replied.

"I love you. Thanks for being you."

"Well, Mika, I wish I could be sweet back. But Jordan Peterson says if you're *too sweet* to your woman, you risk divorce."

"Well, if he says so. Be mean to me."

"You want mean?" I kidded. "I'll tickle you till you scream."

As soon as I made a move like I was going to follow through, Mika took off running to the other side of the bed, laughing as she ran. I pursued her as she faked to one side of the bed, then to

the other. Finally, she screamed, "Ah-nee-***mall!***" *Animal* is a Filipino expression pronounced with the emphasis on the final syllable. It means exactly what you'd imagine given the context.

"So tell me more about our plans for dinner." Mika said, as we
sat back down to our platters.

"We'll get Fish 'n Chips at Ivar's, to start." I said.

"Wait, Ron, I thought we were getting fish and fries."

"They call them chips when they're served with fish. I don't
know why."

"Well as long as us girls get to throw fries to the seagulls, we'll
be happy."

"Us girls?" I said.

"We're not inviting the other newlyweds?" Mika asked.

"Well, I'd kind of wanted to keep it a secret, but at the risk of
being *too sweet*, I'll tell you now. Yes, they're coming."

"What about Jordan Peterson?" Mika asked.

"No, he's not coming." I replied.

Mika's laughter hit my ears like a shot of gin hits the throat:
first a burst of fire then a glowing warmth. I was addicted to her
laughter. It was like strong liquor that takes the drinker by surprise. Who wouldn't want another taste of something that potent,
but without the hangover. But unlike liquor, Mika's laughter had
a healing power. If it were possible, tears of laughter and tears of
joy would be the only kind of tears I'd ever cry again. As the wise
King Solomon said,

*Then I commended mirth, because a man has no better thing
under the sun, than to eat, and to drink, and to be merry.*

But on the other hand, King Solomon said,

*The heart of the wise is in the house of mourning, but the heart
of fools is in the house of gladness.*

Well, I'd been in the house of mourning for quite some time.
And now, I'd be taking up the cause of millions who'd been in
their own houses of mourning. The Ministry of Deacons had two
missions, to bring those who'd been corrupted by the world, *and*

the underworld, to Christ, *and* to keep America out of the hands of tyrants. But now that America had fallen, they surely must have been looking into legal ways to reverse the Covid Coup. My expression changed from sunny to dark. Mika noticed.

"Ron, I want to reach in to give you love when I see your sadness. I know I've burdened you so much in the last few days, talking about things you'd rather forget. I'm sorry."

"No need to be sorry, Mika. You've blessed me with laughter and love, and so much else. *For everything there is a season, and a time for every purpose under heaven: a time to be silent, and a time to speak.* And you did both, in keeping with what the Lord would have wanted. I'm blessed."

"We're blessed." Mika said.

"You're right." I replied. "But there is one gripe I've got with you, Mika. Overseer of the Ministry of Deacons is way too long. So my first request when the Deacons meet will be for them to refer to themselves as Deacons, and to refer to me as the Minister of Deacons, MD for short."

"That's good, Ron, because you're the only MD I'd trust."

"Let's hope America feels the same way, Mika. Because part of my job will be to mock those who've been aiding and abetting in the destruction of America. How better to mock the doctors who've ruined us, who've ruined America and the world, than to take their precious title, and give it to the one who's going to ruin *them*."

Chapter 23

Get Into My Big Black Car

Seattle was still enjoying an Indian Summer so we wouldn't need an umbrella for our night out. But warm weather creatures that Mika and I were, we put on coats worthy of the Seattle nights. When we walked out of our bridal suite, we passed the guard that the Ministry of Deacons had placed, then we went down the one flight of stairs to the lobby.

When we walked into the waiting area, Bruno tapped his temple twice, then pointed to me, acknowledging he'd been told of my new position. Edwin solemnly shook my hand, Bella too. Then Carmelita pulled out her camera that was set to instantly post on X and snapped a group photo that was pre-captioned:

Night on the Town with Bruno and the Nation's Top MD

We walked out of the lobby as soon as Carmelita had finished her shoot. She'd already uploaded more than a few posts; each worthy of the moniker Bruno had given her: Camerlita. And before we'd gotten down the steps to our ride, her first tweet had gone viral.

I'd told Mika my position as Minister of Deacons was not to be kept secret. So I suspect Mika had given Carmelita the words for the caption in advance.

Independent Media would be an important tool in the assault on the Doctatorship, and I'd already been thinking about the legal angles. If Soros could get his dirty work done without breaking a single law, *supposedly*, then we could too. And from what Mika told me, we had more operatives in both the Mob and the FBI than the left did. Ours just needed a boss. Now they had one. I was looking forward to serving the Lord in that capacity. And the risks didn't bother me.

It's easy to put your life on the line when you've got members

130

of your own family waiting to greet you in heaven. It's a win-win. Get epsteined, join your family in heaven. Succeed at saving the nation from tyranny while staying in one piece, go home to your family and enjoy a new America. It even felt empowering. And I knew I wasn't alone in this. The surreal world I'd lived in for the past few years was familiar to others who'd lost their loved ones. One moment your loved ones are by your side. The next, they're in heaven. But the knowledge that they're with the Lord doesn't help with the pain. You can't join them, unless you defy God by choosing your own day to die. But given the state of the current tyranny, thousands had already chosen that route, and just one person taking their own life is too many.

As for the Vax induced heart attacks in young people, they still continued, despite their refusal to put any more poison in their bodies. And to this day, there's no government program to treat vax injuries or any inquiry into their deaths. The cause of excess deaths is a mystery, *at least that's what they say*. Yet those deaths began shortly after the introduction of the so-called vaccinations. But instead of doing anything about it, the CDC is now encouraging parents to give their six-month-old infants the jab. Bastards! Is there some other name for such animals? And yet, much of the public, despite all warnings, remains in a doctor induced state of hypnosis, helped along by the government media collusion to censor truth. How is that even legal, to legitimize killers, but forbid advice that warns of death?

But government agents, or should I say, agents of the Doctatorship, an organization with no legal authority to operate, have no clue as to the fearless kind of opposition they face. Their agents are atheists. What do they know of our belief, that a thin veil separates the living from the dead, and that if you're born-again, you receive your heavenly reward immediately upon death. Bodies are buried, not people. We know our journey ends in life, not death. We don't care how long we live, other than to find new ways to serve the Lord before we go to heaven.

My plan of transparency was acted on by Mika with no more than my mentioning it. I remembered the centurion who Jesus had commended for his understanding of following orders. When I told Mika she had blessed me, it was an understatement. I didn't have to give an order. My word was her command. She made my new position, a position that had been kept secret for nearly 100 years, about as public as it could be. Bruno had been trending on X since Dr. Jensen fell out his window. So to be put into a picture with Bruno, was to be put into the national spotlight.

Diego was waiting for us next to a limo outside the Sortida.

"From here on out, Ron, these guys gotcha." He said.

He pointed to the driver and someone riding shotgun. They both looked like football players except for their Brooks Brothers suits.

"I hope so, Diego. Because I'm flying blind." I said.

"No worry, Ron. They'll take good care of you."

Diego tapped on the roof of the Limo and the guy riding shotgun stepped out and opened the door for us. He must have stood six-foot-six. The limo was big too, with plush leather sofas and plenty of space for all six of us. After the guy riding shotgun got back in, I could see even he had headroom to spare. He kept his eyes on the surroundings, then without turning his head, he spoke.

"Hi Doc, I'm Lenny. And this here is our driver, Ralph."

He nodded his head toward Ralph, still surveying the area.

"Nice to meet you Doc." Ralph said.

Ralph greeted me with what was to become my new moniker, Doc. But our driver and his associate had more important things to do than introduce themselves. Their eyes were scanning every inch of street life outside the Sortida as they pulled out of the driveway.

"The paparazzi are everywhere." Ralph said. "Smile."

Bruno put on a bearlike grin and stared them down. The lady reporter who'd been at the ambulance scene where Bruno saved Dr. Jensen's life, was trotting alongside the vehicle. She came so close that the driver had to stop for a moment. Bruno rolled down his window.

"Haven't you got anything better to do than to follow a retired fireman and his Sunday school teacher?" Bruno said.

"Give me a private interview and I'll show you what else I can do." She replied.

Her liquored breath about choked us as it drifted in the window. Bruno had told me about her, Jessica Whatshername. She'd slept her way to the bottom of nearly every big story she'd gotten.

"Jessica, you have your people call my people." Bruno said.

Then he rolled up the window. I suspect Jessica knew this was Bruno's sarcasm. She knew everything about everyone she followed. The best reporters do.

As we exited the driveway, the paparazzi were in chase. Our stretch limo made it easy to get halfway into each intersection before the light turned red, forcing every paparazzi driver to run at least one light in their pursuit. The only vehicle that hadn't been pulled over by the SPD on our way to Ivar's, was Jessica's. It could have been chance, but I suspect it simply wasn't wise to be pulling over the driver for the City Dump. That was the name they'd attached to Jessica. Sure, most cops wanted the corruption cleaned up in their city, but Jessica's methods were likely illegal. The pressure she exerted on sexual conquests to fess up, while she romped through Seattle's underbelly, was borderline blackmail. And whether her own behavior was prostitution or not, was debatable.

By the time we got to Ivar's, she had camera vans on both sides of the street. With all the directions their cameras were pointing, they looked more like google mappers, than remote TV crews.

Chapter 24

Brides of a Feather

The girls had been chit-chatting on our drive to Ivar's, excited to be outside for the first time in days. But when we got to Ivar's, Lenny advised us to stay in the limo. I didn't blame him. Expecting two guys to protect six passengers from an ant hill of paparazzi would have been unreasonable.

"I'll get fish and chips for all of you." Lenny said.

"Just a durn tootin minute." Bruno said in his faux hick vernacular. "I see my buddies over at the fire station a waving at me. I ain't gonna lose a chance to talk 'em up to the media."

Bruno stepped out of the limo and looked up at the firehouse tower, handing the paparazzi a freebie. Then he walked to the center of the firehouse driveway and shook hands with some firemen. The paparazzi loved it and rushed in to take photos.

Those standing at Ivar's left their place in line to see what was happening. Lenny, now at the front of the line, placed our orders. By the time he brought the food back to the limo, Bruno was finished with his impromptu press briefing and Jessica Whatshername was fuming. Bruno had tied her hands. No official news crew was going to break the law and block a fire station driveway for an interview, not even Jessica's. And from Bruno's sideways grin at her with one eyebrow raised, I knew he knew exactly what he'd done. Bruno had a natural talent for throwing the law in the faces of those who got in his way.

"Are we gonna have fun tonight!" Bruno said.

When he got back into the limo, he lowered his head in silence as Lenny began to pray blessings on the food. Lenny made sure to include a special prayer for our favorite reporter, Jessica.

"May she receive blessings in accordance with your will as we prayerfully seek to be examples of your love this evening."

The juvenile delinquent glow that Bruno had on his face as he'd gotten into the limo, had begun to fade. But as Ralph maneuvered the limo through the ever-present waterfront construction, the glow returned. That's when Bruno caught site of Jessica's crew, frantically setting up a shoot. They were next to the one pier with seats enough for us all.

"The Lord is awfully fast to deliver on Lenny's prayer." Bruno said. "Look at that woman. What is Jessica up to?"

Jessica's crew had set up a raised platform with Seattle's new waterfront attractions in the background. Seagulls were perched on the rail behind her, anticipating the next group of tourists to toss fries from their orders of fish and chips. She'd placed members of her crew on the only available benches and put fences around them to keep the paparazzi from intruding on her turf.

"Have we got a rat?" Bruno asked.

I handed Bruno my Bible which was opened to Matthew 8:5-13, about the centurion's orders being followed.

He read verse nine.

[The centurion said,] I am a man under authority, having soldiers under me: and I say to this man, Go, and he goes, and to another, Come, and he comes, and to my servant, Do this, and he does it.

"So I take it we've got a centurion and they're under orders to set up our poor Jessica." Bruno said.

Mika, looked at her nails as if inspecting a recent manicure, assuring all eyes would be on her, as I'm sure she well knew.

"I would guess that Mika's the culprit." I said. "And I have no doubt she's been in cahoots with your Carmelita, Bruno."

"No." Bruno said. "My Camerlita?"

Bruno tipped his head down looking at Carmelita from beneath his bushy eyebrows. She was inspecting her nails as well, complete with at least one signature smudge.

"I had one of my cousins give an anonymous tip to Jessica." Mika said. "But Jessica must have used the paparazzi as a distraction to get us up to this pier. She may well be what Frank Sinatra called all reporters, but she obviously has some talent."

"Well, maybe." I said. "But is she really that sure we'll behave how she expects us to behave?"

"She's that sure." Ralph chimed in. "I've lived in Seattle all my life and there's nobody as sure of herself as Jessica. She has gotcha questions for all occasions."

"Well, I hope she will turn to the Lord." Bella said. "King David, the Psalmist, wrote, the Lord *leads me beside still waters* and in the next verse he wrote, *he restores my soul.* I really feel bad for those who are caught in a life of sin like Jessica. We really need to pray for her."

This time, it was Bella's husband, Edwin, who prayed.

"Lord, I pray that Jessica would turn her eyes to heaven and call upon Your Name, this day. Amen."

Jessica had taken per place on the raised platform that her crew had set up next to our seating. She had a green screen covering the hundred-year-old concrete pedestrian rail. It was obvious that she planned to fill in the background with whatever she chose, maybe even advertiser promotions. There was no question she had a professional team. Everything was meticulously set up... *except* for the one thing that was out of her control, the seagulls. And she couldn't help commenting on them as her team prepared the area for her show.

"These seagulls are the filthiest creatures I've ever seen." She squawked.

Her team laughed the obligatory laugh. She *was* their boss. But she wasn't finished.

"They should figure out a way to chop you in pieces and cook you in stew." She said to the seagulls.

The seagulls just kept repositioning themselves in anticipation of dinner. They knew it wouldn't be long before the next group of tourists began feeding them. The seagulls considered the benches to be theirs. And as they waited, they left little white droplets, some not so little, on Jessica's no longer clean green screen. She swung her arm at them, scattering them for a moment, but they quickly took their places again.

Then, as quickly as Jessica's microphone was clipped on, her calm returned.

"Ah, we see here Seattle's lovely and stately seagulls. They live in harmony with nature's delicate ecosystem. My dedicated team will do their best to help you and the seagulls enjoy: *A Night with Bruno*."

One thing was sure, Jessica's timing was impeccable. Just as she'd finished announcing, *A Night with Bruno,* Lenny was opening the door for us. Then he reached back into the limo and took out the bag filled with Fish & Chip dinners, setting it next to the benches where we sat.

After Bruno gave the blessing, we began to eat. None of us cared we were on camera, it was dinnertime. We paid little attention to the seagulls who kept repositioning themselves on the rail by Jessica. She was repositioning herself too, for what would be a flurry of pose edits after the shoot. We'd all finished our dinners by now, except for the girls who kept back some of the fries to feed the seagulls.

"Should we start?" Mika said to me with anticipation.

"Sure, go ahead." I said. "Start."

But the second I said start, it was a race. First Bella threw a fry that was caught midair by one of the seagulls, then Carmelita and then Mika. At times, there were five or six seagulls all vying for the same fry. The girls were like kids throwing firecrackers for the first time, having lost sight of anything but the excitement. Luckily, Lenny had three extra-large orders of fries just for the seagulls. He handed them to Edwin who kept resupplying the girls as they tossed them to the birds. Then Edwin tripped, dropping what was left on the ground. The seagulls swooped down to grab them, only to be replaced by more seagulls. Then all three girls threw their remaining fries into the air, and it was an explosion of wings and feathers everywhere. Despite Jessica's being on camera with a live mic, she could no longer contain her hatred for the seagulls. She cursed and stomped on any seagull that dared land on her platform and flailed her arms at the ones on the rail behind her. Then she let out a scream worthy of a stage performance, but this was no act.

"LORD God Almighty!"

Her scream was followed by an eerie silence. It was as if the sound had been turned off in a movie theater as we watched in horror as poor Jessica tumbled backwards, over the rail and into the waters of Puget Sound. As she plummeted, the thin sheet of plastic green screen enveloped her. It made a rustling sound like a flag going down, signaling this was Jessica's last stand. The optics were fantastic, just not for Jessica. Bruno went airborne. Sure, he took a running start and a leap before landing on top of the concrete rail, and then he took a quick look down to make sure there were no impediments to his dive, but in less than two seconds, Bruno was plunging into the water to save poor Jessica, who in answer to Edwin's prayer had indeed looked up to heaven and called upon God's Name, shouting: *"LORD God Almighty."*

The stage lights that Jessica's team had placed around us had blinded us to the huge audience that had been watching from both sides of Alaskan Way, not to mention up and down the sidewalks and from the Ferris wheel on the pier. Bruno had already been trending but the combined total of videos of what had just happened was vying for top position with Tucker Carlson's latest interview. There were shots from every angle, but the Libs wanted to blame Edwin and the girls: two Hispanics and two Filipinos. That went well. But it quickly became clear to everyone who'd seen the videos that it was Jessica's hatred for seagulls, Seattle's beloved waterfront creatures, that caused her fall. And #SPCA, Society for the Prevention of Cruelty to Animals, was trending for third place behind Tucker Carlson and Bruno.

Bruno's dive went viral barely minutes after he'd come up for air, but it continued to trend as new photos and videos posted. Fortunately, or not, for Jessica, the plastic green sheet that enveloped her had prevented her from inhaling any water but had also kept air from reaching her lungs. One pump from Bruno's resuscitator and she was breathing again, but she was still unconscious when the ambulance Ralph called left with poor Jessica in it.

"This is on our tab." Ralph said. "I hope you don't mind, Doc."

"Oh, not at all. We're in the business of saving lives. So, where are they taking Jessica?" I asked.

"Same hospital has Dr. Jensen. Best nurses and doctors money can buy." Ralph said.

And indeed, they were bought and paid for, shooting kids with deadly vaxes for a commission, getting *consulting* fees from Big Pharma to get kids addicted to the latest *harmless* amphetamine or opiate. For some reason, I thought that was called drug pushing, a felony punishable by at least five years in prison. But doctors had an exemption, at least in their minds. If their licensing board gave the orders, they were licensed to kill. And that's exactly what they did with the clot shots, death bed isolations, end of life *meds*, and ventilators.

So Jessica would be keeping Dr. Jensen company. He was exactly the kind of corrupt official she specialized in exposing. But this time she'd found another way to end up in bed under the same roof with a corrupt official. If not for her stomping the seagulls, I'd think she planned it.

Bruno was taken by one of the 24hr construction crews to their trailer where he was able to take a shower and put on a fresh set of clothes. By the time he came out of the trailer, everyone in the area knew about his saving Jessica. For a moment, the cheers drowned out even the sound of the jazz band playing at Pier 62.

When Bruno got back to where we were sitting, he was even more ready for a night on the town.

"And the atheists think the Lord has no sense of humor?" Bruno said. "I don't know what He's got planned for your debut, Doc, but if it's anything like my first public appearance, it's gonna be something."

The local news media had now arrived on the scene, and one of them heard what Bruno just said, so she asked.

"So, this is your doctor, Bruno?"

"Yep, this is my Doc, my one and only Doc. He heads up an entire team. Ask him."

Mika reached for my hand.

"Let's get some privacy first, Ron. It's going to be a fun night. But I'm still hungry. How about that Italian restaurant? Will we be private there?"

Lenny answered for me.

"Oh, they'll guarantee you have privacy. And the press knows what happens to violators."

Chapter 25

The Italian Restaurant

Ralph pulled into a parking stall that faced the loading dock for one of Pioneer Square's oldest buildings. He flickered his headlights and a security guard walked out from the shadows. The guard rolled up one of the corrugated steel doors, revealing another door, the type you'd expect to see at an elegant restaurant.

"Here we are." Ralph said. "Best Italian restaurant in town. We'll be parked right here till you finish your dinner. Don't rush."

Lenny got out to open our door, then walked us to the loading dock steps and up to the entrance.

"See you folks later." He said.

"Later." Bruno answered for us.

Once the maître d' had brought us inside, we heard the loading dock door slam. Lenny wasn't exaggerating when he promised us privacy.

The restaurant had ornate wood with dark accents. Colorful paintings on the walls contrasted with the white tablecloths. The plates and silverware were already laid out. Once we were seated, the waiter added his touch, arranging a mosaic of antipasto platters on our table. Then he gave us a drink menu. It included Italian soda, mineral water, coffee, and of course wine.

The lights were so low that I could barely make out the words on the menu. But the moment our drinks were served, the lights were turned up. Then we could see the rest of those seated in the restaurant.

Mika's father, Cesar, was standing next to our table, his glass raised to make a toast. Mika's eyes were lovingly fixed on him as he made the toast to launch our post honeymoon surprise party.

"To life!" He said.

This was the first time Mika's father had seen her since he gave her to me on our wedding night. He returned Mika's loving gaze. His manliness and confidence were etched in wrinkles on his face, earned by decades at sea, providing a better future for his family.

Then it was Alejandro's turn, the father of Carmelita. He stood, raised his glass, and gave the same toast.

"To life!" He said.

He was every bit as exuberant as when he accepted Bruno as the man who would take his daughter as bride. He too, looked at *his* daughter, Carmelita, with all the love any daughter could hope for.

But there was one more daughter who'd left her father's side on the night of our flight to Las Vegas, and that was Bella, Edwin's bride. Her father, Sergio, made his toast in the same way as the others.

"To life!" He said.

Sergio looked at his daughter as if they'd been apart for years, not just three days, and she returned the same look.

It was an unusual scene for modern day America, where the universities teach daughters to hate, not only their fathers, but all men. These three men stood, holding their heads high, while their daughters looked on, unable to hide their love and admiration.

But it was time to pray blessings on the food, so we bowed our heads, as Sergio said the prayer.

"Lord, we ask that You bless our families, our missions, and our food. In the Name of Your Precious Son, we pray. Amen."

"Amen!" We agreed.

As soon as Sergio had completed his prayer, the three daughters ran to their fathers, embracing them. It was a rare moment to see Mika cry, other than from laughter.

And Bella, the methodical plotter who gave us instructions on how to enter the 5th floor of the hospital, *and* find our way down the hall to Dr. Jensen's office? She was now a joyous mess of tears, as she greeted her father for the first time after her honeymoon with Edwin.

No less a mess, was Carmelita. She was the only one who wore mascara, and now, well, she was still Carmelita, with just a few smudges more.

I'm sure all the grooms agreed as we witnessed the affection between our wives and their fathers, that to have a woman who loves and admires her father, is to have a woman who loves and admires her husband too.

Whoso finds a wife, finds a good thing,
and obtains favor of the Lord.

Each of the brides now motioned their grooms to sit at their father's table, and Mika and I sat across from hers.

"You're an interesting man." Cesar said.

"And we live in interesting times." I replied.

"You jest, but there is truth to the contrast."

"I think so.' I said.

"Either way," Cesar said, "as Christians, we deal in good news. Mika has told me that the two of you agree that a large family is a blessing from God."

"Yes." I said. "It's too bad more people don't agree with us. We're created in God's image. We should want to be reminded of His love through the smiles of our children."

"Yes, I agree." Cesar said. "Mika tells me you're ready for your new duties as Minister of Deacons."

Cesar pulled out an envelope and placed it on the table in front of me.

"The deacons want you to have a high income." He said. "This is a rich ministry. And many of the things you'll do, can't be done if you're not a rich man. That's your signing bonus, along with your first month's salary. Open it. And don't worry, the tax withholding has already been taken care of."

I peeked inside. It was a deposit receipt. It represented no small sum. How could it? That one deposit made me a rich man. But I hadn't accepted the job for money. In fact, in some ways, I hadn't

143

accepted the job at all. I was only being swept along by the current. But it was nice to know that the sole impediment to me carrying out my duties was myself, my diligence, my talent, and my focus, not my money.

"But that's enough of business." Cesar said. "Tonight is to be a celebration of three weddings."

Then Cesar clinked his glass with a spoon to begin the ritual that signals the groom and his bride to kiss. And between bites of food and laughter, Mika and I, and the other newlyweds, accommodated them with nuptial kisses till long after dessert.

Chapter 26

The Dedication

Mika and I woke up early for the dedication where I was to become godfather to the Santos family. I wanted at least a few minutes of practice as this was the first time I'd be taking part in a ceremony as godfather. My kids had godfathers, and godmothers, but Filipino customs can differ from one family to the next. I wanted to make sure I did my part right. I didn't want to offend anyone.

We arrived in plenty of time for practice, and the ceremony went as planned. There were relatives from all over the country, even from overseas. Mika made sure to introduce me to every one of them, telling me which city they were from and other bits of information about their lives. Yes, it was unusual to be chosen as godfather to those who didn't know me. But they knew my dad, and my grampa, or knew of them. So there was a family feel that would have been there, even if someone other than Mika had been doing the introductions.

But Mika and I had been inseparable since we'd met. Astounding what can happen in 3½ days! My life hadn't gotten any less surreal, but this was a different kind of surreal, on the one hand, I was experiencing an overwhelming joy at having Mika. On the other, I was tasked with the responsibility of retribution for what the doctatorship had done, to the nation and to the world over the last four years. And retribution there would be. Maybe the balance would be enough to put old Humpty-Ron together again. But it wasn't so much that I was broken in pieces, but that my heart had been ripped out. Who can lose a son, or daughter, brother, or sister, without losing a piece of themselves? Neither curses nor justice could change the past, but at least justice would fulfill God's command. I had my Bible out and was reading it once again.

The Dedication

Whoso sheds man's blood, by man shall his blood be shed:
for in the image of God made He man. Genesis 9:6

"Ron." Mika's voice broke into my thoughts.

"Yes, Mika?" I said.

"You've been looking at that page in your Bible for so long, but your thoughts are somewhere else. What's wrong?"

"What's wrong doesn't matter as much as what's right." I said. "You, us, your family, my family, those who serve God, there's a lot that's right."

"I'm glad to hear you say that, Ron. Sorry we missed our morning time together. By the way, the food is ready."

I took my seat of honor, a seat I didn't deserve, and we ate with Mika's family around us. This time I raised my glass in a toast I'd heard my grandfather make.

"May our families be..."

Her family finished the toast with me.

"...as rebar in concrete, ever connected and ever free."

"Is this something my grandfather taught?" I asked.

"It's in his book." Mika said.

Then she walked over to a table in the middle of the room with church memorabilia and picked up some books which she brought to me. One was titled:

Toasts for the Speakeasy
by Earl Miller

"Grampa made that toast." I said. "But I didn't realize he'd put together a coffee table book full of toasts. I'm amazed he had time for things other than his ministry."

"Things like this *were* his ministry." Mika said. "He was able to minister to those who were dead in their sins with books like this. Every few pages he'd slip in a Bible verse, but I never understood the toast. How is rebar connected and ever free, Ron?"

146

"Concrete masons recommend keeping rebar free enough so if concrete moves due to heat or earthquake, rebar adjusts with it. Welds are discouraged. If connections are rigid, rebar snaps, and concrete crumbles. The same goes for families."

"My aunt warned me not to be too clingy to my future husband, now I know why. Our union might snap from the tension."

"She's right, Mika. But you can be clingy all you want with me, as long as your *hands* are not *as bands*, as King Solomon warned. I'm sure that's what your aunt meant by too clingy."

Mika grasped my arm and leaned into my shoulder as she ate a taco with her free hand. It was the last night of our honeymoon, but I didn't see that changing anything. Sure, I'd be focusing on ministry duties starting in the morning, but we were newlyweds with no kids to care for. And it would be another month before we'd know if our Full Quiver Family Planning was a success. So until then, the honeymoon would continue.

Chapter 27

Ministry of Deacons

I left my honeymoon suite energized and ready for my Monday morning meeting. It would be my first breakfast with the Ministry of Deacons. But this was no ordinary breakfast meeting. We were boarding a cruise liner that had been refitted as a personal yacht. It was owned by one of the deacons who'd once been a seaman. Such rags to riches tales were not unusual for the crewmen who manned these ships, 25% of whom were Filipinos.

But despite everything that had happened in the last few days, I was still shocked when Mika introduced me to the owner of the vessel, my new father-in-law, Cesar Santos.

"I told you." Mika said. "You're the only thing I ever wanted but couldn't buy. Now you know I wasn't exaggerating."

"I'll bet you didn't know you were becoming the Mick Jagger of Children's book authors when you married my Mika." Cesar said. "Not only did you get a young wife with the deal, but you can take my little boat out for a spin any time you like."

"Yes, take your little boat out for a spin. I'll save a ton on ski boats rentals."

"You certainly will."

Cesar pointed to a ski boat up on one of the lifeboat hoists.

"Wow, who can top that?" I said.

"You can, Ron." Cesar replied. "Success is not just about money. The Ministry of Deacons is waiting to hear your speech."

"Yes, I understand." I said.

I was happy Mika's father had a sense of humor, something every bit as necessary for survival as his lifeboats on hoists. Humor was something I always retained, except when I grieved. In the months after I'd lost my beloved son, I had to grab onto anything to keep me in the world of the living. Helping the desperate was one way I did this. Even then, I got dragged back into the land of the dead. I paid for the hospital bills of an indigent's

148

newborn who later died. But did I need to see her baby in that tiny coffin? It brought back all the anguish of losing my own son, and my brother. The house of sorrow needs our condolences, but the house of the dead is to be left alone. And to dwell on the dead too much comes too close to longing to join them. And that can lead a person to contact the dead, a thing that never entered my mind, but with the depth of my grief, I wasn't about to take chances. That's when I made a conscious decision to stop grieving.

Ye shall not regard them that work with spirits,
Neither fortune tellers:
Ye shall not seek them to be defiled by them,
I am the Lord thy God.

Today I was able to bring myself back from my funk without Mika's help. I'd already expended most of my grief while writing my speech for the Ministry of Deacons.

We were seated once again in a large banquet hall, this time on Cesar's cruiser. I felt as if we were back in the Philippines since there were so many Filipino crew members on board. The sound team had been testing the mics, but now Diego took over. He began our meeting with a prayer and a blessing over the food.

"Lord, we're here to seek your will and to follow it. Grant us wisdom. We ask also that you bless this food as we fellowship here today. In Jesus Name we pray. Amen."

It was an International Buffet and neither Mika nor I had trouble devouring everything on our plates. That's what Full Quiver Family Planning can do for the appetite. The deserts and coffee weren't enough to make us feel bloated either. Just as well, I was the keynote speaker but there were still a few speakers to precede me.

They began with stories about my grandfather and then my father and then Joey, all intended to show a seamless line of succession to me. I knew that there was such a thing as a mantle, a talent or duty that was carried on from generation to generation. But I'd not grasped the seriousness of the duty that had been laid upon me until now. Yes, I wrote stories, because that was in my family. I worked for myself, because that's what we all did. I'd never taken the corporate path, because none of us ever had, except for my uncle, who'd soared to the President of the Bank of Delaware, seemingly overnight. Yes, there are family mantles, and they must be treated with respect. And now I saw mine as clearly as those who'd selected me saw it.

And my duty? Retribution, in accordance with Scripture and the laws that the congress and the legislatures had given us. We would fight because Christians fight. How odd that these deacons, along with Diego, Joey, Mika's grandfather, and my grandfather, had all seen that there was something on me. In earlier times it would have been called an anointing, today, a calling. I took the podium.

Judging from the applause when I stepped onto the stage, there was an expectation. I searched the audience for those I'd met over the last few days. They had taken me the final steps to make sure this was all possible. There was Hank, the airport cop, who smuggled family members in to see their dying loved ones. Diego was standing with Tessie. They'd been married more than 20 years but only last week obtained civil protection for their God ordained union. Their love for their fellow man was evidenced in the way they risked all to save the 17 missing kids. And Edwin, who still knew something about the 2nd floor camera that none of the rest of us knew. And Edwin's wife, Bella, whose know-how got us into the hospital and down the hall to Dr. Jensen's office. Then there was Carmelita, Bruno's happiness in this world, who was snapping photos as I stood, our new media expert. And Bruno, himself, the center of attraction at nearly every event, paying more attention to Carmelita's curves than his best friend on the stage. Such were those who'd brought me here since Mika had planned my trip. And of all those watching as I took that stage, Mika knew me best, as only a stalker can know her man. Chief among biographers and investigators of old Ron, and still, with all she knew, she loved me. The volume on the mic had been set for a political event so I paced my words with a steady voice, but my words came out like fire.

"Let your light so shine before men, that they may see your good works, and glorify your Father which is in heaven. And are we ready to work! Amen?"

"Amen!" Boomed the response from the audience.

"A fools voice is known by a multitude of words so I'll be brief except for some verses here and there. *Behold, I send you forth as sheep in the midst of wolves: be ye therefore wise as serpents, and harmless as doves.* This is, and has been, the verse that has guided the Ministry of Deacons since my grandfather, and Mika's grandfather, set out on a mission to reach not just the so-called civilized world for Christ, but the darkest places on earth, where only Feds and Mobsters dare tread. Well, you're still treading there, so pray always and remember our guiding verse, I'll simply repeat it because I can't say it better than our Savior, Jesus:

Behold, I send you forth as sheep in the midst of wolves: be ye therefore wise as serpents, and harmless as doves.

As you all know, Georgia is the place that was chosen for the prosecution of President Trump. But why Georgia? Because the Georgia racketeering statute allows for prosecutions of those who by the laws of any other state would be innocent. And listen to this, the racketeering law of Georgia allows the DA of any of the 50 Judicial Circuits in Georgia to file a case. That's 50 DAs up for grabs to file cases against anyone who had anything to do with this genocide. And your knowledge of the underbelly of Georgia will be invaluable to us. Many of you already have contacts in Georgia, and why would that be? Well, as our Lord Jesus has told us, the *love* of money is the root of all evil. So, where would the Feds and the Mob be most heavily invested? Where the money is, of course, Georgia. I wondered why so many of our assets were there till I found this on the Georgia Department of Economic Development website. As you see on the screen behind me, they've proudly stated:

70% of U.S. transactions are handled by payment processing firms located in... Georgia!

How many card transactions do you make a day? The average person makes at least one. The Georgia Department of Economic Development claims that of the 30 transactions you make per month, 21 of them made their way through Georgia.

President Trump said he had a *perfect* call with Georgia officials after the election was stolen in 2020. Do you suppose that it makes sense to investigate, whether any of those associated with *Operation Warp Speed Commie Takeover* had a *perfect call*? And with 21 of their monthly transactions routed through Georgia, could there have been disputes that were handled based on white lies provided by those corrupt officials? And would any of those white lies become felonies when prosecuted under racketeering statutes? The answer is yes. For now, I won't name names, but I'm sure you can guess. But let me describe the individuals that orchestrated the communist overthrow of the US government. They are those within government who spread the false narrative that Covid 19 was dangerous to anyone other than seriously ill people. They are the ones who advocated gene therapy which they falsely marketed as vaccinations. They are the ones who recommended isolation through lockdowns which led to drug addiction, suicide, and untreated illness. They are the ones who recommended that our loved ones die alone. They are the ones who decided it was wise to incentivize hospitals and doctors to denounce tried-and-true treatments, who for the first time in history claimed natural immunity did not protect as thoroughly as vaccinations, who denied people early treatment so that they'd go back and infect all their families and return later when their case was too advanced, even for their *so called advanced protocols* to work. Yes, they are the ones who refused to give early outpatient treatment

152

with Ivermectin just so they could get a $13,000 admission, upped to $39,000 when they slapped them on a ventilator. But their deadly work was not done. They prescribed end of life opiates to hasten their victims' death. These are the ruthless corporatists and communists that tripled their money by ventilating too often and too soon. They are the ones who refused to perform community wide antibody tests to determine whether Covid was as deadly as they claimed. Instead, they chose testing that gave false negatives to increase their fake kill statistics. They are the ones responsible for this mass GMO Genocide, marketed as a vaccine, that is still killing young men more than any other cause of death. Since when has heart disease been the number one cause of death for young men? Yes, since the vax. They call them excess deaths, how convenient, they're the ones who claim the world has an excess population and that it must be decreased. These monsters have put themselves forward as heroes, but I seem to remember the words of a Charles Dickens character who voiced similar sentiments about those he hated. "If they would rather die, they had better do it, and decrease the surplus population." It was Scrooge who spoke those words. But unlike Scrooge, the monsters who brought this early death catastrophe upon us will not have a visit from the ghosts of Christmas past, present, and future with a reprieve. No, the crime has already been committed. Tiny Tim is dead from the vax and his brothers and sisters will follow soon. And many of those who have not died are in constant agony from vax side effects. These modern-day Scrooges will have a visit from local law enforcement, not ghosts. And if they want to repent, let them do it from a jail cell or the gallows.

So we'll test Georgia racketeering laws to see how many of the billions of Georgia monthly financial transactions involve any of these modern-day Scrooges. Al Capone was infamous for his gangland killing machine but was prosecuted on tax fraud. And it's Georgia RICO statutes that state when crimes occur under

Georgia laws. What's to prevent us from finding DAs willing to investigate, then prosecute, those who are guilty of genocide? We can prosecute them for minor transactions that when handled as racketeering cases are felonies and can include imprisonment of 5 years and up. When the political climate changes, *the only real kind of man-made climate change*, we'll seek indictments for their more heinous crime of genocide. Till then, we can use the same tactics that have been used against organized crime since the days of Al Capone.

What about your local doctor, or officials from your regulatory departments or anyone else involved in this genocide. How many of their bonuses for killing by vax were processed in Georgia and can be prosecuted as violations of the Georgia racketeering laws? Now why would Dr. This or Dr. That or anyone else call Georgia? Let's take a look at the Georgia Department of Economic Development website once again.

70% of U.S. transactions are handled by payment processing firms located in Georgia! That literally amounts to billions of transactions per month.

Now, you don't suppose that Dr. This or Dr. That might have checked one of their financial transactions during their time in the White House, do you? Certainly, the State of Georgia would not have a law on the books that could cause them to be prosecuted for their own *perfect call*, would they? And what is the recorded message we hear before the credit card company discusses our financial transactions with us? Something about it being recorded to serve us better? I can't name names yet, but we have recorded evidence, and they will be served.

And we're not alone in seeking justice. In Texas, we have an Attorney General on our side. He has a lawsuit against Pfizer for pushing a *vaccination* that he says has been proven to be less than 1% effective, a lawsuit that may open the door for other lawsuits against our beloved neighborhood doctors who take money to shoot our kids with poison, and who accept consultation fees for listening to drug company representatives tell them how to addict the next generation of kids. Now I thought that was the definition of a bribe. Lord willing, we'll soon find DAs who see it the same way the dictionary does.

We'll handle the rest of what we've got to do in small meetings. I'll be available at my table."

I left the podium. Of course there was applause. I was preaching to the choir. And was it loud! There were deacons from every state in the country. The Feds had no clue how deeply we'd penetrated their organizations, and it wasn't a crime. We were simply evangelizing.

The deacons disembarked before lunchtime as we'd already assigned tasks to those best suited to begin work in Georgia and Texas. The rest would continue to brainstorm with me throughout the week as we sought to implement an STD campaign across the nation. STD was our acronym for Scare the Doctors. Now they'd get a taste of their own medicine: fear. But it was one thing to get district attorneys across Georgia, and the nation, to prosecute for conspiratorial *vaccine* transactions. It was another to get it reported in the news. That would take a more clandestine operation, one aimed at the media. I hoped we could come up with a weekly prosecution in every state. Whether the prosecutions had anything to do with the genocide in progress didn't matter, as long as the public and the doctors thought it did. In addition to the payoffs related to *vaccines*, we knew there was more to the Covid hospital payments than had been made public. I personally was aware of billing department heads who'd reported all deaths as Covid to get the incarceration and suffocation payoffs. The financial transactions processed through Georgia, and that was 70% of them, could easily be prosecuted there. But it was important to make sure local media were reporting on local prosecutions as well. And the Ministry of Deacons had the personnel necessary to carry that out. They had about equal numbers of current and former FBI agents as they had current and former members of the Mob. The membership of the Ministry of Deacons totaled around 700, so that would be about 1% of the members of those *highly regarded* organizations. But that number is dwarfed by the number of self-described patriots who'd willingly take up the fight should President Trump give the order... or be taken into custody.

Mika could barely keep track of what was written between the lines on my face. But she had other things on her mind. It was afternoon and the Deacons had left. She squeezed my hand, then said.

"Daddy has a stateroom prepared for us. Let's go."

Chapter 28

The Stateroom

I'd only seen staterooms in pictures, so I didn't know what to expect when Mika led me down the ship's hallway. But I knew it had to be special, everything about Mika was. And this was no longer a cruise ship, but a newly christened superyacht, the Sortida Agua.

Mika held her key card up to the lock and I turned the handle. The suite was two stories. Stairs hugged a curved window with a view of the water. They led to a 2nd floor loft that had a ceiling made of giant skylights. If that weren't enough, it had two bedrooms, a large bathroom, hot tub, telescope, and entertainment center. The 1st floor had a dining room, a huge living room, an office, a galley, and a master bedroom.

But there was no furniture in the master bedroom, only lots of wedding presents. We removed the wrapping to reveal full sized replicas of the furniture at the Sortida. And each piece was right where it belonged.

"It's from Daddy to us." Mika said.

"It's a wonderful gift." I replied. "Now I can remember you as you were on our wedding night."

"As if you need help, Ron. Your memory is like a storybook, made of all your memories no matter how far past."

"That's a compliment I'll accept." I said. "It's one of my most beloved afflictions. But with you? I think my memories will be a blessing, not an affliction."

"Thanks, Ron. I'm blessed in the same way. My mind is a scrap book full of all the things I've discovered about you."

"Our kids are going to be quite the writers between your knack for turning a phrase and my storybooks." I said.

"I hope so." Mika replied.

Mika and I folded the gift wrap from the furniture. It would be a waste to throw away 10 years' worth of wrapping paper. By the

157

time we were done, our lunch had arrived.

"Talk about memories." I said. "It's Ivar's. I wonder how Jessica's doing."

Mika launched into such a beautiful aria of laughs, sighs, and giggles that I had to join in. We'd gotten news already that Jessica was okay, so it wasn't as if our laughter was at her, or was it?

"You should be ashamed of yourself, Ron."

"Yes, Mika. You too," I said.

That was enough to launch us into another spate of laughter till our hunger won out. A lonely seagull was perched on the rail outside our window. This prompted Mika to comment.

"This time I'm going to eat every one of these fries, Ron. These are so yummy. You know, I didn't get a chance to read the plaque at Ivar's. Who is Ivar anyway."

"Well, Mika, the plaque gives a folksy tale of who he was. But I don't know much about him, other than he opened a successful chain of seafood restaurants. He had no children, so he left nearly all his money to the two biggest universities in Washington State. It was just over 10 million. Seems like he would have had a lot more money than that, probably gave it away while he was still living. He paid for the waterfront fireworks every Fourth of July so it's likely he did a lot of good for a lot of people but just kept clam. Anyway, he's a beloved icon in Seattle."

"He was generous with his money but kept his clams?" Mika asked.

"No, keep clam is just an expression that Ivar was fond of. It means to keep your mouth shut so as not to reveal secrets, like a clam keeps its shell closed to keep its pearls hidden."

"Well, that's better yet, Ron. Our Lord said to keep our giving secret, and our Father in heaven who sees secretly, will reward us openly."

That was more than either of us expected to discuss about a tray of fish and chips and the man who made them famous. So I said the blessing and we sat down to eat.

Ron and Bruno

I was used to eating Ivar's Fish and Chips while sitting in the driver's seat of a taxi, not in an elegant stateroom on a superyacht. I'd paid my way through college as a cab driver, back in the 80s, and I used to eat at Ivar's at least three times a week.

Seattle was a hellhole back then, but it had gotten *worse*. It was a gotcha world for cops, who city officials would rather roast than support. Miraculously, the candidate who'd just run for city attorney was caught calling the cops pigs and lost because of it. Was there a chance Seattle was getting better? Who knows? But Seattle was not my problem today. I was eating one of my favorite foods in a stateroom worthy of princes. I had a bride, who if she married up, must have discovered something about me I didn't know. Mika read my mind.

"Daddy was right when he said you became the Mick Jagger of authors when you married me. I've never been in a stateroom like this either, Ron. Daddy was saving this for my wedding present, but on paper, it's a partial advance on my inheritance."

"A partial advance, she says. If this is a partial advance, I can't help asking, if you were to assign a percentage, how partial is it?"

"Oh, maybe 5%, if you include the cost of fuel, personnel, and insurance. You still love me, don't you, Ron?"

"Considering I loved you before I knew your name, of course I still love you. There's no still about it. I'll always love you."

"I have another question for you, Ron. Can we live here till our first born is a year old?"

"Now that's a question I'll have to ponder, Mika. '*A man has to be king of his own ranch style tract home.*' That's my favorite quote from my favorite poor boy rich girl romance comedy, *Who's Minding the Store?* But it expresses King Solomon's words when he said, *A gracious woman retains honor: and strong men retain riches.*"

"I'll sign this stateroom over to you if that makes a difference." Mika said.

"You are really an astounding woman, Mika. We'll figure out

a way to make sure this is my *ranch style tract home*, and that the world we live in is mine. On top of that, we'll make sure our life reflects our dedication to the Lord and your submission to me. As long as all that's taken care of, my answer is yes. We can live here."

"I'm glad you answered like that." Mika said. "Our lives, our family, our everything, will always be under your control with God's guidance as He commands us in Ephesians 5:22."

"Amen." We spoke in unison.

Wives, submit yourselves
to your own husbands,
as unto the Lord.

Chapter 29

A New Kind of Sickness

It seemed as if we'd just arrived, but it was the beginning of our fifth week on board, and today was my second monthly meeting of the Ministry of Deacons. I'd be appointing Bruno as my right-hand man. Bruno had an uncanny ability to spot crooks in a crowd. Who better to keep me from *distractions*. A distraction is a person who turns you off course. Sometimes they're allies with a misunderstanding of time and priorities. Conversations with them need to be delegated out. Others are your enemies and need to be weeded out. Either way, Bruno was the man for the job. He could make a life-or-death decision in half a second, and he could size up people just as quickly. Not that my years of cab driving hadn't exposed me to the criminal element, but street thugs can't compare to those who've managed to keep themselves out of jail, despite a lifetime of crime. And Bruno's ability to judge character was so keen that I was convinced he'd inherited the talent from his dad.

The fact is, I couldn't do the job alone, and I trusted Bruno more than anyone else. And he wasn't going to just be a fancy doorkeeper. No, the Ministry of Deacons needed him as much as I did.

They had put together a most wanted list of dirty doctors, called *The Registry*. *The Registry* contained all the bios that the dirty doctors had posted on the websites of every employer they'd ever worked for. To that was added the Dirty Doctors' misrepresentations of their work history, education, and personal background, plus information about any malpractice suits, or criminal charges filed against them. All of this was done in keeping with my wanting to use parasites to get to the head of the rotting fish. Bring enough lawsuits against the doctors who ran the institutions that benefited from genocide payments, and they'd be willing to turn state's evidence against the higher ups. The Registry was a browsable database that Bruno could use to communicate with the deacons who ran our investigations. This gave him the ability to prioritize who to go after first. If the deacon assigned to the case disagreed with Bruno, they could chat about it via text or live chat. But neither Bruno nor I relished calls with anyone who wasn't related to us. When you go deaf, you realize most people say a lot of nothing. Better to get to the point and have it documented through messaging chats, than grow an organization of back patters and paper pushers.

But the Ministry of Deacons was nothing of the sort. The deacons had been busy with their work, compiling another database. It contained the resumes of cops who'd barely managed to keep their jobs after refusing the vax. Bruno would be browsing that database too and conducting interviews with them. They'd be recruited to go after institutional criminals, those responsible for the deaths and injuries of workers forced to take the vax.

Oh, but they weren't forced, no. They only had a lifetime of retirement benefits to lose if they didn't take the poison. First, they were heroes, essential workers, first responders, but when the humanicide came out, they were painted as villains and anti-vaxers for refusing to be sprayed, I mean shot. I'm trying to imagine an insect staying still while being stabbed with poison. As for our fellow citizens? The hypnotic drone from the media had worked on too many of them.

The media was paid to spread lies by Big Pharma. But the Attorney General of Texas was suing Pfizer now. He said, "Pfizer intentionally misrepresented the efficacy of its Covid-19 vaccine and censored persons who threatened to disseminate the truth." He also said that the Covid-19 vaccine's "absolute risk reduction" was a piddling 1%.

Our work was aimed at multiplying the number of cases against Big Pharma and the doctors who goose stepped to their drumbeat. And Bruno, would be one of our best assets.

I didn't know if it went hand in hand with Bruno's talent for spotting crooks, but he had a photographic memory. And I was anxious to see him get to work. I knew he was getting antsy after his retirement. This assignment was exactly what he needed, and his talent was exactly what we needed.

As a private organization, we couldn't entrap people like the cops could. So Bruno would be putting together a team of cops, anxious to lay traps for those who'd committed genocide.

Imagine officials who are so greedy that poisoning their own navy pilots is nothing to them. Well, we don't have to imagine. Navy pilots who were forced to be vaxed, and that's all of them, were having nearly 10 times the normal rate of heart attacks than before the vax rolled out. It's reasonable to assume that our men in blue were experiencing the same dreadful results.

The cops Bruno's team would recruit, simply had to identify the doctors who got lucrative government contracts, contracts to kill those who'd pledged to protect and to serve. It wouldn't be hard. Cops exchange stories all the time of big shots who think they can break traffic laws with impunity. "Don't you know who I am?" They'd say. Well, the cops knew who they were, because they kept records to make sure they weren't stepping on any politician's toes. A few days of talking shop with cops on the beat, and our embedded officers would have a list of who the killers were by their own admissions during traffic stops. Then they'd entrap them for our deacons who'd send their cases to friendly District Attorneys in Georgia. DAs who weren't afraid to call up a grand jury. The 30% whose financial transactions hadn't gone through Georgia, would be handed over to DAs in their own states to see who could be prosecuted for other crimes. The rest would be handled with civil lawsuits that we would fund. And the civil lawsuits were the path of least resistance. The vax injured were in the millions and the deaths were in the hundreds of thousands if you count from the day vaxes rolled out.

If all went well, we could have enough under indictment and getting sued, that whistleblowers would start coming out of the woodwork. We knew the vax had been a genocidal conspiracy. The question was, what would it take for the rest of the public to know it too, and finally be freed from the spell cast by the Feds, Big Pharma, and Satan himself.

I pitied those who could no longer question authority, until I remembered. These were the same ones who had proudly placed the famous poster on their walls that contained just two words:

Question

Authority

Their sincerity then was no greater than it was now. And once *they'd* taken authority, they no longer allowed it to be questioned. No, they touted authority. The CIA and FBI were lauded by Legacy Media. Well, all this was a call to action, and I was ready for it.

The monthly meeting for the Ministry of Deacons was the only one open to wives. So Carmelita, Bella, and Mika were all there. We'd barely begun our meals when Bella, who was on the other side of the room, started retching, as if her food had been poisoned. Then Carmelita, who was sitting a few tables away began.

And finally, Mika, who was sitting next to me, pulled out a bag from her purse. As the three retched, there was a simultaneous gasp from those in attendance. The room echoed with the sound of dropped silverware. They thought we'd all been poisoned.

Then Bruno stood up and bellowed. "Morning sickness!"

When the guests realized the cause for our wives' conditions, the chuckles, laughter, and finally applause began, as they stood up to congratulate us on the good news. First time I'd witnessed a standing ovation for vomiting. But leave it to Carmelita, our media expert, between her own retches and the others, she was able to get some video clips to throw up on X.

Chapter 30

The Honeymooners

Bruno had reluctantly moved with Carmelita into a stateroom on my father-in-law's superyacht. They stayed Monday mornings through Friday afternoons. Then they'd commute by ferry back to Bruno's ranch. The only good part of it in Bruno's estimation, was that he wouldn't be dogged by a security team every day. Living on a ship took care of both privacy and security. This way, both of us could focus on completing our tasks, tasks which neither Bruno nor I wanted to last beyond the election.

Being godfather to my new wife's family was one thing, but running something that rivaled the office of attorney general in a large state was another. I had Christian children's stories to write, and Bruno had just begun raising grass fed beef. Surely the Ministry of Deacons had their own experts, ones who could take over our ministry work. Yes, I understood that if this was my calling, I had to stick with it. But I wasn't convinced that running a huge ministry was where the Lord wanted me. It was a lot of work, and I had a lot of kids, and grandkids. And Mika was pregnant and... I was blessed. I was enjoying myself so much that I had time to think stupid thoughts. What else would I do? This was where God wanted me.

"Praise God!" I thought to myself as I sat in the lounge chair on the deck outside my stateroom.

This time it was Bruno who read my thoughts. No, he didn't read between the lines on my face. He probably didn't care to look at my old mug any more than I cared to look at his. Besides, we had a sunset to watch from the lounge chairs outside our staterooms. We each had wool deck blankets to cover our legs and the heat lamp hanging from the awning radiated warmth on us. We were sharing a freshly brewed pot of coffee that sat on the table between us, one of those aromatic Seattle blends, the kind with a hypnotic effect.

166

"Yep, we're blessed." Bruno said, replying to my thoughts.

"And to imagine there are Americans who think having kids is a curse!" I replied.

"Welp," Bruno said, "if not for blessings. Well, never mind."

"I'll second the motion. Never mind is right."

It was rare that Bruno and I shut up. But the coffee was good, the service was great, and the crimson clouds that covered the sun were beautiful. Mika had just filled up my coffee cup and dropped off my dessert. Carmelita had done the same for Bruno. Neither of our wives behaved as if their serving us was a chore. They were enjoying it. They could've been singing karaoke, playing music, or taking selfies, but their preferred entertainment was to wait on their husbands and stand at the rail looking out at the water.

The Seattle rain had begun and the few minutes of shutting up was all Bruno and I could take. So we called it a night and headed back to our staterooms.

When Mika and I got back to ours, she said.

"Ron, maybe I'm just a little sick. I might not be pregnant. We better make sure."

"You have a pregnancy test?" I asked.

"Silly, that's not what I meant." She said.

Our stateroom had one of those showers that sprayed from all sides, just like the one at the Sortida. Mika removed my hearing aids and placed them in the charger next to the bed. Then she took my hand and led me to the shower. What can I say? Nothing. I don't kiss and tell.

Chapter 31

A Day at Work

Mika and I had grown accustomed to the brunches at the Sortida, so we continued our custom onboard her father's superyacht. But we were early risers, so we'd start our days with leftovers from the night before, followed by coffee. This way, we were able to continue our honeymoon before my workday began and still have time for brunch together.

As a writer, my custom was to spend two hours of research for every hour I spent writing. Yes, children's books require research. As for the ones I wrote, a good portion of my research was spent reading the Bible. But since my tales were woven into a web of cultural dilemmas, I kept abreast of current events in education. That included updates on what the sewage inspectors had discovered spewing from the boards of uneducation. It was a job few wanted. The sewage inspectors were on the Attorney General's list of insurrectionists, targets for prosecution. Some sewage inspectors (aka parents) had dared confront the boards of uneducation and been jailed.

My research now, was not that much different from the research I'd conducted for my books, except now, much of my research was delegated to the deacons. They'd whittle it down to the bare facts and send them to me. Then I'd speed scan what they sent and decide where to put our assets. Some bad things had just been revealed regarding vax injuries. That was just one of the things Bruno and I would discuss today.

Mika and I had finished our brunch, so I took my daily walk around the deck before heading to the conference room to meet Bruno. He and I would pass each other a couple of times during these morning walks, then turn in for our meeting. We were about to pass each other for the fifth time on our morning walk when Bruno spoke up.

"Ready for our tête-à-tête?" He said.

"I'm ready." I replied.

We turned into the corridor that led to the conference room, then took our seats across from each other. Pastrami, roast beef, cheese, and slices of butter to put in our coffee were waiting for us. We each had a two-sided monitor connected to a Linux. Bruno plugged in his flash drive to his Linux. I plugged my flash drive into mine.

"I'm gonna have to ask *you* to pray today, Ron. We're gonna be looking at some pretty disgusting stuff and I'm too angry to think straight."

"Okay with me, Bruno.

Lord, You know our hearts. Strengthen us and protect us as we seek justice and retribution in accordance with Your Word. You have given us a book of laws and You have given us officials in offices who can enforce those laws. Let our hands be far from lawlessness but kept strong in protecting the innocent."

"Amen." Bruno and I agreed.

"I wasn't exaggerating, old Ron. Here's the latest."

Bruno played a video that told the story of 22 vax injured who'd been flown to NIH for treatment. The video laid out how NIH knew there were more vax injuries but did nothing to help them.

"So, what are these guys up to?" Bruno asked.

"Sounds like Guinea pigs in reverse, Bruno. There was little experimentation involved. The vax injured came in, they were treated, and they went home, mostly cured. But we're just a couple of jokers compared to this kind of government secrecy. Have you got some cops who measure up to this kind of case."

"I've interviewed some geniuses, Ron. And I'm not using the word pejoratively like we usually do. They're real smart guys. I'll talk to them later and see who wants to go after this crowd of, I hate to use so much French, Ron, but there's only one word for officials who have a cure and don't give it to every patient, bastards. The NIH knows people are vax injured. They know how to treat them. But they only treat a tiny fraction of them? I haven't heard of this kind of crime anywhere, and the old man told me about every kind of crime you can imagine. Some of them turn your stomach. But this one, how can they let an entire nation of vax injured suffer when they've got the cure? There are little kids and teenagers suffering, and all the other vax injured. Jeffrey Dahmer is a lightweight compared to these NIH guys."

"It's baffling, Bruno. Well, mass murder is always baffling. So what else you got for me?"

"I've got a list of every member of the World Economic Forum along with where they eat, sleep, and play. Addresses, mistresses, I've got everything."

"Well, that's interesting." I said.

"Hah. Yep."

"What else, Bruno?"

"Some of the cops I've been talking with think it would be a good idea to track down the doctors and nurses involved with vaxing our politicians, Big Pharma execs too. They want to find out if they were getting the real vax or if it was just a saline solution."

"I'm sure you took their suggestion as an order."

"I did. And we're working on it."

"Anything else, Bruno?"

"Yeah, there's some side business that at some point has to be dealt with."

"What's that?" I asked.

"The cops I've been interviewing have been wondering about the 17 missing kids, Ron."

I stepped out of our conference room door and picked up my phone from the slot on the wall. Then I texted my father-in-law, Cesar.

"Council meeting. When?"

"2pm." He texted back.

I stepped back into the conference room, shut the door, and

said to Bruno.

"Okay, it's set. We'll be meeting at 2pm with Diego and all the council members."

In advance of the meeting, Bruno and I brainstormed every possible way to take the 17 missing kids public. In fact, it wasn't the first day we'd discussed it. The problem of keeping the kids incognito had been on our minds ever since Diego told us about them. The biggest question was, under whose jurisdiction would these kids be, once their existence was made public. And who would their guardians be? Diego and Tessie would be most able to answer those questions.

I had my afternoon meal with Mika before the council arrived. Time for family and friends was important to both of us. So, rather than waste unscheduled hours on pastimes during the day, we spent our free time wisely with family, friends, and just being human. Something most people do too little of.

While taking bites of my afternoon meal, I called my kids. As my ears were busy with conversation, my eyes were busy enjoying the view... of my wife. Mika was having her pregnancy glow. Some women have it for the whole nine months. I hoped Mika would too. As for her baby bump, it was likely my imagination. She was barely a month pregnant. But the thought of being a father again made me experience a kind of pregnancy glow myself.

Not all the changes in the world are unwelcome. It was a relief to know that no matter what craving Mika would have, it could be fulfilled within minutes by an app. And if that weren't enough, Chinatown was just a few blocks away. Crazy thing, we both loved food so much that we were always craving something, and for that, Seattle was the place to be.

"We're ready." Diego announced over the intercom.

"I gotta head out." I said to Mika.

"Okay, Ron." She said.

But she wasn't so brief in her send off.

"I really gotta go." I said.

"Okay, okay. Just one last kiss." Mika coaxed me, as if coaxing were necessary.

I wasn't anxious to leave, but none of the people I loved would be safe if we didn't do something about the doctatorship. Mika and I, and all of our ancestors, had a mission, plus all those they'd brought into what had become a huge fellowship of believers. It was made up of not only regular members, but deacons across the country. Funny how people can think Big Guy's the real president, when 50 operatives from the CIA lied without consequence about the authenticity of Hunter Biden's laptop. And that's not a rigged election? The same bunch of liars from the CIA and the FBI had lied about Russian Collusion. But no worry, we were scolded by the talking heads, pay no heed to those pulling the levers behind the curtain.

Mika could still read between the lines on my face but there was too much to read without making me late for my meeting. So she reluctantly pushed me out the door, giving me one last kiss, after the *last*, last kiss.

Chapter 32

The Council Meeting

I sat down in the conference room a few minutes before the meeting was called to order. The monitors were folded back into the table and wide screens at both ends of the room had taken their place. Diego was standing at the podium, ready to give his presentation. The topic was not new. Every member of the council had been brainstorming a solution for the 17 missing kids. Diego had put all the possible solutions up on the screens.

Captain Henry Lewis, Hank to all present, gave the prayer.

"Lord, may we find a solution for the 17 missing kids. Amen."

"Amen." We concurred.

Diego began his presentation.

"We have a lot of possibilities on these screens." Diego said. "A lot of possibilities for what we can do, and when. But whatever we do, it must be clear in the public's mind what we are doing. This process began the moment Tessie and I took the kids out of the hospital and into our care. Take time to look at this list before we discuss it. It includes every idea from every person in this room."

Diego sat down and sipped his coffee while we sipped ours. While we read, there was a knock at the door. The sergeant at arms opened it and was handed an envelope. He then handed it to Diego. When Diego saw who it was from, he quickly opened it. He read through the contents twice, and as he did, he began to chuckle. By the time he took his place at the podium again, he was laughing and shedding tears of joy.

"We're all aware of the heavenly coincidences that have happened to each one of us around this table." We nodded in agreement. Diego continued. "Well, another has just occurred. We have been waiting for our 17th kid to have his adoption finalized, and I have just been handed the approval. Every one of the 17 kids has been officially adopted. And, as adoptions are very secretive, I am not at liberty to discuss where the adoptions took place, what the real names of the children were before adoption, or what those names are now. Nor may I tell you where they reside today. In fact, I am forbidden from telling anyone, including the CIA, the FBI, the Seattle police, or anyone else who might ask the details of these adoptions. Every detail of what happened with the kids between the time they left the hospital till now, by law, must remain a secret. But I can assure you, they are all... safe!"

The conference room erupted with applause. Then we stood as our applause turned into a rhythmic beat: the primal sound that accompanies the capture of prey or the joy of victory. We had won. The 17 missing kids had found safety and any investigation into where they'd gone could be prosecuted as custodial interference. Diego and Tessie had locked the CIA, the FBI, and the media into a box that had no key.

"There is one task remaining." Diego continued. "And that is for Bruno to announce, live, right now, what I have just explained. But we'll go out on deck for this. We don't need any fancy TV crews; Legacy Media is dead. We've got Camerlita, as she's affectionately known, not just to Bruno, but to her millions of followers on X, as well as to those present today. But before Bruno speaks, I'd like Doc to pray."

I stood and prayed.

"Thank You Lord, for using Diego, Tessie, and all those involved in the protection of the 17 missing kids. Thank You also for Your Light, Your Son, in a world of chaos. Lord God, let our enemies continue to be confused and their movements difficult. Let them be filled with the dread of defeat. We thank You also for preparing Bruno for that day, when assisted by Your angels, he saved the 17 missing kids from a fiery death. May this event be a witness to others to turn to You, to be saved from the fiery second death of hell. Most of all, we thank You for Your healing hand, that throughout all this, Diego, Tessie, and the 17 missing

174

kids, have been kept safe. May Your will be done on earth as it is in heaven. In Jesus Name we pray. Amen."

Camerlita was waiting for us on deck. She picked a spot with the best view, and an awning, *in the unlikely event that it would rain in Seattle.* Bruno stood up for his announcement.

"A number of years ago, a 4-alarm fire burned up a building that had 17 kids inside. The kids survived. I didn't know it till a little over a month ago. And now, I have the pleasure to announce that all 17 of those kids... have been adopted. I'll leave it to you to speculate on who they were, why someone wanted them dead, who their parents were, even who adopted them. But by law, none of those involved in their adoptions can say a word. That's how adoption law works in the states where the kids are now. And yes, you can still use pound 17 missing kids to look them up on X. I know all you sophisticates call it hashtag but for us hicks that's one syllable too long. The 17 missing kids are still missing to those of you who love them, and have prayed for them, and they're missing to those who wanted to kill them. But they're safe now."

Camerlita did her work as the professional she'd become. 15 minutes later, Cesar let down the gang plank for the press. They'd already gathered, having been first to receive Camerlita's X posts. But I doubt they appreciated her press corps of one. Camerlita had scooped them once again.

The press was such an ugly sight, knowing what I knew about them, and knowing how they rejected God's love. It didn't matter their clothes or botoxed faces, their hearts were hard, and their master was the world. What is uglier than a child that rejects a father's loving embrace? That's what the world is, and that's what an unbeliever is, an ugly child who refuses our heavenly Father's healing touch. Well, I was torn between throwing pearls to swine and preaching to the choir, but there were certainly some in between, whose hearts might still be open to the gospel. I hoped to find out soon. I missed writing the simple stories that had kept my family fed. Even more, I missed the emails from readers who told me my latest story had led them to a saving knowledge of our Lord and Savior Jesus, the Messiah.

Mika was reading between the lines on my face, again. The moment I noticed, she complained.

"Hey, I was reading *everything*, and when you saw me, half the letters dropped off the page, I mean, your face. Now all I can read is *I love you*. Is that what's written on your face, Ron?"

"It's always written there for you, Mika. You just have to do the word puzzle. Kind of spoils the effort when the answer is always the same, huh?"

"No, Ron, I always love reading *I love you* on your face. I love even more that you can't hide it. I love you too."

Camerlita and Bruno were having no less of a moment. We'd all been blessed with the removal of one of the biggest worries on our minds. It was intoxicating. Diego and Tessie were nearly floating around the deck as every person on board congratulated them.

And for those who didn't share in our elation, there were drinks, free drinks for everyone. But the only ones drinking were members of the press corps. Not only had they been scooped, but by law, they couldn't provide one speck of information more than Camerlita had already posted. It was entertaining to see them in their natural state, blitzed. Jessica Whatshername had gotten a head start, as usual. Yes, she was back in the mix, including the mixed drinks. And the only ones who could tolerate the tales she was telling were others in the press. Her bawdy stories were enough to burn the ears off a decent person. The laughs of her compadres echoed out the doors of the press room. Yes, Cesar had a press room. It saved time for the crew. This way there was only one room where spilled liquor and vomit had to be mopped off the floor. From the looks of it, maybe a man *could* get pregnant. Even the male reporters were displaying signs of morning sickness. I wondered if Camerlita would get a few photos to throw

Ron and Bruno

up on X as she'd done before.

Chapter 33

Nightly Praise & Worship

Jessica had a tolerance for liquor that few could match. And after most of the press corps had left, she was still drinking and bragging about her exploits to those who'd arrived late. The rest of the press corps had already staggered down the gang plank and into taxis, after picking up their indispensable press releases.

That was the state of the news. Press releases could be used in their entirety, or in part, without attribution. Sure, this had been the way the press had gotten their news for the last century. But that's where the real talent began, sorting out the truth from the press releases. At least that's where it used to begin. But decades of college graduates with no real talent, except for copying others' work, along with computers and new technology, started a new form of reporting: copy and paste. It was no wonder when vast sectors of the government, both federal and local, took advantage of these faux educated graduates' laziness by feeding them propaganda. I'd seen lazy students practicing in cheat groups for college exams. I graduated 10 years late, so I can't say whether my generation was guilty of the same. But by the 80s, cheating was the norm. And who knew how many professors were in on the cheating. After all, if they could get dedicated commies to spread their lies, they didn't care if they were *capable commies* or not. And it's not an oxymoron to call them that. A commie is nothing more than a copy machine. If they put out the same propaganda that's put in, they're as *capable* as any *useful idiot* can be.

Cesar had a security detail to deal with stragglers, so he let the press hang out in the press room while we went for our nightly worship service in the ship's banquet hall.

I'd never been part of a church with so many *capable Christians*. And sad to say, that often *is* an oxymoron. I've never seen a man put down a Bible as quickly as a newborn Christian

178

walking out of a megachurch. The pastor becomes his new Bible and matriarchy his new religion. But Cesar's family was nothing like that. In fact, the service on Cesar's ship was half Bible verses and half praise music. And the praise lyrics were as close to the Bible as I'd sung, other than from old hymns books.

Bruno was happy about it, too. I hadn't realized how beautifully he could sing till he sang aboard Cesar's superyacht. And tonight was special. The banquet hall on the ship was full, not just with the deacons and their wives, but entire congregations of churches from across Western Washington. Diego had sent out texts to all the pastors, pastors of churches that had met secretly for much of the past few years.

This was what my grandfather had begun by handing out tracts at the ferry terminal in Bremerton. And it was the conversion of a would-be killer, Uncle Joey, that had brought me here. I wondered who had brought my grampa to Christ. Who was the person who'd shared the gospel with him? But it's never just a man or woman who does that. It's the Holy Spirit as He moves upon the hearts of men and women. I was happy He'd moved upon my heart and upon Mika's.

Mika and I smiled at each other. We were a pair. I reminisced. She read my thoughts. We had a destiny. She was carrying our child.

I wasn't in the mood for tears, even if they would be tears of joy. This was a celebration. I didn't want tears of any kind. I held Mika's hand, we sang hymns, and we read Bible verses.

Chapter 34

A War Had Begun

I'd always hated the word denomination, but in our case, it was a term used loosely. God's Word was our authority. Each man used his Bible. And as many as were capable, were pastors. Every man was the authority over his own family. Those who were not, had not stood with us, but had turned over their families to be vaccinated by the doctatorship.

During the lockdowns, our churches met secretly. When discovered, they were closed, and another was quietly opened. It doesn't take rocket science to open a church secretly, not when everyone in public is masked. As long as there are no snitches, it's literally a matter of minutes. And our grampas, Mika's and mine, set the stage for secrecy when they witnessed to those in the darkest places, bringing them light and hope through Jesus. The fact was, we still had a secret church. We just met in public for now. We could easily go underground again. And even though the 17 missing kids were no longer secret, we still had secrets.

One such secret, is a plan of action in the event of a societal collapse, a societal collapse that the Feds hope to hasten with their cronies in the judiciary and their media mouthpieces. Remove the opportunity for free and fair elections, and yes, you will have a societal collapse. The elites are planning on it, hoping to reap huge profits from a civil war, hoping to make a killing as they have in Ukraine. But there's one problem. The only law breakers are on their side. The United States has seen less than sixty assassinations of public officials in the 250 years since the declaration of independence. Some countries have that many assassinations per year. So if no one on our side is planning an insurrection, who is the elite planning to fight in a societal breakdown? Their plan has long been for the downtrodden to rise up against the ruling class. But they've become the ruling class, and we've become the downtrodden. And now they've given up on class warfare and turned to racial division. So, how's that gone? Huge numbers of young black men, the ones they tried to racially divide, identify more with Trump, the billionaire, than with the Democrat party. Since Trump, Democrats have had to change all their plans to ad hoc attempts to censor him and remove him from the ballot. And the kangaroo court in New York that convicted him on 34 non-crimes? Where did that get them? Within 36 hours of the verdict, Trump raised fifty million bucks, not in spite of the so-called conviction but *because* of it. And that's not including the fund raising of the PACs and the party apparatus itself.

Well, their plans, really aren't a plan at all, they're more of a reaction to revolutionaries. And last time I checked, the revolutionaries are the ones winning against reactionaries. There's little reason to fear that this time it will be any different. And this time: WE ARE THE REVOLUTIONARIES. Anyone hear of Javier Milei? He and others like him are a force that America's progressives haven't prepared for. As the reactionaries that America's neoleftists are, everything they've been doing has been from the playbook of failed dictatorships. Only this time, it's a failed doctatorship. And if Americans simply quit going to the doctor for meds, they'll not only be healthier, but half the funding for neoleftists will dry up. The rest will dry up when gun running politicians stop killing people. We already knew that Ukraine was a money laundering operation for US politicians. But now they've added an extra step, kill people before sending the money out the back door. Oh, I can hear their objections now. It's a war to preserve democracy. Is that why Zelinsky just suspended the elections?

And the doctatorship? They're moving from one poison to the next. They already have over a hundred million obese Americans, guinea pigs, to experiment on with their newest poison: an FDA approved anti-fat pill that interferes with the proper function of the gastrointestinal tract. Now I thought that the gut microbiome protected us from disease, and that it was found inside our gastrointestinal tract. Mess with that, and you mess with our natural immunity. But what do doctors care about natural immunity. There's more to be made off poison than making people well.

But even with all this, plus their AI, they're still losing the battle of predicting what will happen next. They know, and their AI is programmed to know, that history repeats itself. But you can never tell which part of history it will be. Maybe this time it will be the French revolution with mass beheadings. Or might the targets of an angry electorate be doctors and drug company executives, responsible for cheat by mail voting and death by vax. How would a trial in a red state go for them? We'll find out.

And the civil suits will offer them no protection by pardons. We've been taking note of their methods against Trump, and we're improving on them. Only we're using their tactics against the real racists and killers, the ones who recommend ivermectin for non-European immigrants to the U.S. as a harmless dewormer, but when old white men want to use it for more serious contagions, they refer to it as horse medicine. How many died for lack of immediate treatment with ivermectin? Some estimates put it in the millions. And that's just in America.

Well, we know the plans of the Feds, because their assets are loyal only to themselves, to a sexuality, or a victimhood. By definition, a diversity hire is not promoted for the content of their character, and the federal government is full of such hires, chosen not for the content of their character, but for the color of their skin, or their rainbow. At the highest levels in every sense of the word high, they think only of themselves, their victimhood, and their sexuality. They can no more keep their plans to attack the citizenry secret, than they can keep their pronouns secret. Yes, we know their plans. But do they know ours?

If there were any old school assets still left in the CIA, or the FBI, surely, they would know our plans. It would be easy. Pick up a novel, read a few lines of an angry post, or count the numbers of service men refusing to rejoin the military. Problem for them, is there are too many plans for them to get a good read. There are literally hundreds of peaceful plans that can be carried out in the event of a societal collapse. But the Feds have only one plan: Get Trump. And if they succeed? Even RINO David Brooks says, "Ivy League judges taking Trump off the ballot would cause this country to explode." But David Brooks has it wrong by two letters. Implosion is the word, not explosion, because citizens will simply stop complying without one shot being fired.

Chapter 35

Anything But War

Mika was still experiencing her pregnancy glow. Her morning sickness was gone, and our days and nights were anything but war. We'd developed that deeper trust that comes with time. We didn't have much to complain about so we ad libbed fights to keep the fire going. It's easier than it sounds. She'd behave her worst and I'd behave my best, scolding her when she didn't go along with my wishes. With her art for laughter and my art for writing, the fights never lacked a good story line, or a happy ending... in bed.

I'd been able to return to writing through strict time management. I spent 56 hours a week on ministry, 56 hours a week for uninterrupted nightly sleep, and 56 hours a week for eating, calls to my family, time with Mika, story writing, and a day of rest.

It was a blessing having Mika as a sounding board for my stories. I used to call my kids and read them my rough drafts, but now I called them to read them my prepublication versions. But their skills had become so polished that their input would still require one final edit.

Bruno's organic ranching had come along too. He had several large herds of grass-fed cattle that he grazed on cutover timberland. He'd picked up nearly 500 acres at a bargain price. The grass had cropped up naturally and since it had never been grazed, his beef had more nutrients than any this side of the 19th century.

Bruno was not one to be idle either. So if he wasn't doing work for the Ministry of Deacons, he was researching cattle care. And Carmelita made sure to interrupt him at just the right times to keep him from getting bored.

So Bruno's and my itineraries were full. But they didn't require we stay in one place. And as if reading our minds, Cesar walked in on us while we were doing Ministry planning.

"Hope I haven't caught you at a bad time, have I?" Cesar

asked.

"Not at all." Bruno said. "What's on your table?"

"Speaking of which." Cesar replied. "How are your herds?"

"They're awaiting their final act of altruism." Bruno said.

"Well, we wouldn't want to prevent them from committing a selfless act. That's why I keep ordering from you. But I'm wondering, are you two up for a change in scenery?"

I didn't have to answer. Cesar knew I hated Seattle. I hadn't moved to Phoenix for the rain. And Bruno hadn't moved across Puget Sound for concrete. He hated Seattle just as much as I did. And neither of us had been off the ship in months, other than Bruno's trips to tend to his herds.

Cesar looked at us, then said.

"I'm getting tired of Seattle too. And I'm getting tired of seeing two old men get older who just months ago, were as young as any I'd met. We're headed out tomorrow. Does your ranch require anything other than cowboys and a vet?"

"Nope." Bruno said. "Except for a few kind words from me."

"Okay, Bruno, we'll add a cow cuddler. The Ministry of Deacons will pick up the tab. And don't worry, Bruno. We'll keep your buyers supplied. Are you in?"

"I'm in." Bruno said.

"Me too." I said.

"You don't want to know where we're headed?" Cesar asked.

"Who cares. Anywhere but here!" Bruno and I spoke as one.

"Well, then it's settled. We'll reach Panama in two weeks and in a month, we'll be in Venice. From there we can wing it. Not literally, I'm too spoiled living in this castle on the water."

"You mind if I ask you a money question?" Bruno said.

"Not at all." Cesar replied.

"I know a ship captain is paid well, but it doesn't add up to hundreds of millions. Could you share with me and old Ron, how you came to have so much dough?"

"Certainly." Cesar replied. "I don't sow what I don't want to

185

reap. I don't want to reap perversion, so I don't invest in Disney or companies like them. I don't want to reap idolatry, so I don't invest in sports teams. I don't want to reap military interventions, so I don't invest in military stocks. I don't want to reap poison, so I don't invest in Big Pharma. I don't want to reap medical corruption, so I don't invest in medical facilities. I don't want to reap egotism, so I don't invest in entertainment. And I don't want to reap lies, so I don't invest in Legacy Media. And the Lord has blessed me for my choices."

Cesar wasn't one to multiply words. He'd just described in 45 seconds the investment strategy that had made him a millionaire. And it amounted to forsaking the world.

For what shall it profit a man,
if he gain the whole world,
and lose his own soul?

Neither Bruno nor I could focus on work after Cesar told us about the cruise, so we called it a day and returned to our staterooms.

Mika and I spent the rest of the day as if it were a holiday, just hanging out. We ordered from the Sortida for old times' sake. The food was great. The coffee was too. The rest of our afternoon, and the evening, was indescribable. And considering I don't kiss and tell; no description is necessary.

Chapter 36

The Deacons Return

We'd reached open waters by the time Mika and I woke up. There was a misty rain lightly blowing against the windows. The morning fog on the sea was breaking up and blue skies were rising to the south. I was glad our course was set for warmer weather. The rain would soon disappear.

Mika and I had just stepped out of the shower when the intercom chimed. I hadn't heard it, but I could see that it did, because Mika's movements were the same as the last time it rang.

"Room service."

Mika repeated what the person on the other end said.

"He'll be right there." She replied.

Mika had faced me and kept her head steady as she spoke. She knew I'd be hearing with my eyes. You wouldn't move a book around if you were holding it for someone to read. The same applies when you're speaking with the deaf. But we don't literally read lips. That's just an expression. The deaf hear words with their eyes. Muted words are instantly converted from visual to audio.

After Mika spoke, I grabbed my robe, ran a brush through my hair and put on my hearing aids. Then I opened the door. A steward was standing next to a food cart.

"We didn't order breakfast." I said.

"Yes, Sir Ron. Mika's father sent it. He said to tell you there's a buffet this morning in the banquet hall."

"What's the occasion?" I asked.

"The deacons and their families boarded last night, while you were sleeping."

Mika overheard and came out of the bathroom, proudly wearing her new maternity dress.

"Hi Reggie. I didn't recognize your voice on the intercom. Ron, this is my nephew, Reggie. He was one of your biggest fans,

187

even before you became Doc. He grew up reading your children's stories. My father is training him to be a sea captain. He's starting from the ground up. Or is that the deck up, Reggie?"

"You're the expert in English, Aunt Mika." He replied.

"Nice to meet you, Reggie." I said. "And I apologize. I usually exchange names with those I meet."

"Oh, it's okay, Sir Ron. I'm sure my coming here so early took you by surprise. If there's a way I can improve your time onboard, let me know. Being locked up for your safety must be hard."

"Locked up?" I asked.

Reggie looked nervously at his aunt, realizing my captivity was still a secret.

"Ron." Mika said. "We didn't want to interfere with your work by telling you about the death threats. Besides, you hate Seattle so much, I never had to tell you to stay onboard."

"Death threats?" I asked. "What about my kids?"

"They're okay." Mika said. "Some have joined us on the cruise. The rest are well out of harm's way. It's good your grandkids are homeschooled. They're having a wonderful time. It's an adventure for them."

"Man can my grandkids keep a secret!" I said.

"Sir Ron, it was easy. Diego just told them to read your story, *The Clandestine Clan*. You know, from your series, *Patriot Kids of Desert Ridge*."

"I hadn't thought of it, Reggie, but at times, my stories do follow real life a little too closely."

"Oh, that's what makes them great, Sir Ron. When I was a kid reading them, it was like I was all grown up. I imagined I was part of every story you wrote. But now that you're in the spotlight for taking on the doctatorship, you're more famous because of those who hate you, than those who love your books. I'm glad you're here on my grandfather's ship, there are so many people who hate you now, and not just on X. They really hate your guts."

"Well, thank you, Reggie. Nothing beats hearing people hate

my guts." I chuckled.

"Oh, but I admire you, Sir Ron. You too, Aunt Mika. When people ask me what I think about all the Covid lies, all I have to say is, Doc is my MD, and Mika is my aunt. Then they know whose side I'm on. You're both famous."

"Well, I'm glad to know it's not for the wrong reasons." I said. "How better to be famous than for being hated. Jesus warned us that it's the false prophets, who everyone loves:

Woe unto you, when all men speak well of you!
for so did their fathers to the false prophets.

But none of this is because of me, Reggie. God uses us as He sees fit."

"I don't want to disagree with you, Sir Ron, but Aunt Mika told me about your humility. And there's nothing wrong with it. But isn't it true that the Lord praises those who follow his orders? Jesus even used a parable to describe His joy when we obey Him. He told the story this way:

His lord said unto him, Well done, thou good and faithful serv-
ant: thou hast been faithful over a few things, I will make thee
ruler over many things: enter thou into the joy of thy lord.

You were already faithful over a few things, Sir Ron, and now the Lord has made you ruler over many things, you're the Minister of Deacons, the MD, Doc!"

"Thanks, Reggie. And please, call me Ron, or call me Doc, but no need for Sir Ron."

"Yes, sir! I mean, yes, Doc! I've been looking forward to calling you that. Is there anything else I can do for you, Doc?"

"Not that I can think of, Reggie. How about you, Mika?"

"No, Ron, this is already a nice surprise. Thanks for bringing brunch early, Reggie."

"You're welcome, Aunt Mika. Nice meeting you, Doc."

"Nice meeting you too, Reggie."

Reggie returned to his duties, shutting the door behind him as he left. I walked over and locked it.

Mika had begun moving our breakfast from the cart to the table. The smell of food made my mouth water, but my appetite was for her. She was always trying to please me which increased my desire. She kept busy for a wife with no children. And busyness was something I always noticed. When you're deaf, you're all eyes, and laziness doesn't escape detection. But Mika was on the other end of the spectrum, busy all the time. If she wasn't busy pleasing me, she was at the gym playing badminton with Camerlita, or working out. If she wanted to chit-chat, her aunts worked in the galley where they taught her to cook while sharing family news. And of course, Mika and I spent at least an hour a day reading the Bible together. That pleased me more than anything else. Many wives avoid reading the Bible with their husbands. But for Mika, reading the Bible was just as much about pleasing me as pleasing the Lord. She knew that if she ignored reading the Bible, she'd be a dime a dozen, just another pretty face, just a cliche. It doesn't take long for an ignorant Christian to become an ignoramus. And neither one of us wanted that to happen. It was a joy to immerse ourselves in God's Word – God's Love – together. Too bad reading the Bible had become a rare trait among *lockdown compliant Christians*. Now there's an oxymoron.

To some, my joy at the good fortune and happiness I was experiencing might seem shallow. I called shallow Christians, Ladee-da Christians. But shallowness often comes from an easy life. And who wouldn't want their family to have an easy life. We certainly can't blame those who are blessed for the fact they lack a deep understanding of suffering. Nonetheless, a little bit of Bible reading can make a spoiled heart softer and wiser. I wished my family could have had nothing but blessings. But there was one blessing that could never be taken away from us, our joy of salvation.

But we knew grief, despite our attention to God's Word. There are no guarantees. As for joy? For me, it was only because Mika did such a good job keeping me out of depression that I was even experiencing such joy. And of course, the Lord's loving hand was on my shoulder, having given Mika to me in the first place.

And my kids? Well, I hope seeing their father march on, despite having twice suffered what they had, gave them solace, that along with my telephone calls to keep our ties close. And they had kids too. What a joy for them *and* me.

To whom much is given, much shall be required. I wondered how much more would be required of me and my family. Might the Lord spare us more tragedies? I could only pray. *Only pray?* Talk about oxymorons. It is never *only praying*. It's asking our best friend and Savior, the King of kings, for help. That's a lot more than *only*.

Mika tugged at my arm. She had apparently been reading between the lines on my face. She was praying. I prayed too.

"Amen." I said.

She concurred, then quoted.

"For where two or three are gathered together in my name, saith the Lord, there am I in the midst of them."

Mika seemed to care only about loving me and being loved by me. Yes, I know, *Love is a Verb*. But to her, my being there, looking up as I wrote my stories and did my research, smiling at her, those were the only verbs she needed... outside of the bedroom. But pleasing her was even easier than loving her. She'd learned her love making from textbooks, not hookups. The books told her, *say plainly what you want*, and she did. There was no coy shyness about her. Mika was 100% real, well, 99%. And when we entered the Master's Bedroom, as she called it, she was mine, in every sense of that word. But like Esther approaching the king in the Book of Esther, all she need do was to step into my presence, and I'd grant her request.

Mika had gone back to arranging our food on the table, and my loving gaze had become a blank stare across the waters. She took me by surprise when she nuzzled my ear and whispered.

"Let's eat, then dessert."

I knew the meaning.

Then, the fact that my kids were on the ship hit me.

"My kids!" I shouted.

Mika was ready for my delayed response, so she wasn't startled.

"Yes." She said.

"Which ones?" I asked.

Mika showed me a list of her text messages that read:

"Your dad just found out you're here. We don't want to wake you up, so we'll meet you in the banquet hall at 10am."

I prayed blessings on the food, then we ate. Between bites we conversed.

"I hope you're not angry that I texted your kids that we'd meet them later, Ron. We can go now if you want."

"No, no, we can wait. They know I have a regimen in the morning. I eat first, then have coffee, then I read my Bible."

A knock at the door interrupted our conversation. I figured it was Reggie coming back for the food cart. But when I opened the door, I was nearly knocked down by my granddaughter. She jumped out of her mom's arms and into mine. My daughter, Kaya, added to the weight, nearly climbing up into my arms herself.

"I had to see you, Daddy." Kaya said.

I hugged her, kissing her on the forehead as my granddaughter kissed me all over my face.

"This is my daughter, Kaya." I said to Mika.

"Nice to meet you, Kaya." Mika said.

"Nice to meet you too, mom." Kaya replied.

"And this," I said, still holding my little granddaughter, "This is Jenny."

"Hi, Gramma." Jenny said.

Mika instinctively reached out to hug her. I expected Jenny to draw back and cling to me as she always did when meeting new people, but she held onto Mika, so I let go.

Mika's face now outshined her pregnancy glow and Jenny would have been happy remaining in her arms, if she hadn't noticed our stairway to heaven. At least that's what our stairs that wound their way up toward the skylights must have looked like to my little Jenny. When she jumped out of Mika's arms, I knew I had to keep a strong grip on her. I didn't want her tumbling down the stairs, so I used every parent's secret weapon: distraction.

"You're huge." I said. "You've grown like a giant. I can't believe you're so big!" I was now lying on my back on the carpet, bench pressing her like a barbell. "You're giant like a building. Don't come down and gobble me up!" I said.

Jenny was giggling now as I pressed her over and over into the air. But I knew my daughter Kaya must be hungry, so I gave Jenny back to her.

"See you in the banquet hall." I said.

"Oh daddy." Kaya clutched me. "I missed you so much."

"I missed you too, Kaya."

"I love you, Daddy." She said.

"I love you too Grampa!" Jenny said.

I replied to both of them with my customary send off.

"I love you and I love you and I love you and I love you."

Then I blew kisses to them as they walked out of the door. They caught their kisses in their hands and placed them on their lips. Then they blew kisses back to me and I did the same. Kaya smiled like the little girl she would always be to me, forever my daughter.

I closed the door, locking it for the second time. Then Mika grabbed me, held me against the door, and kissed me.

"I love you too... Daddy." Mika said.

"That's the first time you've called me that." I replied.

"Well, you are Daddy. That's your identity. To your kids, your grandkids, the kids who read your stories, and the Ministry of Deacons. You were chosen for a reason, Ron, and that's the reason."

I blushed. It was the first time I'd blushed since the night we met, when Mika's father said Mika had fallen in love with me. And as for compliments, this was the best I'd ever gotten.

We sat back down to continue our feast. We only enjoyed *early* feasts on Mondays, when the Deacons gathered. I ate mine at the deacon's meeting. Mika usually ate hers with Camerlita, in the Crow's Nest. That's what Cesar called the cozy dining room that sat atop the ship. It had a rotating floor just like the ones at the Space Needle and the SeaTac Crowne Plaza. But today, Mika and I were happily feasting together, hours before our daily brunch.

It's not like we deprived ourselves the rest of the week. It's just that our regular breakfasts were leftovers from a 5-star dinner, instead of fresh gourmet breakfasts made to order. But that was *our* choice. We simply didn't want to let a 5-star dinner go to waste. Both of us were taught the adage, *waste not, want not.* I guess that made us white supremacists, along with saving the wrapping paper from the furniture Cesar had given us.

Everyone in the ship's galley knew our tastes in food so they took pride in listing all the healthy ingredients for us. Today's meal was:

Prime Rib marbled with fat.

Ground Rib Eye Nuggets with spiced butter dipping sauce.

Organic Spinach drowning in blue cheese dressing.

Baked Potatoes with melted cheddar, butter, and sour cream.

Naturally Sweet Pumpkin pie with egg yolks added - crust of pecan flour, beef tallow, and salt.

Baby Coconut Pie - crust of crushed macadamia, egg whites, coconut oil, and salt.

Except for the egg whites, potato, pumpkin, and spinach,

everything we ate was full of saturated fat, the exact opposite of what the lying Ancel Keys passed off as a healthy diet. I'd accidentally NEVER followed his diet. It simply never made sense to eat crap. And since eating what I liked kept me thin, I had no reason to search for crappy substitutes. But now that I knew the benefits of saturated fats, it was no longer an accident. I deliberately followed a high fat diet.

The lies about saturated fat had been just as insidious as the lies about vaxes. When the Lord speaks of the fat of the land, it's a good thing. The Lord wouldn't create a metaphor for goodness with a food that was bad. No, the fact is, Americans don't eat enough fat, then they cook with oils that are cancerous if heated, replacing healthy saturated fat with dangerous seed oil. What does a fat person put in their shopping cart? Pink capped milk bottles, lean cuts of meat, and too much bread, aka, sugar. But it's Ancel Keys who convinced doctors to tout this dangerous diet. He's right up there with the vaccine killers, lies for money instead of health for money. The obesity epidemic wouldn't have been possible without the *epidemic of lies* from American *doctors*, *doctors* who turned Ancel Keys' recommendations into a liturgy of false medical doctrines. Other than surgeons who provide life-saving interventions, MDs are no more doctors than lying politicians are public servants.

These *so-called doctors*, belong to a club that prevents real health experts from receiving licenses as Medical Doctors. Only if they first attend universities where they're indoctrinated to push drugs, instead of prevent illnesses, are they allowed into the club. And the few so-called preventative measures they allow, are for diseases that don't exist. Even if they did exist, the cure is worse than the disease. 27% of all meds approved by the FDA are pulled off the market within 15 years of their approval. The stats show you're simply better off staying out of the *doctor's* office unless you need surgery. The sole purpose for this government sanctioned club is to keep the incomes of licensed drug pushers, aka,

MDs, high. The push for licensing MDs didn't begin until the late 1800s, and it took till the 1930s before every state gave them a monopoly on the prestige attached to a license. They were now required to be graduates of schools that taught to dose with drugs, not to treat underlying causes. Apothecaries didn't disappear, they were simply renamed Clinics and the concocting of formulas outsourced to pharmacies. Only the universities that touted drugs stayed in business so that by the 1940s, most of the naturopathic universities had closed their doors.

Medicine Doctors is what MDs have been from the start. And the medicine they push is poison. These Med Doctors have never been more than middlemen between Big Pharma and pharmacies, nothing more than licensed drug pushers masquerading as honest members of society.

And no marvel, for Satan himself
is transformed into an angel of light.

I knew the cholesterol *myth* was exactly that, way back in the 90s, when my insurance agent explained it to me. He said clients started asking him the price for life insurance with high cholesterol. So he called management to find out why it wasn't factored in on their price quotes. Management sent him to one of the company's actuaries. They're the ones who determine rates based on actual risk factors, not wives' tales. My agent said that the actuary told him:

"We don't ask about high cholesterol because it has no bearing on longevity."

A couple of years later, the question about cholesterol popped up on his application for the first time. So he called the same actuary and asked her if they'd discovered that cholesterol shortened life. She answered,

"No, not at all. Even the doctors prescribing statins know that."

196

Then he asked,

"Well then why are we asking about cholesterol now?"

And she said.

"Because doctors prescribe meds for cholesterol and 27% of all meds are recalled for harmful effects within fifteen years of their approval. These high cholesterol patients don't need to be patients at all, but now that they are, we can be sure the doctors will give them something that has a 27% chance of hastening their deaths. They have a higher chance of death not because of high cholesterol but because doctors are putting them on meds."

But the fact is, 99% of the population needs no drug other than the ones naturally produced by our own bodies: dopamine, serotonin, endorphins, and oxytocin. They're produced when we exercise, etc.

And the etc. was the part that Mika and I enjoyed most. It was a natural consequence of our Full Quiver Family Planning. And since we'd finished our breakfasts, and had our morning coffee, we were ready for what Mika had referred to as *dessert*.

Chapter 37

You are Daddy

Video calls are not the same as being with someone. I wanted my family with me and now they were. When I walked through the banquet hall, I hugged each of my kids as well as grandkids. We shed healing tears of joy at being together again. I could see that Mika had understated how many were there. *All* of them were there except for three: the two who'd gone to heaven before leaving the womb, and the one who'd joined them later, my firstborn, the one doctors had killed. The husbands and wives of my kids were there too.

My grandkids lost interest in the food after someone let it slip there was a play area. So Mika and I excused ourselves to take them there. The grandkids could catch up on food later, it was a grandpa's perk to spoil the grandkids. I shoved some snacks into one of their backpacks, and bottles of water into another. Then we set out for the play area.

There's something about a child's hand when given in complete trust. Some of my grandkids hardly knew me, but they knew what my kids told them, and that was enough for them to trust me. But I didn't have enough skin on my arms for them all to latch on, so the rest of them grabbed hold of Mika's arms.

"What should I call you?" Adaleah asked her.

"You can call me Gramma or Gramma Mika." She answered.

"Yes, and she's the hottest gramma of all." I said.

"I'm sorry, Gramma. You have a temperature? You wanna go inside and sit down." Adaleah said.

Mika looked at me crossly which was very much out of character.

"I'm sorry, Adaleah. Grampa shouldn't have said that. Hot just means beautiful." I said.

"Well, then of course you should have said it. Gramma is super beautiful. I think she loves you because you're old and know a

198

lot. Is that why you love Grampa?" Adaleah asked.

"Yes, and there's a lot of other reasons too." Mika said.

One of my other grandkids whispered in Adaleah's ear.

"Whoosh!" Adaleah said. "Course Grampa kisses good. He's in love."

"He's in love." Another of them mimed.

"Get back to playing on the monkey bars." I said.

When they noticed I wanted to change the subject, they saw even Grampa could be a target for teasing, so they sing-songed:

> *Grampa and Gramma sittin in a tree,*
> *K - I - S - S - I - N - G.*
> *First comes love, then comes marriage,*
> *then comes Junior in a baby carriage.*

This set Mika off, and I mean like fireworks. Her laughter was operatic in no small way. Then my grandkids joined in, and you'd have thought a choir was onboard. But instead of singing words, they were laughing on key. They couldn't have followed Mika's tune any better if they'd been professionals.

By the time the laughter had subsided, my grandkids were all over Mika.

"How'd you do that?" One said.

"Yeah! How'd you do that?" Another asked.

"It's her talent." I answered for Mika. "Some people sing, some dance, and some write stories like Grampa. Your Gramma Mika laughs."

"Wow, that is too cool." One of them said.

"Too cool!" They repeated, skipping around the playground.

"I'll bet you made Grampa feel *real* good the first time he heard you, just like you made us feel." Another said.

Mika was nearly in tears from all the compliments, till one of my grandkids said:

"I wonder if she's ticklish?"

"Okay, okay, enough of this." I said gruffly. "The Lord has blessed Gramma Mika with a wonderful talent. Let's make sure she only laughs when she wants to. Deal?"

"Deal!" They said at once.

Little Adaleah was glued to Mika. The rest of the grandkids were playing. And Mika's pregnancy glow wasn't waning. If I'd had a glass of anything in my hand, I'd have made my favorite toast.

"To life!"

Chapter 38

To Life

Cesar was a gentle character. He had a dozen children and did his best to keep them near him. He'd been a seaman for 40 years, 30 of those as captain. That was when he got busy having kids. Being captain allowed longer stays at home, something he knew was important to keep his family intact.

Mika was his youngest child. His wife died giving birth to her. It would have been a normal birth, but while Cesar was away at sea, his wife's doctor convinced her a cesarean was needed. It wasn't. And the doctor who performed the surgery lost her medical license. But that wouldn't have happened if Cesar's brother hadn't been well connected. The doctor would have kept her practice where deaths rivaled kidnapped Covid patients on ventilators. A hundred percent of her patients were cesarean. She hid that fact by having several clinics where other doctors assisted those who couldn't afford her expensive surgeries. Mika was fortunate to have survived her mother's C-section. And her mother, as a born-again believer, was fortunate to have her passage to heaven paid for by the blood of our Savior, Jesus.

Yes, a thin veil separates the living from the dead, and if you're born-again, you receive your heavenly reward upon death. Bodies are buried, not people. Our journey ends in life, not death, our sins paid for by the blood of our Savior, Jesus.

But losing a loved one is devastating when their death is sudden and unnecessary. And so many of us who've lost loved ones are constantly reminded of it by something we can't avoid. For the death of my brother, it was a landmark mentioned on the news every day. For the death of my son, it was a hardware store found in every community. For the death of Cesar's wife, it was his name: Cesar.

Cesar was hosting my children in his Crow's Nest Restaurant when Mika and I returned from playing with the grandkids. The families of the deacons, along with Bruno, Camerlita, Edwin, and Bella, had joined Cesar too. So I left Mika at the Crow's Nest and returned to the banquet hall. The deacons had just finished watching the video I'd produced with my staff. It was a summary of all the crimes that had been committed by both private citizens and *so-called* government officials since 2020. That's why everyone but the deacons left before it began. It was simply too much to watch. The draconian measures and poisonous *vaccines* had devastated the nation and the world, ruining hundreds of millions of lives and destroying millions of businesses. And the killing fields were still fertile as far as greedy health officials were concerned.

Most people didn't know the jab was gene therapy, not even close to a vaccine. The CDC even changed their definition of a vax midway through the humanicide, to cover their tracks.

When I stepped up to the podium to speak, the mood was somber, like what you'd expect in a courtroom for a murder trial.

"You've just seen our ministry video that took months of work by dozens of our staff. It's an odd thing when you pour your heart into a job, and it renders no joy. Yet it was the horror of what has happened, and what is still happening that kept us working, hoping we might provide some relief, some justice, to those who have been harmed. Much of the harm was caused by the jab, and it is rightly called a jab, for it wasn't a vax at all, but a gene therapy intended to damage. On top of that, instead of the normal method of delivery, those giving the jabs were instructed not to aspirate, in other words, they were told not to worry about whether they injected toxic MRNA directly into a vein instead of muscle tissue. Because of this, it's estimated that 1 in 20 vaccines were injected intravenously with harm done to over half a billion of our fellow human beings. And for those who did not suffer a direct hit, the MRNA still made its way into every organ of the body. It just took longer to do the damage. The reason we haven't seen more lawsuits is because the liability for this vaccine is handled differently than the liability for other vaccines, it's handled by government bureaucrats. And those injured, simply cannot afford the attorney fees to sue a government unwilling to pay for the damage they've done. So instead of millions suing for injuries, there are less than 10,000. But death statistics do not lie. You and I have seen the charts showing excess death spikes that follow injection rollouts. Part of our job will be to make sure the public becomes so well informed that they are immune to being gaslighted that all this was an accident. We must never forget; this was and is a deliberate genocide. The places where gain of function is done are not medical facilities. They are bio-weapon labs. Why are there such labs in Ukraine, on the border of Russia? Why was there such a lab in Wuhan, and why were the American people unwittingly funding it. We are dealing with genocidal maniacs. We must keep that clear in our minds. The lockdowns had no scientific basis and did nearly as much harm as the myocarditis caused by the MRNA jabs. I am still grieving my son's death. Many of you are still grieving the loss of your loved ones. We've prayed that there would be something, anything, to keep us on this side of the veil between life and death. Yes, our wives and children have salved our wounds as best a human can. And we have done our best to salve their wounds. But some of us, have only been kept sane by documenting the horror of the atrocities committed: doctors locking loved ones out of the hospital during their loved ones' dying days, recommending jabs for no reason other than to receive bonuses, denying admission to those who were not vaxed, forbidding early intervention and treatment with Ivermectin while the CDC recommended Ivermectin for all African immigrants. Apparently, it's good enough to proactively protect against River Blindness in Africans, but not to proactively protect against Covid in Americans or for Joe Rogan. When it's Joe Rogan taking it, it's horse dewormer. And to the FDA, Africans are no more than cows, based on their, *You Are Not a Cow,* anti-ivermectin campaign. Government is nearly always the originator of misinformation, not the public. This is one of many messages we must get across to our neighbors. Their fellow Americans are not their enemies. Their enemies are the ones who have infiltrated the honorable offices of the United States government for the sole purpose of destroying America and replacing it with what America has always stood against, tyranny. And tyranny is always accompanied by slavery, but this time, they have at their disposal bioweapons that can change the very nature of what it means to be human. We cannot let them. With tyranny comes the motivating force, money. And as we've discussed before, we know most of the money makes its way through Georgia.

We consulted with each other as to how much to include in this video and the unanimous answer was everything. And as time permitted, we did. But did we have to include the babies in caskets just days after receiving their jabs? Did we have to include pregnant mothers convulsing just weeks before delivery? Few wanted to. I didn't want to. But we all knew we must. You saw the videos and photos along with doctors' descriptions. And this, my friends, is preparation for a prosecution. We've discussed that when expedient, we can prosecute these doctors and nurses for crimes other than their atrocities, but that will not preclude us from prosecuting later for their actual crimes against humanity, crimes they knowingly committed. Yes, there were some doctors who spoke against the jabs and documented the genocide. But most doctors participated in it. And we haven't forgotten the pharmacists who refused to fill prescriptions for Ivermectin while giving out free jabs! All these will pay the price: A trial by peers. And if found guilty of crimes against humanity, crimes resulting in death, they will receive the maximum penalty the court shall impose. And what about those who conjured up this diabolical plan, these Dr. Jekylls who have committed treason against their countrymen, the men who right now sit in positions of power working against all the laws and even the constitution of the U.S. Government? Well, what happens to traitors? Do I need to speak the words? But there is a crime worse than treason for this crime has crossed borders. Did we allow Germany to claim immunity for their doctors of death who experimented on fellow citizens under Hitler's reign? We didn't. And we will not in this case either. There will be a time that justice prevails. And it will happen in such countries that permit prosecutions despite immunity. We *will* prosecute.

We knew what was done to America was evil. But we didn't know all the details. And now that we know just a mere 1% of the details, we can testify that it was horrific. The last three years, and the next three years, will result in more deaths and collateral damage from these lethal injections, than all the wars of America put together. And even the wars did not produce the degree of torment that the vax injured are still suffering. From seizures, to pain, to unending itches, to mental confusion. Nothing in the history of America has rivaled this. And why did all this happen? So that the beloved *gain of function* experiments could reap profits for drug makers, the law makers who've invested in them, and certain unelected officials in government. But they're not through. Their next step is to launch us into new wars, with bioweapons that are in violation of the Geneva Convention, and then pretend that more weapons disguised as new and improved vaxes will cure us from the diseases they've created. And their *cures* will be more lethal than the diseases, as has been the case with these so-called vaccines. But we're not going to let that happen. There are nations that have had 5 times as many deaths from what they call unknown causes than they had from Covid. Some of their assemblies have voted for full investigations while Western politicians have chosen to coverup the genocide. We have all the data to back up every claim in the video you just watched. I'll end this presentation with a verse.

When the wicked rise, men hide themselves:
but when they perish, the righteous increase.
Proverbs 28:28

May the righteous increase."

Unlike my first speech, the applause was light. We were all too horrified by the video to do anything but mourn, not just for our countrymen, but for those killed and wounded around the world.

Diego now took the podium and spoke.

"Today we vote on whether to move to the next step, which is to seek prosecutions. The vote is yours. We have the resources. We have a quorum. We've discussed the direction we want to go with this. The question is, will we?"

Diego handed out the ballots along with pencils. They were just small white pieces of paper. No questions necessary. A yea or a nay was sufficient.

It didn't take long. Diego walked back through and picked up the votes. There was one word written on every one of them: Doc.

Diego stepped back to the podium to explain the vote.

"Ron, when you became the Minister of Deacons, the MD, Doc, you became our chief prosecutor. This is not a committee. This is not a legislative body. There are times for that, and this isn't one of those times. Yes, every one of us here is willing to sign on, not rubber stamp, but go along with anything you decide, but it is your proposing it, not our endorsing anything, that matters to us. You have the anointing, the mission, or whatever you want to call it. None of us know why, you just do. And all of us are in agreement with that one fact. In no way are we rubber stamping anything. We are judiciously coming to a verdict and the verdict is that Doc is the one who will determine our direction. If you delegate, so be it. If you change directions, so be it. You are the chief prosecutor, not in the legal sense but as the guiding force. No elected official, no matter how great his ability, can do the job either. In this nation, leaders of that sort are called mayors and governors and presidents. But none of those has ever concurrently carried the mantle of prosecutor. And there is no other person in this nation who is overseeing a collection of men such as we have here today, to end the doctatorship. For now, you have chosen the route of instilling the fear of prosecution in our enemies, from the hospital administrator who profited by requiring every employee to be vaxed, to the pharmacist who refused to fill prescriptions for Ivermectin and Hydroxychloroquine. But if you take a different tack, so be it. The decision on what actions we'll take belongs to you.

There was a prosecutor chosen during the Nuremberg trials. He had no law degree. He had never prosecuted anyone before. He recently died at the ripe old age of 103. You're very much like him. We know who's been chosen for this job, and it is you, our Doc.

We understand that you and Bruno have been working tirelessly and you need a break, as many of us do. But the plans you, Bruno, and the Ministry of Deacons have already put in place can go forward, despite the short time off that you and many of us will now take. We have friendly DAs in nearly every state who are ready to begin prosecutions from parking tickets to homicide. To begin with, it may be that most prosecutions end with nothing more than 30 days in jail for contempt of court. But that will be the minimum we seek. We look forward to months and years of fear put into the hearts of our enemies, and death to those who have shed man's blood. We'll close this meeting with a Bible verse, Exodus 23:27.

I will send my fear before thee, and will destroy all the people to whom thou shalt come, and I will make all thine enemies turn their backs unto thee, and flee from thee.

May the Lord's words here be fulfilled for us as well. Amen."
"Amen!" The Deacons shouted.

Chapter 39

A Burden Lifted

Vengeance is mine saith the Lord, even so, God's Word describes the laws and processes that may be used *to do judgment and justice* as the Lord requires, for *whoso sheds man's blood, by man shall his blood be shed.* But the Ministry of Deacons was large enough to proceed with the task of finding courts *to do judgment and justice,* regardless of how many of its deacons were on vacation. So I was ready to take the short time off that Diego had announced. It had been a long time since I'd taken anything you could call a vacation. But there was no better place than Cesar's cruise ship with all my family and so many friends.

I was sitting on the deck chair outside my stateroom considering all that had happened, and my father-in-law, Cesar, sat down in the deck chair next to mine.

"You know, Ron." Cesar said. "When pastors I support have needs, they rarely call. I know their needs. I don't know how, I just know. Then after I've made a deposit into their bank, I send a text that reads, *needs met.* You have a need, Ron, but it's not money."

Cesar picked up his phone and sent a text. My phone immediately buzzed that I had a message.

"Check your phone." He said.

"Your text to me reads: *needs met.*"

"Ron, your needs have been met since September."

"I know what you're saying, Cesar."

"I'm sure you do, Ron. Mika is your asset, your healer, with the Lord's help."

"Even so, Cesar, I don't want her beautiful laughter to turn to sobs in my darker moments. I'm concerned."

"Ron, Mika has been bringing light to my darker moments since she could say goo-goo, and that's no exaggeration. When I see her read between the lines on your face, I'm reminded of what she did before she could even talk, let alone read. That's when I was in *my* darkest moments, *after I'd lost her mom*. Mika has the gift of face reading and a healing laughter. She healed me, still does. And now she's healing you. But what you don't know, Ron, is that Mika's mother had the same gift. My wife's name was Siloam, like the Pool of Siloam in the Bible. And just like Siloam means sent, both Mika and her mom, were sent to heal."

"I believe it." I said. "I mean, that Mika's gift for laughter and reading my face is a healing power from God."

"I'm glad to hear that, Ron. So don't worry about your living in the house of mourning. Mika will take care of you, for herself and on behalf of the Lord."

"Yes, she has been, Cesar. You raised her right."

"I did my best, Ron, but don't be too sweet to her. She can be ruined by sweetness like any woman. But you know that."

"As much as I wish it weren't true, yes, I know that. And by the way, Cesar. I really would like to make it out of this house of mourning. Lord willing, I'll be out soon."

"Oh, you will, Ron, you will, come June. That's the due date for my grandchild, isn't it."

"Yes, it is, Cesar. Mika and I are looking forward to our child's arrival."

Chapter 40

Not *Just* a Millionaire

By now we'd passed through the Panama Canal and refueled in Saint Martin. I was tempted to ask Mika the cost to top off the tank but did an Internet search instead. I soon realized that Cesar was not *just* a millionaire. The cost to refuel his ship for the first two weeks of our cruise was already in the millions. Mika noticed what I'd searched.

"Come with me." She said.

We walked to the freight elevator and took it down one floor. In an instant, we'd passed from the luxury of a cruise liner to the belly of a cargo ship. The sounds of clanging metal blasted into my hearing aids. I yanked them out and turned them off. Then I put them back in, this time to block out the sound.

"Sorry, Ron, I didn't expect all the noise." Mika said. "There must be worms ahead. They're moving apes in sections."

"Worms ahead? Moving apes in sections?" I asked.

Mika was barely able to hold back her laughter as she typed a note on her phone to show me. It read:

"Storms ahead. They're doing freight inspections."

This time it was me who began laughing. Mika took it as her cue to laugh with me. When we regained our composure, I looked over the rail from the corrugated steel platform where we stood. Cesar's ship held thousands of container cars.

I gave Mika the thumbs up, and we went back up the elevator. When we were in our stateroom again, I turned my hearing aids back on.

"Somehow I'd thought this was a former Cruise ship." I said.

"Then Daddy did a good job. But I hadn't realized you were that deaf, Ron. There's a lot of noise coming from below deck."

"Well, I didn't hear much of it, and what I did hear, I figured was normal. I didn't have anything to compare it to. I've never been on a cruise ship *or* a container ship. So now you know. Even with hearing aids, there's a *lot* I don't hear."

"Have you thought about learning sign language?" She asked.

"Mika, I studied French, Spanish, Chinese, and Filipino. Not to mention, all my stories are in English. Then what happened? I went deaf. If I studied sign language, I'd probably go blind."

I squinted my eyes and moved my hands as if I were signing. As I did, I walked back and forth bumping into the walls of our stateroom. But Mika was quick with a comeback.

"Well, Ron, that might encourage you to learn braille."

"Now you sound like my mother, always the optimist."

"Oh, comparing me with your mother, Ron? Does that make you a mama's boy?"

I took her taunt as a request to subdue her. I obliged, chasing her to the master's bedroom, *as she called it*. And master, I was.

Chapter 42

The Italian Castle

It had been weeks since we'd passed through the storms, if you can call them that. They were mild compared to the ocean storms I'd seen on socials. Even so, I'd gotten in the habit of checking the weather on my phone, so I picked it up.

"Clear skies and 45° in Porto Marghera." I said.

"Porto Maghera, Ron? We're in Venice? Yehey!"

"I'll ask the obvious, Mika. Does that mean we'll be taking a gondola ride?"

"Oh, no, Ron. Not on the canal and not in the air."

"In the air?" I asked.

"Yes, there are lots of hot air balloons up in the Swiss Alps and they have gondolas too. But I'm not interested in that, I just want to play in the snow. We're only an hour and a half by jet from the Swiss Alps. Can we go? Please?"

"Sure, but how?" I asked.

"I already told Daddy. He said if you agreed, he'd take care of the transportation. I'll let him know it's a go. We'll leave this afternoon. That way it won't be a rush to get ready."

"So how are we gonna get to the snow, Mika? I can't believe there's an airport on top of a snowcapped mountain."

"Our bus will take us to the Venice Marco Polo Airport. And our private jet will fly us to Sion. By the time we arrive, our other bus will be waiting to take us to Château-day. The International Balloon Festival just ended there, but there will still be lots of balloons. We can play in the snow while the hot air balloons light up the sky. Look, Ron, they're like huge Christmas ornaments!"

Mika showed me a video of the colorful balloons. When a pilot pulled the rope to ignite the flame for the hot air, the designs on the balloon would light up.

It had been years since I'd taken an interest in such worldly events, but Mika had sparked a spirit of adventure in me. And hey, I was supposed to be on vacation, and we weren't paying someone to risk their life. Mika said the festival was over. We'd just be watching those who couldn't get enough of flying their balloons.

I did a search for *hot-air balloons Swiss Alps*. There were lots of places offering rides. It must be a thing there. Maybe it is everywhere. It is in Arizona.

"I'm all in." I said. "As long as we don't get into one. Recently, four people died in a balloon accident near Phoenix. It's amazing to think they're flying them up in the Alps. I've got to see this."

"I agree." Mika said. "They're much too dangerous to ride in. But the kids will love playing in the snow while watching them."

"The kids?" I asked.

"Well, you wouldn't leave your family behind while you went off on the trip of your life, would you, Ron?"

"Well, I did before, Mika."

"Ron! That was an emergency."

"Okay, it was an emergency. The stalker had to cart me off to Las Vegas." I kidded.

"Ron, did you tell them I was a stalker?"

"No, but the truth is, Mika, they probably figured it out. That's always how I end up married."

"As if you had nothing to do with it." She said.

"Well, really, what did I have to do with this marriage, Mika? But I don't care. I'm unbelievably blessed that you stalked me *and* pounced on my heart. I'm not getting lost in sad thoughts anymore. The Lord used you to heal me."

"I'm so glad He did, Ron. And the Lord used you to complete me. I can't wait to see our baby this June."

"I feel the same way, Mika. But hurry up and text your dad. There might not be any charters left."

"It's okay, Ron. When I said our bus, I meant *our bus*. This ship holds a lot of stuff. As for the private jet, that's Daddy's private jet. He chartered it to tree-huggers from Seattle on their way to Davos. His plane is here at the airport getting fumigated from the stinky tofu... I mean, serviced."

This time I was the one who launched into an aria of laughter. Mika quickly joined in.

We'd grown more alike as newlyweds should. And laughing was the second most effective exercise we practiced daily. As if we needed practice.

Then there was food. This morning's breakfast was delivered straight from the chef's galley.

In keeping with Mika's and my tastes, our breakfast was heavy on the meat, eggs, and dairy. The ship's 5star chef was Mika's cousin, Abel. He'd built a castle with Rack of Lamb. The sections of meat met to form walls and the ribs pointed up like battlements on a fortress. Glazed cheese crust was used for mortar.

The castle sat inside canals filled with colorful sauces. Baked potatoes sliced in half and scooped out, served as gondolas. They floated on the colorful canals to celebrate our arrival in Venice.

Chef Abel, like all of Mika's family, had more than a touch of artist in him. As I got to know Mika and her relatives, I wondered what kind of genius we should expect come June, when she would give birth to our first child. As we ate, we talked.

"I hope the last few months have been as good for your dad as they have for me." I said.

"They have, Ron. He says that seeing me pregnant and with a good husband like you, has given him closure over the loss of my mom. And like you, he grieves for a very long time. He's looking forward to the arrival of our baby."

"I'm looking forward to our baby too, Mika. When I hold you close, I can only think of life. How much more will my thoughts be of life when I'm holding you and baby in my arms."

"That will be beautiful, Ron."

Mika and I finished our food without conversation, then drank the Italian coffee that came with our meal. Much of our relationship had been silent: Me, watching Mika busily clean, or add feminine touches to our stateroom. And Mika, looking up to catch me watching her, as I wrote my stories or did work for the Ministry of Deacons. Sometimes lovers are perfectly matched. But I'm not the one to tell anyone how to find such a match. I've never chosen a lover. They've always chosen me. But three is a charm and this was my third marriage. I was enjoying the longest honeymoon I'd been on, and judging from how we approached our relationship, our honeymoon might never end.

We'd finished our Italian coffee, and today, Mika took the lead when it came to dessert.

"Ron, we have a long day ahead of us and we haven't had dessert." She said.

Mika held out her hand. I handed her my hearing aids and she put them in the charger on the nightstand, then she added.

"We forgot our morning shower, Ron."

My eyes heard her words.

"Won't that melt our dessert?" I said.

"Yes." Mika answered. "Just like it does every time. I like it better that way."

Chapter 42

The Swiss Alps

It was just past noon when we boarded our bus for Marco Polo Airport. All my family, as well as the deacons and their families, were with us. Cesar had talked to me about the possibility of two flights. He didn't think it wise to put all my kids on one plane. So I left it up to my kids to figure out who would go on which flight, but none of them wanted to be left behind if one of the planes went down, so we went together.

Cesar's jet wasn't small like the one we flew to Las Vegas. It was a 747-8, and it was as luxurious as it was big. We stepped inside and were met by stewardesses unlike those on commercial flights. Each had the manners of a maître d' in a fine restaurant. They seated us at mahogany tables with ornate inlays.

I couldn't have imagined riding on such a plane when I booked my economy seat to Seattle. And my memory of it prompted a sense of loss. I forgot to cancel my flight from Seattle back to Phoenix! I lost 140 bucks! But my sense of loss vanished as quickly as it came. A set of heavenly coincidences had whisked me out of a world where economy seats had any bearing on my daily life. 140 bucks? Cesar could lose 140 million and he'd still be flying high.

Chef Abel provided the 5star dining. And when it came to dessert, those of us who weren't still kids had a chance to be kids again. Chef Abel's creation was a Matterhorn of chocolate with ice cream peaks. Sheer rock cliffs were chiseled into huge chunks of Swiss chocolate. Grissini breadsticks held strawberries dotted with frosting above gondola baskets carved out of frozen mangoes. And all this, atop a glazed ice cream cake with chocolate ice skaters. I wondered if Chef Abel had molds to form all the pieces, or had he done each one by hand. But none of that mattered when it came to the giants sitting around this miniature Swiss Alps. Every table had one and even the adults couldn't resist ransacking this land of Lilliput transported to a mountain-top.

Man had I gotten into food. Eating 5star food on Cesar's ship had turned my imagination into a recipe book of stories. Next, I'd be writing poems to prime rib! Mika interrupted my thoughts of food.

"It's getting easier to read between the lines on your face, Ron. My cousin Abel is a fantastic chef, isn't he?"

"That's an understatement." I replied.

"I'm glad to see you're happy." Mika said. Then she whispered in my ear. "But we both know it might just be a manic phase."

I whispered back. "I've been thinking of that too, Mika. And I'm sure it's partially a manic phase, mostly a happy phase, but best of all, it's a phase without grief."

I looked around me at the tables. Every one of my children and grandchildren were there. I'd spent a long time grieving but now it was time to celebrate. The Lord had answered my prayers. Yes, the country and the world still needed justice, and millions still needed healing. And after my vacation I'd return to my duties as Doc. But my eyes, and Lord willing, the eyes of my family, would be on today and tomorrow, not yesterday.

Mika tugged my arm.

"Ron, there's something you reminded me of when I showed you the cargo area of Daddy's ship."

"What's that?" I asked.

"Daddy said there's more to deafness than meets the eye. He said your Grampa had a special talent."

"I'd put it another way, Mika. There's more that meets the eye of a deaf man than meets the ear of a hearing man."

"Unconfuse me, Ron."

"Mika, godless men have lying lips. And hearing people rely almost entirely on their ears to determine if someone is lying. But the deaf don't rely on what they hear with their ears. We hear with our eyes. And the pursing of the lips, the swagger, the stance, the crossing of the arms, the tapping of the foot, the movement of the eyes, silently tell us a man's true intentions. Cab drivers can also judge a man's character by sight. They must decide if it's safe to pick up passengers before they even hear a sound. When I quit driving taxi it took years to get over sizing up people with my first glance."

"Well, why did you want to stop sizing people up, Ron."

"Mika, it's not a pleasant job to constantly judge people. But when you're protecting your life, you have no choice."

"Maybe that's the reason the deacons chose you to lead them. You saw past lying lips. You weren't fooled by Covid lies."

Chapter 43

Doc's Debut

When we touched down in Sion, our bus was waiting. Ralph, our limo driver from Seattle, was now the bus driver. And as before, Lenny rode shotgun.

Lenny handed me a license to carry.

"Are we expecting trouble?" I asked.

"No." He answered. "But I was a Boy Scout when they were still straight. Their motto is *Always be prepared*. And what was it that our Lord said?"

"*Wise as serpents, harmless as doves*." I quoted.

"Yeah, that one, Doc. Just go heavy on the wise and light on the harmless."

Then Lenny handed me two 45 caliber revolvers inside of two upside-down shoulder holsters, the kind I wore as a cab driver.

"Try these on, Doc. I know they're your favorites. But put on these snow fatigues first."

I followed Lenny's instructions.

"Yeah, this looks good." I said. "A couple of black 45s hanging outside my white fatigues."

Lenny responded by handing me a ski jacket.

"That's better." I said.

Then he continued his instructions.

"Your 45s are loaded with 230 grain hollow points. They'll stop anything short of a bear. I don't trust automatics either, no matter what they say."

"Well, what about that Uzi you're holding?" I asked.

"That's for appetizers, Doc. If a taste of this doesn't satisfy the bad guys, I got these."

Lenny opened his ski jacket to reveal his own pair of upside-down holsters. Each held an oversized pistol called The Judge.

"I got a couple of Judges, Doc. And they can be jury and executioner if need be."

219

"Aren't those a bit heavy?" I asked.

Lenny peered down at me. Now, I'm taller than most men at six-foot-one, but Lenny is midway between six and seven foot, and built like a football player. His pistols looked like toy guns next to his huge hands.

"No disrespect, Doc. But no matter what Jordan Peterson says, there are such things as dumb questions."

"Duly noted." I answered in Jordanese.

It was good to be part of a brotherhood of fanatical evangelicals who treated each other with no more respect than drinking buddies, but no less loyalty than comrades in arms.

Ralph finally woke up from his power nap and said.

"Excuse me, Doc, Lenny. Can you two stop brandishing your weapons long enough for me to open the door and let the rest of these gentlepeople in from the cold?"

Lenny and I scooted away from the door so that everyone else could enter. After they'd all boarded, Lenny stood at the front of the bus looking nothing like an airline steward and loudly recited our pre-trip safety instructions.

When he was done, Mika and I handed out the white fatigues and ski jackets her aunts had wrapped in plastic with name tags.

The road was covered with snow and chains were required. Our security team trailed us up the mountain, but there was nothing unusual. Even the overconfident SUV driver who'd careened into the ditch was no surprise. She was demonstrating to passersby that she could spin all four wheels on her SUV every bit as fast as two, and still remain stuck in her rut.

We arrived at Château-day barely half an hour before sunset. The girls jumped out of the bus first. They were first to throw snowballs too, but my kids and grandkids quickly joined in. Then Ralph opened the storage bins that were filled with toys: snowball makers, catapults, shields, sleds, and more. Their snowball fights stopped long enough for everyone to pillage the bus. Then they returned to their battle stations and escalated the conflict.

Lenny took me aside for a moment and said:

"Doc, we've got a lot of targets to protect here. I'm assuming you and Bruno can take care of yourselves for an hour or two."

"No Problem." I said. "It's just another episode in the life of Ron and Bruno. But seriously, Bruno, and I can handle it."

"Well, for you it's just an episode, Doc, but I've been doing this for 20 years."

"I have nothing but respect for you, Lenny. Thanks."

"Don't mention it, Doc."

Lenny was a lot brighter than his rough exterior let on. He had to be, 20 years of protecting high profile targets. Then I realized for the first time the seriousness of our situation. I was a target. Mika was too, and the rest of the families. The sooner we got off the mountain, the better. Then I thought of something.

"Lenny, see these hearing aids, I mean, I know you can't see them, and nobody else can, but they're in there." I pointed to my ears. "My hearing aids are Bluetooth. They're paired with my phone. If you're on a call with me, you'll hear everything I hear as well as everything going on around me. Bruno's got the same setup for his hearing aids. Have the guys in our surveillance van call us. Once we're connected, we'll just keep the line open. Do I think Bruno and I can handle everything? Yeah. But if we get into a situation, you're our backup."

"You're a genius, Ron."

"Yeah, I know." I replied casually.

I knew I'd get a chance to get Lenny back for his comment about my dumb question. Trading barbs, subtle or otherwise, is an art form between friends. And Lenny, who'd spent 20 years protecting lives, was the best kind of friend I could have.

I strolled over to watch my grandkids throw snowballs. Looking around us, our security team was anything but small. We had over a dozen men scanning the terrain. It looked like a stake-out for a drug bust. Enough so, that most of the tourists who'd been enjoying the snow had gone inside after our bus arrived.

Obviously, our presence was unnatural. Well, two hours of play time and we'd be on our luxury bus back to our stateroom.

Then out of nowhere, Jessica Whatshername walks up to me.

"Fancy seeing you here." She said.

"Yes, fancy. Are we doing impersonations of Bruno now?" I asked.

"Speaking of Bruno, Doc. Bruno didn't want to have a drink with me. But I'll bet you will." She said.

My phone was now buzzing in my pocket, but I couldn't answer it. It was in the pocket of my snow fatigues covered by my ski jacket. I hated these phones, full of too much personal information to risk carrying in an outside pocket, and too hard to answer if kept safely hidden. Then I remembered, if I bumped my right hearing aid in the middle of a call it would disconnect. These hearing aids were supposed to answer calls that way too. I rubbed my hand past my ear as if by accident since it never worked when I did it on purpose, and it worked! I heard Lenny's voice on the other end of my phone, whispering.

"Say something, Doc, so we can test the mic."

"I'll pass, Jessica." I said. "I rarely drink."

"Perfect." Lenny whispered. "We'll mute our side."

My security team could now hear every word we exchanged. Then a familiar face appeared. It was Dr. Jensen. He'd come up behind me.

"Jessica just bet you'll have a drink with her. I'll bet you will too."

Dr. Jensen was holding what felt like the barrel of a gun to my spine, and despite being armed, there wasn't much I could do. Nothing about Dr. Jensen was the same as when Bruno and I first met him. The animation in his face was gone. He had a stare like the wannabe passengers I'd chosen to pass up driving taxi. But I didn't have the luxury of ignoring Dr. Jensen, considering what he was holding to my spine. So I accompanied Jessica Whatshername and Dr. Jensen to a table outside the lodge.

"You know, Dr. Jensen." I said. "My mother used to poke me in the back with her finger, just like you're doing. She did it to speed me up. We're sitting down now. Any chance you can remove that thing from my back?"

"We're still in a hurry... Doc! That's what you like to be called now, isn't it, old Ron. Yeah, you still let Bruno call you old Ron. You and him must be pretty close. But you're about as much of a doctor as a ham sandwich. And if the FBI has its way, that's what you'll be."

"I was just about to tell you the same thing, Dr. Jensen. But you're a lot more than a ham sandwich. Nobody has to trump up charges against you like they do with a ham sandwich. I'd say you're a potato sitting on The Chair, waiting to be reincarnated as french fries, compliments of Old Sparky."

"Ha, listen to the storyteller. Nothing but a gypsy storyteller. Old Sparky. When were you born? I didn't know they were still using electric chairs for executions. Not as creative as what we've got planned for you."

As Dr. Jensen was finding his groove with his criminal bluster, we were met by another doctor I recognized.

"I can't remember your name." I said. "But aren't you..."

"Yes, I'm the doctor who kept you out of the hospital where your son was being treated."

"I've been wanting to ask you about that, Doctor...what's your name?"

"What's in a name?"

"Impressive, you know Shakespeare. Then you also know, *a butcher by any other name would still smell of blood.* But you must have a name, and I couldn't just call you Dr. Whatsyourface, that would be impolite, so Dr. Butcherface, it is."

"Call me whatever you like, you and your white supremacist friends."

"I see, so I'm a white supremacist. You see any faces among my kids that don't contrast with the snow, Dr. Butcherface?"

"You know, as well as I do, that you don't have to be white to be a white supremacist. Thomas Sowell, Clarence Thomas, and Candace Owens are all famous white supremacists."

"So, is that why you held my son hostage? Was he a white supremacist?"

"Your son wasn't being held hostage. He was a patient."

"I know. If he hadn't been a patient, then *I* would have been holding him. Did you let anyone in to see him?"

"Of course. We let his primary physician in. He was under treatment with Adderall."

"Under treatment with a drug that's made of a combination of four amphetamines, Adderall? That's treatment?"

"I know where you're going with this, Mr. Miller. Your adult son was an addict."

"Who said he wasn't an adult? Was the pusher who got him hooked an adult too?" I asked.

"Nobody pushed it on him. And by the way, I wasn't the one who prescribed it for him."

"Who was?" I asked.

"Does it matter?" Dr. Butcherface said.

"Maybe not. I took photos of all his prescriptions when we found him dead. Maybe they're still available on one of my old phones."

"Go ahead, Mr. Miller. Find the prescriptions. It's not illegal to write prescriptions."

"Yet." I said.

"So, what are you getting at?" Dr. Butcherface asked.

"Nothing at all. You're the ones who invited me to the party."

"Yes, it is a party." Dr. Butcherface said. "And we've got a little entertainment planned. Let's go on a ride. I've been taking a *crash course* in balloon piloting."

"A *crash course*, huh?"

"Yeah, once you get them airborne, they float real nice. But landing them safely, especially in the Swiss Alps, *can* be a problem. You know, Mr. Miller, I'm an atheist, but I'm still asking myself how the Lord could have made it so easy for us: a man as hated as you, going somewhere as dangerous as the Swiss Alps."

Dr. Butcherface escorted me, Jessica, and Dr. Jensen over to the gondola of a balloon. The tie downs were decorated with colored ribbons like ropes on a maypole. I remembered the nursery rhymes I'd read to my grandkids about maypoles.

> *Boys and girls danced round the tree*
> *Singing loud as e'er could be.*
> *Leaves of fluttering ribbons hung*
> *The maypole dance had just begun*

Dr. Jensen's shout at the balloon pilot brought me back to the present.

"Get out!" He shouted, waving a pistol with his free hand while still holding the barrel of his other gun to my spine.

The pilot jumped down to the snow and sprinted away, then Dr. Jensen went back to talking like a novice thug.

"Get in and don't try anything funny!"

"The only thing funny around here is the clown walking behind me." I said.

"Once a gypsy, always a gypsy." Dr. Jensen said. "Talk about clowns, making kids smile with your little fairy tales. Then you scare the hell out of 'em claiming there's some kind of a bogeyman, a deceiver called Satan. You oughta be ashamed of yourself, scaring them, then having them sing *Yes, Jesus loves me.*"

"So, Dr. Jensen, what made you throw away a promising career as head deceiver, I mean physician? I really can't figure that out. Maybe you're just... no good."

I continued my banter, hoping he'd be distracted and move his gun off my spine, if only long enough for the security team to get in a shot.

Lenny had begun whispering through our phone connection again:

"Camerlita's had you live streamed on X since you met up with Dr. Jensen and Jessica. You're coming through like a Hollywood movie shoot, including the video from the surveillance van's cameras. Wave to your audience. *No wait*, don't wave, keep cool."

I couldn't believe Lenny was kidding around while I had a gun pressed to my spine. But it was reassuring he was calm enough to kid around. Then Lenny answered what I would have asked.

"Our snipers are still trained on Dr. Jensen. But we can't risk a shot while he's got that gun glued to your spine. We're gonna mute our side again. We don't want to distract you, Doc."

By now, I was in the gondola with Jessica, Dr. Jensen, and Dr. Butcherface. None of them seemed quite normal. But could any of them have seemed normal while kidnapping someone? Well, I have to admit, Jessica seemed entirely normal. She was sauced to the gills as usual.

Dr. Butcherface let out the tether, so we were now about six feet above the ground. Then he cuffed my hands above my head to a bar on the flame-burner. This prompted Dr. Jensen to drop his guns to the floor.

"Toy guns." Dr. Jensen said. "Shows how smart you are, Mr. Miller. But you dried up my cash flow. And that wasn't smart. My wife went to the judge and opened all my banking records. But we can fix that. A lot of people want you dead. This will be a simple ballooning accident, and I'll be richly rewarded by those who know it's not. So, you see, Mr. Miller, I got nothing to lose."

Just then, Bruno reached over the edge of the gondola, grabbed Dr. Jensen, and said.

"Except your teeth!"

After Bruno had punched Dr. Jensen, Jessica jumped down from the gondola. She managed to walk about twenty feet, then passed out.

But Dr. Butcherface, who wasn't anxious to meet Bruno, had begun tugging on the chain that fueled the flame-burner for the balloon, bouncing the gondola till Bruno could no longer hold on.

My grandkids, oblivious to the situation, saw what looked like streamers coming down from the balloon and began shouting.

"Maypole! Maypole."

Then they took off running for the tethers that tied down the balloon, but their parents scooped them up before they could get close.

It had been all of 45 seconds since Dr. Jensen first put his toy gun to my back. And rounding up nearly a hundred people playing in the snow wasn't easy for the security team, not without clueing in my captors, making them more desperate than they already were. Even so, the security team was making progress.

Dr. Butcherface's tugging on the chain that fueled the flame-burner was putting more and more tension on the tethers that held the balloon down. But Dr. Butcherface wasn't happy about the progress. He wanted that balloon off the ground and he wanted it now. So he gave a desperate tug, breaking the chain to the balloon's flame-burner.

But Bruno wasn't happy either, seeing his old friend getting kidnapped. He'd climbed up the side of the gondola again and was about to jump in when Dr. Butcherface threatened him with the chain he'd broken.

"I've been waiting 40 years to get my hands on someone like you." Bruno said. "Go ahead, swing that thing!"

Dr. Butcherface swung the chain at Bruno who put his arm straight up. The chain wrapped around Bruno's wrist. And what happened next to Dr. Butcherface was a dream come true, just not for Dr. Butcherface. Bruno tightened his grip on the chain and jerked that scrawny butcher's face toward him. Then he let him have it, chain and all. I wasn't surprised. Bruno had a knack for delivering a clear and concise message.

Then I realized the bar that held my handcuffs was broken, so

227

I slid my cuffs over it, grabbed the keys off Dr. Butcherface, and uncuffed myself. Bruno saw I was free, so he let himself down by the chain that was still wrapped in Dr. Butcherface's limp hand. When his feet touched the ground, Bruno gave the chain a jiggle and it came loose.

"Now I got *me* one of these souvenirs." Bruno shouted.

"You earned it." I shouted back.

Bruno walked back to the bus where Camerlita and everyone else was waiting to give him a well-deserved hero's welcome.

By this time, Dr. Jensen was pissing his pants, quite literally. And as I moved to keep my snow fatigues clean of it, I noticed there were more passengers than the two quivering doctors and myself. Nurse Casandra, the charge nurse for Dr. Jensen's floor, was bent over, looking more like Gollum than anything human. But instead of coveting a ring, she was bent over a vial of multi-dose Covid-19 vaccine. It was empty, but her syringe was full. She held the syringe as if it were a sacrament in an unholy initiation and had my pant leg rolled up about to vax me!

"You bitch!" I screamed, jumping out of the way of her jab.

My curse echoed off the mountains and my kids and grandkids who were watching from the bus heard it. I've never seen so many gaping mouths in my life, such a word from out of the mouth of a Christian storyteller!

It startled poor Dr. Jensen too, and that, along with my rocking the gondola when I jumped back, caused him to fall between me and Nurse Casandra. Then she started to talk, repeating the words she'd said that day in front of the emergency room when Dr. Jensen was admitted. It was then that I realized she was just as crazy back then as she was today holding that syringe.

"Now what does your recent memo say about unruly patients?" Nurse Casandra began. "Oh yes, upon scanning patient code, if patient history does not indicate drug interactions, sedate the patient from the approved list of medications. Yes, that's what it says. And Dr. Jensen, your history indicates no drug interactions whatsoever. You're not on any meds. In fact, you're not even vaxed. Well, I've run out of sedatives. But this is an approved medication."

Then Nurse Casandra jabbed Dr. Jensen's leg with her syringe, and he screamed a word that made mine sound like it came off a Sunday School vocabulary list.

The jostling in the gondola had loosened the balloon from its tethers and it was 30 feet off the ground by the time it passed over our bus. I grabbed onto one of the tethers and swung down onto the Plexiglas roof as everyone inside watched. They'd gotten a little bit more entertainment than the snowball fights and mountain views we came for. But I didn't want them to lose sight of the balloon either. As I stood on the roof, I pointed to the balloon as it continued to climb in altitude. It was beautiful. It's not every day you can see a huge Christmas decoration like that. And it went up quicker without me. Nurse Casandra looked over the side, a smile on her face, then she lit up a cigarette, her excuse to remove her ever-present mask. She was singing an anti-war song. Odd song for a genocidal maniac. "Where have all the flowers gone." But even villains will sing.

The mountain rescue team kept firing their rescue rope launching gun, but by now the balloon was well out of range. Besides, it'd be nearly impossible to bring the balloon safely down without help from those inside. And Nurse Casandra seemed more interested in her cigarette and her song than anything going on around her.

Lenny and Ralph helped me get off the roof and into the door of the bus. There was no applause. I was simply met by the same gaping mouths that I'd seen through the window when I used a bad word, except for Bruno, who clapped slowly while nodding his head and displaying his giant grin. It was his way of saying he knew old Ron would escape somehow, even if it was by the skin of his teeth.

Camerlita still had me live on X, and I wasn't above theatrics.

So I took off my coat to reveal that all the while I had two 45s holstered under my arms. That's when the applause began.

I sat down next to Mika and my daughter, Kaya. She was holding little Jenny, my granddaughter, in her lap. I wasn't hearing well so I unpaired my phone from my hearing aids. Then I noticed my call with Lenny. It had only lasted 2 minutes and 58 seconds. I couldn't have been in the balloon much more than half that time.

"Look at this, Mika." I said, showing her the call record.

"Yeah, I noticed it. It seemed like forever, Ron. I love you. I didn't take my eyes off you the entire time. I'm so proud of you. You look great on video."

"That's it? I look great on video? Weren't you worried? What about in person?" I objected.

"It's not what you look like in person, Ron. It's what you do. And you do it well. And as for worry? I gave my life to the Lord Jesus a long time ago."

"Amen." We both said.

We sat watching the balloon through the skylit roof. Dr. Butcherface had bent the lever for the flame-burner when he broke the chain. The flame was locked on and the balloon was getting hotter and going higher fast.

Jessica had been fortunate enough to have escaped the balloon, and as I saw it, she likely had nothing to do with the medical terrorists' plans. In fact, it would have been unusual for her not to turn up at our first stop after we left Seattle. We *were* the story that gave her a worldwide claim to fame, or should I say, infamy. She could no longer work in Seattle since she'd cursed their beloved seagulls. But alcoholic or not, she was tenacious. I didn't see her career ending soon.

Mika and I held hands as we started the trip back to Venice. This time, we'd travel all the way by bus. And this bus was every bit as luxurious as Cesar's jet, not to mention its huge Plexiglas roof.

Ralph was just about to pull out of the snow-covered parking lot when Mika asked.

"Can we have one last blast of mountain air?"

"Ralph, did you hear that?" I said.

"Sure, no problem, Doc. Everyone, zip up your jackets."

Ralph hit the button to open the Plexiglas roof. The chill was a reminder of how much I missed the Phoenix sun. I'm sure my kids and my grandkids missed it too. We looked up at the black night of the Swiss Alps. Stars painted the alpine sky. It reminded me of the desert sky outside Phoenix. The mountains were nearly invisible without the moon to light them up.

While we were enjoying our last few minutes of mountain air, Edwin was testing the onboard karaoke. But before he began to sing, the balloon with the medical terrorists came into view again. And as we watched, Edwin sang.

"By the time I get to Phoenix, she'll be rising."

And like the operatic laugher that she was, Mika let out a laugh that echoed off the mountains, muffling the rest of Edwin's song. It wasn't a happy sight to see: three corrupt members of the medical profession who'd launched themselves to their own deaths, no happier that is, than to see three murderers hung on the gallows. But Mika's laughter was infectious. The safety team for the lodge must have set off strategic explosives before the balloon festival, because Mika's laughter, and the laughter of everyone with us, was enough to start an avalanche. We had reason to laugh, as did everyone watching on X live. These three villains had executed their own countrymen for hire, and now, they were about to suffer self-inflicted executions. Was it a sin to laugh? Not according to God's Word. *The righteous shall see, fear God, and laugh.*

We watched as the balloon continued to rise, then it burst into flames. And when it did, ***it went down faster than Dr. Jensen flew out the window, and down to the roof of Julio's food truck.***

Psalm 52:1-6

Why do you boast in your mischief, O mighty man?
The goodness of God endures forever.

Your tongue devises mischief, like a sharp razor,
working deceitfully.
You love evil more than good, lying more than truth.
You love all cruel words.
O you deceitful tongue. God shall destroy you forever,
He shall take you away, and pluck you out of your dwelling,
and root you out of the land of the living.

And the righteous shall see, fear God, and laugh.

Back on the Sortida Agua

We arrived back at our ship a couple of hours before midnight, and despite the fact we were in Venice, we were home. We'd been on the ship just shy of five months, and we were no longer living out of suitcases. Our stateroom had all the hallmarks of permanence. It was elegantly furnished and had more electronics than most homes. Yes, material things don't make a home, but they do provide a sense of the familiar. And in a world where each day became less familiar, our comforts were a reminder of America, a land where even a deckhand could become Captain, owner of an ocean liner, and billionaire many times over. I hoped the America I'd grown up in, part fairy tale, but mostly real, would not become a distant memory.

Mika and I had gone to sleep exhausted for the first time from something other than honeymoon activities. And we weren't used to a ripple in our routine. So, when we woke up, I sat down at our dining room table, and *Mika* opened the refrigerator to pull out leftovers from the night before. Of course there were none. We'd eaten on the bus ride back. But on cue, the intercom chimed.

"Yes?" Mika spoke into the intercom.

"Breakfast, compliments of Chef Abel." The voice announced.

I opened the door. It was Mika's cousin, Reggie.

"Congratulations, Doc!" He said.

Then he rolled the food cart into our stateroom.

"Congratulations for what?" I asked.

"Chef Abel's cake says it all." He replied.

Then Reggie uncovered a huge cake. It was a replica of Mount Rushmore, but there was only one president, Trump. The other heads were Russel Brand, Julian Assange, and me.

"Is this a riddle?" I asked.

"Take a guess." Reggie said.

"Something tells me that between checking in to the Sortida

Hotel, and returning from the Swiss Alps, that I raped someone."

"Yes, yes!" Reggie said gleefully. "It's a badge of honor to be falsely accused of rape nowadays. See, your face is right there between Julian Assange and Russel Brand."

"Yes, I'm honored. But will the charges be dropped?" I asked.

"I'll let Aunt Mika give you the details, but yes, even if you'd done it, no charges could be brought."

"Ah, some kind of diplomatic immunity. Well, I'll have to eat breakfast and have my coffee before hearing the details on that."

"Yes, you need to eat first. And Chef Abel made sure to give both you and Bruno superhero breakfasts. After all, who swings from a hot-air balloon onto the roof of a bus, or gets hit with a chain, without getting hurt. It was like you and Bruno were stars in an action thriller. Grampa Cesar had the X livestream up on the banquet hall movie screen. He kept replaying it till you got home.

And some of the haters on X have changed their minds about you. What guy with two 45 caliber revolvers escapes without firing a shot! #Docmightberight started trending early this morning on X. It was started by one of your biggest critics. And Doc, *you look great on video!*"

"Yes, thanks for the kind words, Reggie."

Now I was really beginning to think I must look horribly old off camera. Well, at least I was photogenic. But as for what really mattered, I had no complaints. Mika and I were about to have our first child, and every day was a blessing.

Mika had already taken our breakfast from the cart and put it on the table. Only the cake of Mount Rushmore remained.

"I'll take this cake back to the kitchen for the brunch party." Reggie said.

Then he placed the lid back over the cake.

"Party?" I asked.

"You'll find out later." He said. "Aunt Mika will clue you in. I gotta get this cake back to the kitchen before it melts."

"Okay, Reggie. See you later."

Reggie pushed the cart out. The moment the door shut, Mika pressed me against it.

"Seems like this is becoming a habit." I said.

"Habit? What? Let me go! You rapist!"

Mika barely got out the words before her laughter began. We rolled on the floor laughing in each other's arms till we cried. Still gasping for air from laughter, we managed to take our seats at the dining table.

"Let's pray." I said.

Our prayer included giving thanks for a lot more than the food. We'd been kept safe, while those who wanted to do *us* in, did *themselves* in. I was now as infamous as Bruno was famous. What is it they say, all publicity is good publicity? If that's the case, Jessica was one of the most blessed women in media by now. She'd become as infamous as anyone can, short of committing a crime. Nice to know we weren't the only ones who had something to be thankful for. And Mika's and my families? They were a network of support that few could boast, outside of those with a political dynasty backing them. Then I realized, I was the lightening rod at the top of a political dynasty unlike any in recent history. I was a novice when it came to the intrigue of the underworld. Mika wasn't. What that woman knew was beyond her years. I peeked at her as we prayed. Her eyes remained shut. Other than her laugh lines, there wasn't a wrinkle on her face. They say all women marry up. Well, Mika wasn't stupid, so there had to be things about me that Mika knew but I didn't. I prayed the Lord would open my eyes to the things Mika saw in me and give me a hint of what was to come.

"Amen." We closed our prayer.

A rush came over me. The Lord had immediately answered my prayer. I now sensed the anointing that everyone said was on me. Sounds crazy, but I felt bigger, as if a string that held whoever I was together, had been loosened, and that I had grown to fit into a new larger self.

"Oh, there it is again." Mika said.

She stroked the hair on my arm.

"Daddy said you were a Silverback and that I'd see you change each time you reached new heights. I guess swinging from the rope of a hot air balloon onto the roof of a bus counts. You're worthy of more than a stalker, Ron. I'm glad you accepted my proposal."

Normally, I would have denied there was any change or that I was anyone special. And of course, nobody *is* special except that we're created in God's image. Even our love for Him is because He first loved us. But what just happened? Something in me had changed. Whether one millimeter of my body was even the slightest bit different, didn't matter. Today, I had a new skin, and I'd grown to fit into it. Cesar had told me about Silverbacks, a kind of ape. And how those who accomplish great things are like them. They say that there are genetically no Silverback Apes, that they all begin the same. But when one ape survives the onslaught of every other ape to win the top spot, he grows. The silver begins to grow at his spine, then covers his scalp and becomes the crown visible to all. He becomes the Silverback, unbeatable, at least within his realm. But he's powerless when an intruder of another kind appears, as we're powerless except for the power of God's grace. I prayed to the Lord again, this time, to grant me the wisdom to rightly use whatever this anointing was.

I'd been given honor, honor I didn't deserve, and families that loved me, in ways I could never repay. I looked up to the Lord in heaven and smiled in thanks. All these blessings were from Him.

Except the Lord build the house, they labor in vain that build it.
Except the Lord keep the city, the watchman is wakeful in vain.

Mika and I finished eating our Superhero breakfast, and were on our second cup of coffee, so I was ready to hear what I knew would be a long answer to my question.

"What's this diplomatic immunity I've got, Mika?"

"Daddy took care of it. Well, let me qualify that. He took care of it with a little help from your uncle: Edwin P Neilan."

"Now, you know we're forbidden from communicating with the dead, Mika, and I don't think your dad would break that commandment, so clue me in."

"Well, Ron, remember how your uncle Ed was one of the Vice Presidents of the ILO."

"Yes, he used to send me postcards from places all over the world. I've still got them somewhere. But I never quite understood what the ILO was or why he traveled so much."

"ILO stands for the International Labor Organization, Ron. It's an organization within the UN, but it existed before the UN. They can even issue passports that provide diplomatic immunity. Many members of the WEF have diplomatic immunity through NGOs within the UN. It makes sense for members of the Ministry of Deacons to have diplomatic immunity too. Your passport says who the issuing authority is. Here, take a look at yours. Daddy got diplomatic passports for all of us before we left from Seattle."

I looked at it. I'd never heard of the organization that issued it.

"But you still haven't told me what the ILO does and why my uncle Ed was associated with it, Mika."

"The task of the ILO, Ron, was to help workers, employers, and governments make progress toward more freedoms and better working conditions. Your uncle was its most famous vice president and its most famous member, ever. He was also the employer delegate for America. Those combined positions required him to travel to nearly every nation. He was already well known for his outspoken criticism of corruption in America. You have the letter he got from Senate Majority Leader Mike Mansfield, who was infuriated that your uncle Ed called congressmen: *con-men, bagmen, patronage peddlers, and gravy ladlers*. And because of that, he was trusted by small businessmen and workers around the world. He was also trusted by... let's just say, insiders.

And he learned secrets that to this day the CIA doesn't know. There are still people who want to pay him back for all the good he did for them. And since you're his only male heir, one of them contacted Daddy when he heard about the Feds interest in you. He knew you might be framed, and us too. That's why he issued diplomatic passports to all of us onboard Daddy's ship."

"So, Mika, you're telling me, that on top of our grampas' deep penetration of America's darkest places, with a type of organization I never could have imagined, that there's a guy out there who knew my uncle Ed, and he's working to protect me?"

"Um, Ron, it's not just one guy. And your grampa, Peter, who owned the vitamin company? You already know that he found out the hard way what Big Pharma is up to. They ruined him by claiming zinc was unproven as a protection against illness. It wasn't until 1974, four years after your grampa Neilan died, that a daily recommendation for zinc was established by the National Academy of Sciences. Ron, your grampa was helping people with vitamin supplements, long before their healing effects were known to the general public. But the Feds put him out of business when he was forced to remove the most effective ingredients."

"Mika, next thing you'll tell me is there's an outfit bigger than the Ministry of Deacons, set up by Grampa Neilan and his son, my uncle Ed, to penetrate Big Pharma, Big Guns, and the CIA."

Mika was silent.

"Mika. Mika? Aye, aye aye!"

That was enough to set Mika off. And as usual, her laughter was contagious. By the time we'd finished laughing, we'd broken a sweat. Mika pulled out my hearing aids and put them in the bedside charger. Then she took me by the hand, and we headed for the shower that sprayed from all sides.

Proverbs 1:22-33

How long, simple ones, will you love simplicity?
and scorners delight in their scorning,
and fools hate knowledge?
Turn at my reproof:
behold, I will pour out my spirit unto you,
I will make my words known unto you.

You who have refused, though I called,
I have stretched out my hand, and no man regarded.
But you have set at nought all my counsel,
and would none of my reproof:

I also will laugh at your calamity.
I will mock when your fear cometh,
When your fear cometh as desolation,
and your destruction cometh as a whirlwind,
when distress and anguish cometh upon you.
Then shall they call upon me, but I will not answer.
They shall seek me early, but they shall not find me:
Because they hated knowledge,
and did not choose the fear of the Lord:
They would none of my counsel: they despised all my reproof.
Therefore, shall they eat of the fruit of their own way,
and be filled with their own devices.
For the turning away of the simple shall slay them,
and the prosperity of fools shall destroy them.

But whoso hearkeneth unto Me shall dwell safely,
and shall be quiet from fear of evil.

The Nuremberg Code (1949)

1.The voluntary consent of the human subject is absolutely essential. This means that the person involved should have legal capacity to give consent; should be so situated as to be able to exercise free power of choice, without the intervention of any element of force, fraud, deceit, duress, over-reaching, or other ulterior form of constraint or coercion; and should have sufficient knowledge and comprehension of the elements of the subject matter involved, as to enable him to make an understanding and enlightened decision. This latter element requires that, before the acceptance of an affirmative decision by the experimental subject, there should be made known to him the nature, duration, and purpose of the experiment; the method and means by which it is to be conducted; all inconveniences and hazards reasonably to be expected; and the effects upon his health or person, which may possibly come from his participation in the experiment.

The duty and responsibility for ascertaining the quality of the consent rests upon each individual who initiates, directs or engages in the experiment. It is a personal duty and responsibility which may not be delegated to another with impunity.

2.The experiment should be such as to yield fruitful results for the good of society, unprocurable by other methods or means of study, and not random and unnecessary in nature.

3.The experiment should be so designed and based on the results of animal experimentation and a knowledge of the natural history of the disease or other problem under study, that the anticipated results will justify the performance of the experiment.

4.The experiment should be so conducted as to avoid all unnecessary physical and mental suffering and injury.

5.No experiment should be conducted, where there is an a priori reason to believe that death or disabling injury will occur; except, perhaps, in those experiments where the experimental physicians also serve as subjects.

6.The degree of risk to be taken should never exceed that determined by the humanitarian importance of the problem to be solved by the experiment.

7.Proper preparations should be made and adequate facilities provided to protect the experimental subject against even remote possibilities of injury, disability, or death.

8.The experiment should be conducted only by scientifically qualified persons. The highest degree of skill and care should be required through all stages of the experiment of those who conduct or engage in the experiment.

9.During the course of the experiment, the human subject should be at liberty to bring the experiment to an end, if he has reached the physical or mental state, where continuation of the experiment seemed to him to be impossible.

10.During the course of the experiment, the scientist in charge must be prepared to terminate the experiment at any stage, if he has probable cause to believe, in the exercise of the good faith, superior skill and careful judgement required of him, that a continuation of the experiment is likely to result in injury, disability, or death to the experimental subject.

"Trials of War Criminals before the Nuremberg Military Tribunals under Control Council Law No. 10", Vol. 2, pp. 181-182. Washington, D.C.: U.S. Government Printing Office, 1949.]

Footnotes

https://doctatorship.com

The evidence is piling up so rapidly for the claims made in this book that a website was needed to provide documentation. Keep up to date on all the evidence.

https://doctatorship.com

Notes

Notes

www.ingramcontent.com/pod-product-compliance
Lightning Source LLC
Chambersburg PA
CBHW050413260626
47156CB00003B/987